Miracles, Inc.

T. J. Forrester

SIMON & SCHUSTER PAPERBACKS
NEW YORK   LONDON   TORONTO   SYDNEY

Simon & Schuster Paperbacks
A Division of Simon & Schuster, Inc.
1230 Avenue of the Americas
New York, NY 10020

First Simon & Schuster trade paperback edition February 2011

SIMON & SCHUSTER PAPERBACKS and colophon are registered
trademarks of Simon & Schuster, Inc.

For information about special discounts for bulk purchases,
please contact Simon & Schuster Special Sales at
1-866-506-1949 or business@simonandschuster.com.

The Simon & Schuster Speakers Bureau can bring authors
to your live event. For more information or to book an event,
contact the Simon & Schuster Speakers Bureau at
1-866-248-3049 or visit our website at www.simonspeakers.com.

Designed by Meredith Ray

Manufactured in the United States of America

10 9 8 7 6 5 4 3 2 1

Library of Congress Cataloging-in-Publication Data
Forrester, T. J.
    Miracles, Inc. : a novel / T. J. Forrester.
        p. cm.
    1. Spiritual healing—Fiction.   2. Swindlers and swindling—Fic-
tion.   3. Life change events—Fiction.   I. Title.
    PS3606.O74865M57 2011
    813'. 6—dc22   2010004238
ISBN 978-1-4391-7558-3
ISBN 978-1-4391-7560-6 (ebook)

For those who never have the chance to grow old

Miracles, Inc.

Chapter 1

ONTRARY TO NEWS REPORTS, I, Vernon L. Oliver—brother of Lucy K. Oliver and son of parents who raised their children on corn and Christianity—am not insane. Admittedly, my attorney claimed otherwise in my trial against the great State of Florida. I played along, spewed nonsense to the psychiatrist's questions, rolled my eyes and lolled my head in front of judge and jury, but in the end, I bear no ill will against the justice system. I made a series of choices that led to nowhere good and those choices landed me in a six-by-ten cell with concrete walls and a steel frame bed.

At one time, not too long ago, I was revered—a man who treated his followers with kindness, with love, a man whose heart was open to all. They still send me letters, pleading in their blindness for my innocence, for they cannot believe I committed so heinous a crime. The letters come in bunches, sometimes a hundred or more a day, and I've requested that the guard only bring a sampling—no more than ten, no less than five. I spend my afternoons writing in careful strokes, assuring believers that faith is not an illusion. What else can I do? My acolytes want bright lights and speaking in tongues, they want paraplegics jumping around the stage, they want the hum that permeates their souls when my voice tumbles over the auditorium. So, I give them what I can. It's the least I can do.

Terrence Sandoval, my attorney, is the one who suggested I write an autobiography; a tell-all about Vernon L. Oliver's fall from grace. He wants money (more than I have) now that the IRS has foreclosed on my property, frozen my assets, sold my private jet. The money that was left over—the $2 million the government allowed me to keep for legal fees—is long gone. When Sandoval suggested in that persuasive way of his, "Write the book, sign over the proceeds, or find a public defender to file your appeals," I said I would think about it and get back to him.

And I have thought about it. I've woken with it on my mind, I've thought about it while eating the gruel that Florida calls breakfast, thought about it while watching the clock on the wall, listening to it tick toward the time when the guards will enter my cell and take me on the long walk to the chamber where they will strap me to a gurney and plunge the needle into my arm.

I have no desire to stand nakedly before accusers and believers alike, but I dread the damn clock, hate the thought of my footsteps on that cold linoleum floor. Most of all, I dread not knowing what's on the other side.

My attorney says he's here for a visit, to see if I've accepted his proposal. In a suit, with a tie knotted against his scrawny neck, he sits outside my cell in a chair pulled up for his convenience. I prop open the horizontal slot in the steel door and sit on the floor so I can see his eyes. He wears cologne, a sweet smell that reminds me of windblown flowers, the sweep of a woman's breast, of red lips on my pelvis. He peers down at me, all teeth and dimples, asks if I'm getting along all right.

"That cologne," I say.

Sandoval speaks in a moribund tone, like a bored teacher after a long day of classes. "Do you like it?"

"It reminds me of this guy I knew back in high school. He sucked dick behind the gymnasium in exchange for cigarettes."

"I can see we're in a foul mood today," Sandoval says. "Maybe I should come back tomorrow."

I don't want him to leave, yet I don't want to give him the satisfaction. The satisfaction of what, I don't know. Maybe I'm lonely.

A quavery voice comes from down the block, a convict bitching about nothing in particular. John T resides five cells to the left, and he's here because he killed a woman who sold him the wrong foot cream. If anyone should have gotten off on insanity, it was John T.

Sandoval glances at his watch, and I despise him for his insensitivity. He has places to go, things to see, a life to live. I'm stuck here, in this orange jumpsuit, staring at these four walls until the State decides it's time to end my miserable life.

"If you change your mind, start with your childhood," he says. "It'll create sympathy in the reader."

"I'll leave the carving of the stone tablets to Moses."

He rises and offers a half wave, a resigned move, like he topples his king at the end of a brutal chess match. His footsteps echo out of hearing range, and silence returns to my cell. I go to my bed, lie on my back, and face the ceiling. The paint is gray and without cracks, and the light in the center burns with mild intensity. I stare until spots float before my eyes, get up and sit at the desk in the corner. I have decided to give my attorney—that bloodsucker with the ingratiating smile—what he wants. I pick up my pencil and begin the first chapter.

Lucy was born with a genetic illness. She died when she was seven, a skinny little girl with knobbed knees and a bucktoothed smile. We loved each other like life itself.

I write for three hours, scratch out every sentence but the first three, scrawl a three-word ending.

Screw you, God.

Does the in-between matter? I was sixteen when she died, and I spent my adolescent nights thinking about God and the fairness of the world. I had a choice and knew it. I could believe or deny his existence. I chose to believe.

Why?

It is impossible to hate something that does not exist.

So, I will not write about my sister in this autobiography, I will not commercialize the name of Lucy K. Oliver. I will begin on a day when I received an offer I couldn't refuse. Should I have turned it down? Maybe yes, maybe no. I only know one thing for sure.

There are no innocents in this story.

Chapter 2

Pastor Yost and I waited in a curtained room inside a hot revival tent pitched in the middle of an Ohio field. We worked for Tabernacle Carnival, this Holy Roller outfit on its northern swing. The year was 1996, and I had recently celebrated my twentieth birthday.

I lit a cigarette and peeked through a slit. Watched Mrs. Yost sit at the organ and riffle through sheet music. She ate Valium like kids eat chocolate-covered raisins, and she glued plastic fruit to her hats. Today, a grape cluster dangled off the brim and settled close to her ear.

Yost squirted minty-smelling spray in his mouth, ran through a stretch of voice exercises that ended with the musical scale, shook out his arms to loosen his joints. He was closing in on sixty and combed his thinning hair across his scalp. His shirt was buttoned to his throat, an effort to hide the port-wine stain on his neck. I'd never seen the entire birthmark, but what peeked above the collar looked like an upside-down Florida.

"You should give those up," he said, and pointed a crooked finger at my cigarette. "The devil's own handiwork."

I imagined my hands around his neck, lifting him off the floor, saw my fingers squeeze until his face reddened and his head exploded. A harmless fantasy, one I indulged at least three times a day.

"Tuck your shirt in," he said. "You look like a bum."

I hitched my pants, returned to the slit.

Yost had once confided he had dreamed he was interviewed on *60 Minutes*, and how, in the wake of the publicity that followed, he had been offered a television show and preached to millions every Sunday. Subsequently, I needled him on a daily basis.

"Hey," I said. "I just saw Mike Wallace."

He ignored me and took out his flask. Swallowed a shot. He'd been a chaplain during the Vietnam War and told stories about brave soldiers who had taken shrapnel for their country. I'd discovered early on that he despised men who wore long hair, thought they were no-good hippies. I was born in 1976 and had never even *seen* a hippie. I wore my hair to my shoulders because my girlfriend liked it long, something I never told him, figuring it was none of his business. My height exacerbated the tension. I was six four last time I measured, which meant he had to crane his neck when we talked. When we were together, aside from the service, where clearly he was the boss and I was the subservient, people gravitated toward me instead of him, especially women, who often commented on my cheekbones and black-as-night eyes.

He handed me the flask. I took three swallows of his whiskey.

"Give you punks an inch, you take a mile," he said.

Mrs. Yost played a slow rendition of "Shall We Gather at the River?" and her husband handed me the offering plates. The plates were deep—scalloped bottoms covered in felt—and the rims were worn smooth. I swished the curtains to the side and walked out to the front of the stage. Birds fluttered overhead, among the network of poles that supported a canvas so faded the color reminded me of a dried-out orange. Three hundred and fifty seats formed a semicircle in front of a metal stage. I knew the count because I folded and unfolded chairs whenever the carnival moved to a new spot. We'd been here three days, and the previous congregations had trampled the grass. Transformed it into this yellowing carpet. The only breeze came from the flapped opening, and the stench of rotted flesh and leaky colostomy bags swirled over the faithful. The tent was half full, below-average attendance for an afternoon service. Stage lights flickered on, and Yost walked to the pulpit. He spread his arms as if to embrace every onlooker.

"God is with us today," he said.

Amid a shower of "Amens," I walked down the center aisle and passed the plates, watched fives and tens flutter downward like birds to the roost. The congregation was made up of locals, and the healthy among them were dressed in their Sunday best— flowered dresses for women, cheap black suits for men. Firm hands held Bibles and supported the sick, patted shoulders and adjusted hospital robes.

"God," Yost said, "has told me a great healing is upon us. God has told me to ask my brothers and sisters to open their hearts. God has told me we must fill that offering plate with our twenty-dollar bills."

A woman in curlers rolled on the grass. Her dress hiked to her knees, and fleshy legs thrashed the air. Peggy Brougham sold trinkets in a booth when she wasn't speaking in tongues and warming up the congregation. She shouted out what sounded like a blend of baby talk and Portuguese, and a collective "Hallelujah" filled the air. Whispers of "Hosanna on high" came from joyous lips. These people weren't idiots, yet they came willing to exchange money for a chance at a miracle. I pinned their herd mentality, their sheeplike bleating on hope. Hope that the man onstage would take away the pain and sickness, hope that Jeffery would breathe without coughing blood, hope that Bobby Sue's leg bone would heal. Hope. That's what we sold twice a day, and this congregation was about to get a major dose.

Mrs. Yost played a yearning melody that increased in decibels until it filled the tent with its power. Babies cried and men shouted, women ran their fingernails over their arms and lifted their voices in screeched platitudes. The music subsided into an incessant beat. Keystrokes that drove Yost from one side of the stage to the other.

"Praise the Lord," he said, and raised his voice. "I feel the Holy Spirit. He is upon us."

I emptied the plates in a box at his feet, estimated we'd cleared over six hundred dollars. Not bad for the first pass.

"I feel the power," Yost said. "I feel the *power*."

I selected Frankie Ford out of the front row and guided him up the steps. Frankie wore dark glasses, and he carried a white cane. He was an expert at disguise, and the second time we worked together I'd mistakenly picked a truly blind man out of the congregation and that had pissed Yost off so much I almost got fired. From that day on, Frankie sported an upside-down flag pin so I wouldn't mix him up with someone else. Today, he wore a droopy mustache and ratted yellow hair, looked like someone who stood on street corners and asked for spare change. The pin gleamed proudly from the pocket of his camouflage shirt.

Yost dabbed at sweat running down his face and walked the stage, prayed mightily that God—in his infinite justice and mercy, in his kindness of heart, in his ability to see all things good— would extend a helping hand and heal this poor blind man right here, right now, right here, right now, right here on this stage in front of these witnesses, these lovers of all that is holy in life and in truth, these people who understand God's work comes at a price and without their help we might as well pack up this tent and this stage and become vagabonds like this poor man who has lived in darkness since he came out of his mother's womb. Frankie lifted his arms and turned up his palms. Amid murmurs and rustles, Yost laid his hand on the offered head, and Frankie, like a weary traveler, sagged to his knees. He took off his sunglasses, and when he spoke, he had tears in his eyes.

"It's a true enough miracle," he said.

"Amens" thundered toward the ceiling.

"He was blind and now he can see," Yost said.

Shouts of "Praise the Lord" followed the "Amens."

Frankie sat behind Yost. There were two seats, which meant we had one more miracle on tap. This was around the time in the service Mrs. Yost's age caught up to her, and she slowed down the beat until it was hardly moving. Mr. Yost glared at her. She bent over the organ, and the music resurrected itself.

A man wearing a John Deere hat jammed his crutches under his arms and lurched toward the steps. He had a bad right foot. Like maybe it got crushed in farm machinery and hadn't healed properly. I turned him around and assisted him to his seat, pointed at a skinny woman who had been carried in on a stretcher and lay motionless on white sheets. Yost came down off the stage and shouted for the demon to leave this woman.

"Begone from this holy world!" he said.

Yost prayed and the crowd prayed, and he laid his hand on her head. Nothing happened, and for a nightmarish moment I thought I had picked out someone who was actually sick. But then

Valerie Bentley, "auto wreck survivor," began to move around. She had taken drama in high school and thought she was a hotshot actor, so she milked her time in the spotlight more than most. Eventually, she patted her legs and said she could feel them for the first time since she walked across that street back in Dallas and the UPS truck had run a red light and flattened her like a runaway dog. She walked onstage and leaned over the microphone.

"I had the devil in me," she said. "But now my heart is as clean as fresh snow. Praise Jesus, I can walk."

I swear to God, the congregation stopped breathing. I swear to God, I thought some of them were about to have heart attacks. Yost, who didn't like actors to go overboard after the healing, which meant shut up and sit down, angled her into the seat next to Frankie. She folded her hands and issued a smile.

A woman crawled toward the steps. She wore a stained choir robe, smelled of urine and rose perfume. I'd worked this job for three years and had not contracted a communicable disease, and I planned to keep it that way. I folded an empty chair, held it down at my legs. She clawed at my shoes, turned around, and crawled back to her seat.

I fended off two more forays in the next five minutes, passed the offering plates as Mrs. Yost played "Amazing Grace." The congregation filed out and I lit a cigarette and walked the rows. Picked up empty drink cups, a quarter that had missed the plate. Pastor Yost answered his cell and talked in a low voice. He snapped his fingers to get my attention.

"Miriam wants to see you," he said.

Those five words meant one thing to a Tabernacle Carnival employee. Your ass was about to get terminated.

"What?" I said.

"She wants you to turn in your employee badge. Tomorrow night, end of the workweek."

"What did you tell her?" I said. "Did you say something about me running late this morning?"

I stepped onstage and walked up to him, stood there until his head tilted upward. Mrs. Yost, on the organ seat, nervously tapped her foot. I leaned over and whispered in his ear, "Go to hell."

The color in Yost's face deepened, and he exhaled a harsh little snort.

"Up yours," he said.

I walked out of the tent into afternoon sunlight, squinted, and waited for my eyes to adjust. Getting laid off was one thing; how to tell Rickie was another.

The carnival was set up in the shape of a wagon wheel—the tent was the hub and the booths, butted end to end, branched like spokes toward the periphery. Outside the barbed wire fence, a highway led to towns where advance teams had tacked flyers on light poles. The week had started slow and stayed slow. Rumors of a layoff had circulated for months, so getting the ax wasn't a total surprise.

I walked a big sweep around the tent, dodged tie-downs and stakes, and came up on aisle E, subtitled WORD OF GOD & JESUS JEWELRY. Aisle E was busy even on slow days, and I heard snatches of a testimony about how Pastor Yost had healed a woman on a stretcher. Soon as that testimony died another sprang up, this from a fat-necked teenager who allowed how the Holy Ghost came over her and she had talked in tongues like never before.

Someone shouted, "His Holy Name," which brought a peppering of "Hallelujahs."

I spotted Rickie at her Bible booth and hung back in the crowd. Rickie was short and slender, and she wore a cotton dress that fell demurely to her ankles. A man in a white shirt and black tie walked up to her and said he needed a King James magnum edition. Rickie cocked her head and smiled. She had these wide eyes, brown lashes the color of her hair, and most men who stopped and talked opened their wallets. My girlfriend worked on commission, and the more she flirted, the more money she made. What no one saw under the dress, which was a good thing because we were required to project a conservative persona at work, was the piercing in her left nipple. A silver strand glided from the stud, swooped over her breast and down her stomach, curved upward and docked in a belly button ring. She'd told me one night, after a sprint of margaritas and a ten-mile run of vodka collinses, that she wore the chain to break up her symmetry, that before the adornment she could draw a line down her center and not tell her good half from her bad.

I wondered when she would feel my gaze, since we had that kind of connection. Rickie always knew when I was around. She turned in my direction, and I ducked behind a booth that sold Jesus watches. I'd had my share of lovers, but Rickie was my first full-blown relationship. She didn't want me; she wanted *all* of me. I didn't mind saying it. My girlfriend scared the crap out of me.

Later that night, after the booths closed and the carnival darkened, Rickie and I walked to her RV, where I took off my dress shirt and dress pants, changed into faded jeans and my favorite T-shirt. The shirt had a chromed chopper on the front side, and its rider stared fiercely at something in the unseen distance. I wrapped a Harley bandanna around my skull. Tied the ends into a square knot. Rickie got me a beer, and I sat at the table and spun my lighter in circles.

In the three years we'd been together, we had spent time and money fixing up this place. The curtains were blue, her favorite color, and they were cut off at the bottoms to fit the windows. We got the couch cheap because it was supposed to unfold into a bed, but that part was broken and now it was simply a brown couch and a couple of brown cushions. The commode, this energy saver that used minimal water to drown a turd, was our latest purchase. I hadn't complained about the cost. If Rickie wanted to save the planet, who was I to argue? On the walls, nailed into every available space, were shelves holding textbooks she'd used in college, along with novels she'd purchased at yard sales.

Rickie had been raised a foster child somewhere in Colorado and never talked about her real mother and father. She graduated high school early, attended Boulder University when she was sixteen. She took literature courses and quoted Robert Frost. Her favorite poem was about two trails diverging in the woods and how the adventurer had taken the one less traveled, which to her translated to quitting after sophomore year to join the carnival at seventeen. She never elaborated about her childhood or inquired about mine. Without coming out and saying it, we had decided our pasts were off-limits.

Rickie brought me another beer and I kicked off my shoes and watched her cook omelets. She used real ham, not that chopped-up swill sold in the 7-Eleven, and she browned her onions because I liked them that way.

She carried over the omelets, and we ate and drank. Then she cleared the table, tore a page out of a Bible, and rolled a joint. We had smoked our way through Matthew and Mark and were now well into Luke. Rickie lit the joint and the paper burned an inch up the side, so she wet it with saliva to stop it from burning clear to her mouth and scalding her lips.

"You should have rolled it tighter," I said.

I toked the joint and unbuttoned her shirt. Fingered the silver strand where it attached to her nipple. She'd changed into a green blouse, and the bottom tucked into jeans low on her hips. I unzipped the jeans, and she pushed my hand away.

"Off-limits for three days," she said.

"You got your period?"

"Gushing like Old Faithful."

We'd had a condom fail a couple of weeks ago, so the period was good news. We drank more beer, Rickie got out the Scrabble board, and we picked tiles out of the velvet bag. Halfway into the game, I laid down seven tiles for a fifty-point bonus.

"*Nainsook* is not a word," she said.

"It's a word."

"Use it in a sentence."

"You want me to use it in a sentence?" I said.

"Indulge me."

"'*And yourself,* she thought in her nainsook, *you want him to be Uncle Remus goes to war, then the old happy fishing patriot.*'"

She got out a pint of Jim Beam, and we sipped and contemplated the word. I pointed to the bookshelf below the kitchen window, told her the sentence came out of *Yonder Stands Your Orphan,* a Barry Hannah novel.

"Page twenty-six, twenty-one lines from the top," I said. "*Nainsook* is the third word from the left margin."

Rickie knew better than to waste her time looking. I remembered everything I'd read, and I'd read all the books in the RV, which meant I knew every word in every book.

"Nainsook is a soft lightweight muslin," I said.

She sipped her beer and smiled. "I'm playing Scrabble with a goddamn dictionary."

We finished the game and she totaled the score, rolled up the paper, and threw it in the trash. I'd beaten her by 142 points.

"I think I'm losing brain cells." She toked the joint and exhaled. "Picking up your bad habits is wonking me out."

We drank more Jim Beam and toasted diminishing brain cells. When I was young and a foot taller than my classmates, I would have given anything for fewer brain cells. In junior high, I'd grown adept at writing illiterate essays, speaking in grunts instead of sentences, muddling algebra problems I'd solved when I was seven. My deception fooled my peers, who quit calling me Beanpole and accepted my averageness with metallic grins and open arms, but my teachers were incensed and requested monthly teacher/parent consultations. My father told me to study harder and maybe my grades would improve. I told him Rome wasn't built in a day. Continued my ride on the Flunk-Out Express. Eleventh grade, my teachers passed me despite a .7 GPA. I was determined to do better, and the next year finished with a big fat 0. My transformation was complete, my popularity at an all-time high.

Rickie tugged me to the couch and rested her head in my lap. I ran my finger along the curve of her ear, over the shiny opal in her lobe. One of the things I liked about my girlfriend was not having to hide how my brain worked. She was not intimidated or jealous, simply accepted me for who I was.

"What would we do if I got laid off?" I said. "Hypothetically speaking."

"She's not going to lay you off."

"I'm saying what if she did. What if I got laid off tomorrow night?"

"Don't even say that," Rickie said.

She rolled another joint, and we smoked it. I ran out of cigarettes and smoked butts out of the ashtray. Rickie's eyes were bleary, and her words sounded rubbery. Like the consonants and vowels bounced off her lips instead of coming straight out to open air.

"Did you say something?" she said.

"I don't think I did."

"I thought you said something." She clapped her hand over her mouth and yawned.

"I said I'd go crazy hanging around here with nothing to do. It'd drive me nuts."

"I didn't hear you say that. I swear I didn't hear that."

I swished beer cans and found one that was a quarter full. "Well, that's what I said."

She closed her eyes, her chin nodded to her chest, and a snore fluttered her lips. I picked up a magazine and leafed through the pages. Rickie wanted to live on the beach, and she bent the corners of pages that had pictures of sea and sand. She got a mysterious feeling when she thought of the ocean, said the feeling came from her bones, like the ocean was part of her and that's where she belonged. I stopped on a page where a glossy hog glided on open road. The model sat on a Harley-Davidson Springer Softail and had the same fierce, far-off expression as the rider on my shirt, like he was going somewhere important. I imagined myself on that bike, hair whipping in the wind, knees straddling that cobalt blue gas tank. That was the sum of Rickie and me. She wanted the beach, and I wanted a bike.

I dropped the magazine and closed my eyes. I should have told her the truth about tomorrow. I could be such a bastard sometimes.

In the morning, Rickie walked into the kitchen and puttered around. She had on these shorts that rode up her legs, and her bare feet made sucking sounds on the floor. I went outside and stood in the cool air. To the east, clouds were stacked on top of each other, and the bottom layer was silvery red. Rickie brought me a cup of coffee, and we watched the sun creep above the browned earth.

"You're quiet this morning," she said.

Red-haired Johnny Bentley came out of an RV, stumbled across the field, doubled over, and threw up. He drank wine and rolled his own cigarettes, checked the tent every morning and made sure none of the tie-downs had loosened. He staggered down an aisle and a few minutes later the clang of a sledgehammer on a metal stake broke the stillness.

"Tabernacle Carnival is a brontosaurus choking on comet dust," I said. "One of these days it'll give one last heave and roll belly-up."

I blew across my coffee, inhaled the roasted aroma. "We should go get some real jobs, something more high tech. Jobs that'll be around five, ten years from now."

"I make good money selling those Bibles."

"Which you never fail to remind me of," I said.

"When have I ever said that?"

"When have you not said it?"

"I might have suggested you should try to get a booth job, something on commission, but I don't recall saying what you just said." She spun on her heel and stalked back to the RV. "Onward, Christian Soldiers," someone's idea of a joke, played over the loudspeakers. Johnny Bentley wandered past, and I asked if he had a cigarette. He rolled me one and marched onward. I thanked him, went back inside, and plunked my cup on the counter. Rickie watched me, her lips pressed into tight thin lines.

"What did I do?" I said.

She bent over the sink and washed out the cups and didn't say a word. Which was okay with me. When she got her period, anything I said was like dangling a cape in front of a bull. I left without saying good-bye, headed to the time clock, punched in with thirty seconds to spare. I walked down aisle B, to where Johnny and his sledgehammer stood behind a display of silver crosses and Holy Ghost paperweights. Johnny had a stare that made patrons nervous, so he didn't make much money over the counter. To compensate, he sold bootleg cigarettes and fake Cuban cigars to carnival employees. I bought two packs and watched him unscrew a thermos lid, pour wine into a cup.

"Taking Communion early?" I said.

"Wiseass."

Johnny had worked the carnival longer than anyone and told stories about the old days, before Miriam fired the midgets who performed nightly shows. According to Johnny, there was major money in midget fucking. Not so much in peep shows. People would only pay a quarter to see a peep show, but they had coughed up the bucks to sit in bleachers and watch midgets hump for an hour or more. When Johnny talked about midgets, his expression turned wistful, like he wished he could go backward in time.

I lit a cigarette and stood around for another few minutes. When I wasn't in the tent, I worked security and kept a lookout for shoplifters, a ridiculous occupation for someone surrounded by the faithful. The pious may have been clueless, but they weren't thieves. I began my serpentine route, up one aisle and down the other, each time avoiding Rickie's aisle when it came into view. At noon, I stopped for pizza and fried ice cream, took a long break, then headed toward her booth.

"I want to talk to you," she hissed.

I studied an imaginary point over her head.

"I want an apology," I said.

"I'm down here, dipwad."

I lowered my gaze an inch at a time. She rang up a sale, brushed her hair out of her eyes. She grinned, and I grinned back. I never could stay mad at Rickie.

That evening, I helped her close her booth, told her I'd catch up in a few minutes. I headed toward an Airstream parked in a lonely section of the field. Miriam was an enigma among her employees. She owned multiple businesses and only showed up at the carnival every couple of weeks, leaving the running of things to Yost. She arrived in different rental cars. Talked to no one when she walked the aisles. Rumors followed her everywhere she went—lesbian, stuck up, rich, slept with everything on the East Coast so she's headed west—name it and I heard it about Miriam.

I knocked on the trailer door, and she invited me inside. The Airstream had sloped walls and thick carpet. Chrome counters in the kitchen. She offered me a seat in the recliner and chose a position across from me on the couch. I forced my gaze up the black dress, over the belly and mounded breasts, to the curve of her throat. She had timeless skin, wrinkle-free, a woman I judged somewhere between forty and forty-five. I studied the slim line of her jaw, the green eyes that accepted my once-over. She wore her hair tucked back, and jade earrings reflected the lamplight when she turned her head. Her voice had a confident lilt with a touch of pride mixed in, not enough so it came off as bragging, but it was there just the same. It wasn't vanity, although she was certainly a beautiful woman. Miriam's pride came from her accomplishments. She had worked her ass off for what she had, and I couldn't help but admire her for it.

A burned smell came out of the kitchen, and she got up and removed what looked like brownies from the oven. She brought me one, along with a Coke, and sat back down. The brownie was hard enough to chip a tooth. I nibbled and swallowed my drink to wash everything down.

"I've only been late to work a total of 2,587 seconds," I said. "That's hardly a reason to lay me off."

"I'd have to agree, Mr. Oliver. 2,587 seconds is hardly a reason to lay someone off."

"And I've never stolen so much as a nickel from the offering plate."

She opened a yellow folder. Flipped a page. "Says here you flunked out of high—"

"I'm not the sharpest tool in the shed but I work harder than most."

"Mmmm," Miriam said. "IQ of 157, took your SATs despite flunking out."

"Seemed like the thing to do."

She flipped another page. "Perfect scores, interest from Ivy League schools, yet you wound up in my carnival."

"One of life's tragedies," I said. "A mystery that will forever go unanswered. Did we really go to the moon?"

"Excuse me?"

"You have an unusual way of letting someone go—not that I've had experience in this game. I prefer football to fencing. Larger crowds, beer on tap, cheerleaders shaking their pom-poms, that sort of thing."

"But you fence very well, Mr. Oliver. A man with superb épée skills."

"Do you always investigate your employees?"

"It's my job to see behind the scenes, to really find out what's going on; so yes, every Tabernacle Carnival employee has a file. Does it bother you?"

I shrugged.

Miriam took my plate and can to the sink. She didn't like being cooped up in the trailer and suggested we go for a walk. Under the black sky, she chose a direction away from the carnival, toward a corner of the field I had not previously ventured. We came to a gate and draped our arms over the top rung. Lights above the booths went out one by one, and the parking lot emptied as cars and trucks spilled onto the highway. A necklace of red taillights expanded in opposite directions. The lights were on in Rickie's RV, and I hoped she was starting supper. That lump of charcoal Miriam had passed off as a brownie had reminded me I was hungry.

"Do you have any aspirations?" Miriam said. "Do you want to do anything except work as a front man for Yost?"

The breeze picked up, and I smelled rain. Wondered if Rickie had the windows closed. Lightning sliced downward, branched into a three-pronged fork, spread across the sky. Thunder rolled over the carnival.

"I'm getting married," I said.

"To the beautiful Rickie Terrell, I presume."

"We've talked about it." Rickie had talked. I had listened.

"Does the happily married couple plan to live in an RV for the rest of their lives?"

"We're going to buy a beach house," I said. "Probably down in the Bahamas."

"Harbour Island is beautiful. I love the pink sands on the eastern shore."

I had read about but never seen Harbour Island and its beaches. "Harbour Island, Eleuthera, Nassau, Grand Bahama, Andros, we'll wind up somewhere. The Cayman Islands are also an option."

The sky was blackest to the west, where the storm gathered strength, but overhead stars lit the night. A meteorite swept eastward and flamed out at the end of its arc. Rickie loved shooting stars, thought they were nature's way of perking up the night. I saw them for what they were. Hot coals that may, or may not, land on someone's head. Chances of that happening were slim, but who knew when cosmic destiny might come a-calling. Miriam said something about needing money to bring dreams to fruition.

"We're saving up," I said.

Rickie and I had six hundred dollars in the piggie bank last time we counted. Miriam was quiet for a long time, and I thought the conversation was over.

"Listen," I said. "Let's cut out the bull—"

"I want to help you out, Mr. Oliver."

"What?"

"I want to offer you a promotion," she said. "I'm talking more money than you ever dreamed, I'm talking so much money you can buy a beach house anywhere in the world. I'm talking so much money you'll live in the lap of luxury for the rest of your life. The lap of luxury, Mr. Oliver."

A sprinkle landed on my arm, and I wiped away the wetness.

"Televangelism, Mr. Oliver. Think Nick Wheaton big."

She had caught me off guard, and I sensed her delight.

"You have the looks," she said. "You have the charisma. The rest we'll teach you."

Preachers like Nick Wheaton, slick talking heads for mega-congregations in megasanctuaries, repulsed me. How these scammers could return to the scene of their lies Sunday after Sunday was beyond me. They symbolized the New Pentecostal, a religion as stagnant as a dying fishpond. If I had to choose, I preferred the Old Pentecostal and their tent ministries one step removed from snake handler days. At least at Tabernacle Carnival the faces in the seats changed week to week.

"I'm afraid I wouldn't do well in a church setting," I said. "All that counseling, having to patronize parishioners."

"I'm talking fast and light, Mr. Oliver. No permanent sanctuary, low overhead, high-tech stages. I intend to create something new in the Pentecostal world, a show so exciting it will make headlines all over the globe."

"Are you serious?"

"Serious enough to have scheduled you a flight out tomorrow morning," she said. "To our training facility."

"I haven't said yes."

"I want you enough to pay out a ten-thousand-dollar bonus."

The offer sounded like easy money, so I stuck out my hand and we shook. Miriam moved close, and her breath warmed my neck. She was only a silhouette in the darkness, but I felt the energy between us, and if I hadn't been involved with someone else I might have kissed her. I backed off a step. I could discount one Tabernacle Carnival rumor—Miriam was not a lesbian.

"I make you nervous," she said.

"Temptation is the devil's own handiwork."

She laughed and so did I.

"One thing," she said.

"Yes?"

"I advise you to steer clear of Yost."

"He was up for this job?"

"Let's just say he thought he was in the running."

I walked her back to her Airstream. She filled me in on my weekly salary and how long I'd be away, ended by saying she'd send a driver to pick me up tomorrow morning. I told her I'd be ready and started across the field. The wind howled and the rain turned into hail and I broke into a run. Lightning struck a pole on the highway, and a fireball formed and ran down the power lines. Out of the darkness came the roar of a locomotive, only there were no tracks and I knew what made that noise in the middle of a storm. I was almost to the RV when lightning spit out of the clouds and lit the sky and I saw the twister snake toward the carnival. I threw open the door and Rickie jumped back from a lit candle on the table. I grabbed her and blew the candle out and threw her on the floor and jumped on top. I waited for the chaos to stop, but the tornado sounded like it was about to rip open the door and suck us into the night. Rickie held on, fingernails digging into my neck, and I squeezed her so tight I couldn't breathe.

Seconds later, like the twister had never happened, the RV went silent and we were left clutching each other on the floor.

The rain and wind stopped, and we stepped into the night. The clouds blew over and the stars came out, and we studied the firmament like we could not believe it was real. We walked through the wet grass to the center of the carnival, held hands, and looked around. Canvas, stakes, ropes, stage, organ, seats, offering plates . . . all ripped up and carried into the Ohio night.

Johnny staggered up and mumbled something only he could understand. Mr. and Mrs. Yost milled around. In different circumstances I would have worked my promotion into the conversation, but now was not the time. Miriam walked up, and she and Rickie looked at each other. Something passed between them. Some sort of connection I couldn't fathom. Rickie turned away and headed toward aisle E, told me over her shoulder she had hamburgers in the oven. Hamburgers? Rickie could think of the strangest things. Johnny said the aisle lights were isolated from the tent circuitry and might come on if he reset the main. Miriam told him to give it a try, and he disappeared into the night. A few minutes later, the first row of metal halides flickered to life.

"Mr. Oliver," Miriam said. "This doesn't change a thing. You fly out as scheduled in the morning."

"You gave *him* the job?" Mr. Yost said.

I couldn't figure out why Yost was upset. The young elbowed past the elderly, that was the natural way of things, one of the reasons life survived on this planet. I patted his rigid shoulders and said, "I'll say hello to Andy Rooney for you."

The light came on above Rickie's booth, and I could see her wiping the counter. I went over and helped her out. Satisfied that nothing had been harmed, we walked the aisles, soon realizing the twister had set down precisely in the middle of Tabernacle Carnival, ripped out its showpiece, and left everything else intact. Rickie kept saying she couldn't believe it, but I'd seen tornado damage in a town near where I grew up in Silvington, Indiana, and I knew twisters had minds of their own. Sometimes they stayed on the ground, and sometimes they touched down here and there. This was a here-and-there twister, a good thing for all concerned. I slid my hand to the small of Rickie's back. Guided her home. She seemed dazed, like her mind had gone on vacation and hadn't returned.

Inside, she changed into a T-shirt and white panties, and I slipped into boxers, ran a bath towel over my hair. She dropped a coffee can on the kitchen floor, knelt, and stared at the spilled grounds for the longest time.

"I was listening to the radio," she said, "and the announcer read this warning that there were twisters in the storm and I waited for you to come and you never did."

She swept up the coffee grounds, got two six-packs out of the fridge, and we guzzled beers one after another.

"Where were you?" she said, and slammed a can on the table.

"I was talking to Miriam. Down by that gate on the other side of the field."

"You were talking to Miriam?"

"She offered me a position," I said.

"Did she give you a booth job? Did she put you to work on commission?"

"Not exactly." I got out the bong and filled it with water, and we traded hits for the next hour. Rickie changed into her pajamas, and I stared at her top, at the ducks paddling across blue cotton. There must have been hundreds, thousands, maybe millions. She poked me, wanting to know what Miriam wanted.

"I told you," I said.

"Tell me again."

"She offered me a televangelist position, said she was going to make me rich and famous." I closed my eyes and woke to a wet face. "Hey, did you throw water on me?"

"Apple juice."

I wiped my forehead, licked my fingers.

"Did you sleep with her, Vernon?"

I blamed Rickie's jealous nature on abandonment issues. And who could fault her? I could only imagine life in foster care. She went to the sink and turned on the water, poured in some Dawn dish detergent. Threw a cup that whizzed past my ear and hit the wall. The cup fell to the floor and broke into three pieces. Rickie had played shortstop for a church league, and when she hurled dishware it did not idly sail through the air. I jumped up and held her until the stiffness left her arms.

"I'm sorry," she said.

"Well, I didn't."

"I said I was sorry."

I took a shower and washed off the apple juice, followed her into the bedroom and set the alarm clock.

"I thought you'd be happy," I said. "I thought we'd celebrate and maybe decide where we wanted to move."

"You don't know her like I do."

"I didn't think you knew her at all."

Rickie's strained look told me that was all I was getting out of her.

"It's a twelve-week course at a Pentecostal seminary in southern Florida," I said. "Somewhere around Lake Okeechobee."

"Twelve weeks?"

"I'll be back before you know it."

She rolled over, and from the way she jerked her legs seeking a comfortable position—something she did when she was upset—it took her a long time to fall asleep. I could quote enough Nietzsche to bore someone into a coma, solve mathematical problems so beautiful they'd make Pythagoras cry; I could talk so much bullshit the listener didn't know if I was coming or going, but I had gotten to know Rickie well enough to realize that I had no idea how a woman's mind worked. I stared at the shadows and wondered if I was doing the right thing, asked myself if our relationship could stand three months apart. Eventually, I concluded I had no clue. We might last, and we might not. I forced that thought from my mind, tunneled under my pillow, and fell asleep.

In the morning, I packed my duffel bag while Rickie made coffee. I drank a cup, and she came over and sat in my lap.

"Call me," she said, holding up her cell. "I want you to call me every day. Call me collect if you have to."

"Okay."

"I want you to promise. I want to hear you say it."

"I promise," I said.

A car drove up, and the driver flashed the headlights. Last night was the first time Rickie had accused me of screwing around. Crazy bitch. No way was I sleeping with Miriam. Not even if she offered herself on a silver platter.

Chapter 3

DREDGE, THE CONVICT WHO lives in the adjacent cell, believes death row inmates wind up buried in the prison graveyard. Dredge is a slow-talking guy, and he's here because he raped and murdered four boys. He nailed them to wooden doors and cut their throats, has another ten or so years before he makes that walk. John T, the loon who killed the woman for selling the wrong foot cream, is not so lucky. He's scheduled to die tomorrow afternoon, and he's spent the last few minutes describing the meat he ordered for his last supper. On his plate, he has roast beef, fried chicken, New York strip, and barbecued ribs.

"They sent me beef ribs and I distinctly asked for pork," John T says. "I distinctly asked for pork. I remember very clearly."

"You should ask for your money back," Dredge says.

John T hollers for the guard and no one comes, which is not unusual because guards rarely get off their fat asses. Death row is a cushy job. The guards bring breakfast at seven, lunch at noon, supper at six. Trays enter and exit the slot in the door with barely more than a grunt from the hall. Vegetables are soggy and salty, meat grainy and bland, eggs runny and cold, the orange juice too tart to drink. I'd cut off a finger for those ribs on John T's plate, and so would every inmate on this row. Dredge beats on his door, and the metallic vibration resonates through the wall.

"Fuck you!" John T says. "And fuck everyone else in this place! May your mothers rot in hell."

"Same to you!" Dredge says.

Dredge likes to heat the pot until it boils. When things get too hot, he usually twists the knob in the opposite direction. Usually. I speak in a loud voice. "John T, may the Lord have mercy on your soul."

I have been here six months, and those are the first words I have directed to anyone besides my attorney.

"Fuck you, Preacher!" John T says, a sentiment inmates echo until it booms up and down the hall.

My cell has a window in the rear, and through it I can see the graveyard and its rows of tiny markers. Farther out, armed guards man the towers that overlook two fences running the perimeter. Razor wire tops the fences, and guard dogs patrol the exterior. Beyond, in the free world, palmettos and short oak trees grow from sandy earth. Florida scrubland. Full of rattlesnakes, blue-tailed lizards, and beer-drinking rednecks.

Earlier today, a man drove a backhoe into the graveyard and thrust the shovel into the earth, piled dirt alongside an ever-deepening hole. The man took a break at three o'clock, ate a chicken leg, then shoved a tape measure into the abyss. He climbed aboard and dug for another half an hour. Now, late in the afternoon, the backhoe is silent, immovable, and the brown mound it created shimmers in the setting sun. John T and I live on the same side of the block, and I wonder how he felt to see that dirt removed scoop by scoop.

I cannot endure the idea of maggots eating eyeballs, of fingernails growing long and curved. I cannot stop thinking about my mummified remains sinking through a rotted wooden bed. Next time my attorney visits, I will ask him to assume responsibility for my body. I have not thought beyond cremation, I only know I do not want to wind up in that graveyard.

Guards enter the hall, marching side by side. Shiny black boots strike the floor in unison. John T screams, and Dredge hollers something I can't make out. The block erupts but does not drown out that march. My hands clench and unclench, a fisted metronome that keeps time with the thud of determined leather soles. The beat consumes me. Fierceness that threatens to destroy me organ by organ. I wish for a cigarette, but the warden has deemed them unhealthy and his prison is a tobacco-free environment. An ironic proclamation, given death row is on perpetual lockdown and the exercise yard is off-limits. I feel myself dissolving into an organic puddle, a miscellany of putrefied DNA that was once Vernon L. Oliver. Here is when and where it ends; the floor is where I will exist for eternity. The marching stops, a cell door slides open, and the block quiets down.

"I distinctly asked for pork," John T says.

The block has a resigned feel, and I suppose every inmate wonders how he will act at this moment. The marching begins again, not as crisp as on entry. John T stumbles past. He has a pockmarked face and his eyes flit wildly, like he's trying not to miss anything in this second-to-last day of his life.

Twenty-four hours before the execution, the State of Florida transports the convict to a holding cell in the main prison a few miles outside Starke. We're three hours to the south, in a death row overflow that was added to a prison built back in the 1930s. Not imprisoning us where we die is the height of bureaucratic inefficiency, but it does enable us to escape these walls one last time.

I try to envision a convict's last ride, think of grass and two-car garages, of clouds against a blue canvas. I see cars and trucks flowing down the road, drivers oblivious to the unfolding event. I do not hold their naïveté against them. Their children attend school, their mothers and fathers grow old on wooden rocking chairs. These people work five days a week and spend Sundays in church. They have no idea of the horror that awaits the prisoner in the van.

John T has chosen the needle over the electric chair, and tomorrow he will feel the first pinprick at 5:45 p.m. A second needle, a backup, will be inserted into his other arm. Fifteen minutes later, the doctor will turn a knob and a sedative will drip down the long tube. Florida, the great moral authority that it is, puts its prisoners to sleep before killing them. This has nothing to do with humane treatment and everything to do with creating a tolerable atmosphere for AP reporters. Who besides the victim's family wants to watch a prisoner suffer? Who wants to hear the screams, the profanity? Who wants to see the mouth shape itself into an anguished oval?

Once John T is sedated, the State will send pancuronium bromide zooming into his vein. Not only will PB make John T piss on himself, it will stop his diaphragm and his ability to breathe. That alone is enough to do the job, but the ever-efficient State follows with a megadose of potassium chloride. PC stops the heart.

PC is the knockout punch.

In the morning, I wake before the lights come on. A hum escapes the vent high on the wall, the turn of a fan in a faraway location.

We live at a constant 72 degrees Fahrenheit. Someone down the block turns on a radio, and Garth Brooks comes over the airwaves. The breakfast tray arrives, and I drink tomato juice, eat the eggs, skip the bacon. I think of John T in the holding cell, isolated from the world, and wonder what his night was like last night. He has eleven hours left on this earth. Eleven hours. That is an amazing thought, and one I do not dwell on. John T's misery is his to suffer. I want no part of it.

From nine to twelve, I work on my book, then eat a cold cut for lunch. I stand at the window and sip milk out of a cardboard carton, watch sparrows circle over headstones and settle on the mound. The birds are so tiny it's difficult to believe they can fly at all. But then they are off, brown dots that disappear across the field.

In the past, I changed into a clean jumpsuit and tidied the cell in preparation for Sandoval's visit. I combed my hair, I wore my prison issue shoes and knotted the laces in neat figure eights. I thought about pleasantries we would exchange, worked out conversations beforehand. I did all this because that's what civilized people do. Now, I pick up a comb and gaze into the mirror, study the eyes that recede into dark sockets, the hair that falls in black tangles over my shoulders and down my chest. I drop the comb and turn away. I am in a cage on death row, barely more than an ape. Efforts to impress my attorney are a facade, a futile attempt to convince him we stand eyeball to eyeball on the evolutionary scale.

Sandoval sits in a chair in front of the door, and I assume my position on the floor. He wears a shirt open at the collar and short at the sleeves. It's a relaxed look, like he's headed for the coffee shop soon as we're done talking. He smiles, and I hate him for his white teeth and forays to the dentist. I brush twice a day using prison-issue paste, and my canines are turning yellow.

"Four hours," I say.

"Excuse me?"

"John T has less than four hours to live." I am a gorilla trapped in a rising tide. Water laps at my mouth and nose. I tilt my hairy head and breathe, treasure the air in my lungs.

"I think we might have a movie deal," Sandoval says.

"Yeah?"

"But first the autobiography. We need to finish it so the screenwriter has something to work from."

"Did you know they dug his grave the day before the execution?" I say.

"I didn't know the prisoners could see the graveyard from their cells."

I realize he's never seen prison from my perspective.

"Only this side of the block," I say.

Sandoval smiles that smile of his, the one he used when he talked to reporters on the courthouse steps.

"Listen, I've filed the paperwork for our first appeal."

"It's a waste of time."

"We must try."

"I signed a confession, I laid it all out."

"There are considerations," he says. "Questionable interrogation practices, extenuating circumstances—"

"I don't want to be buried in that graveyard. I want to be cremated and my ashes spread somewhere else."

Sandoval rises. "Keep the faith, Vernon. This isn't over yet."

"You bet," I say. "That's the spirit."

If I could slam the door, I would. If I could walk to another room, I would. The best I can do is turn and head for the far corner of my cell. In prison, even good-byes are beyond my control. He says he'll be in touch. I wish him well and go back to my countdown.

At 6:00 p.m., radios turn off. I have never heard the prison so quiet. At six thirty, the warden opens the slot, and his somber gaze seeks mine. He wears a wedding band and appears around forty-five, a veteran of state executions. I have not seen him since my second day of incarceration, when he dropped by to welcome me to the prison. I asked if he'd forgotten his fruit basket, and he'd laughed and moved on. For some convicts, the warden is the symbol of their incarceration and inspires hatred. Not me. To me, he's just some guy doing his job.

"Pronounced dead at six twenty," he says.

He goes cell to cell and repeats his words. Later that night, a pickup drives into the cemetery, and men dressed in blue uniforms remove the coffin from the bed. In the headlight glare, they lower John T into the ground, working quickly, like they have lovers at home.

I get out my pencil and paper. Writing keeps me sane; it's the only thing that keeps me going. Screw John T and his ribs, screw Sandoval and his appeal, screw his screenwriter who wants me to hurry along. This is my story, my life. The telling of it will proceed at my pace.

Chapter 4

THE HELICOPTER LIFTED FROM the tarmac and flew westward out of Miami, toward the seminary that awaited me. Buildings grew small under the skids, and cars on the asphalt ribbons shrunk into little more than toys. The Everglades took shape. A green mat that stretched horizon to horizon. Here and there, sun glanced off water, and slick surfaces shone blackly orange in the morning light. An hour later we began a descent into a yellow cloud. The rotors forced wind downward and the cloud parted and buildings on an island in the swamp appeared. The helicopter settled on a concrete pad, and I jumped out. Happy to have terra firma underfoot, I ducked away from the blades and headed toward a man wearing a cowboy hat. The helicopter lifted off, clearing a tunnel to the blue sky, and then the whirling blades were gone and the vapor reshaped itself. A bitter taste settled in my throat.

"Welcome to Bible Camp," Alton Pierce said, and spit red mucus into a handkerchief. A small man, he had lines on his forehead and appeared close to fifty. The hat had this turned-down brim, and yellow soot coated the crown. A feather drooped out of a black band. The feather was old and used up, like its owner.

"I love what you've done with the air," I said. "Puke yellow is my favorite color."

"We burn sulfur to keep the mosquitoes away."

"Carcinogen for breakfast, lunch, and dinner," I said. "No wonder you need a faith healer."

"Check the wit at the door, Mr. Oliver. I'm too busy to waste my time with banter."

I thought about asking for a claim check. Left it alone.

He suggested I leave my bag while he showed me around. I propped it against a building and followed him past the dorms, cafeteria, chapel, and classrooms. The architecture, Sharecropper Deluxe, looked like it had originated in the early 1900s. I studied the slatted wood on canted walls, shingles on lopsided roofs, the gray paint that peeled in strips and hung off eaves like embarrassed Spanish moss. A shiver came over me, a dog shaking off water, and for a strange moment I felt like the only human alive in a dying world.

We stepped off the sidewalk onto black dirt. Followed a footpath slightly downhill. I did not see a tree or plant or blade of grass; apparently nothing could live for long in this cloud. We walked another five minutes and came up on a crusted stovepipe that rose from the ground. Yellow smoke spewed upward and outward. I pictured a demon under the dirt, coughing and snorting, expelling this vile concoction to clear his sinuses. We continued on the path until we came to an electric fence. On the other side, in the bristling swamp, cypress and saw grass meshed into an impenetrable tangle. An animal thrashed, and a white heron shot upward and sailed out of sight. Movement in the water and an alligator surfaced.

Alton pointed to where a moccasin crawled across a mossed-over log, slithered up the slope, and stuck its head through a bottom link. White light flashed, an explosion of electricity, a sizzle that reminded me of frying sausage. I blinked. Watched the snake writhe down the slope. The head was charred beyond recognition, yet the body slapped against the dirt like it hadn't realized life was over. Water boiled, and white-rimmed jaws came together in a snap loud as a slammed Dumpster lid. Swirl of a long reptilian tail, a scaly exclamation point, and the alligator sank out of sight.

"Son of a bitch," I said. "I'm held hostage in Jurassic Park."

"Not to worry, Mr. Oliver. That fence is there to protect us from the creatures. You may drop out of Bible Camp anytime you wish. Of course, there is the bonus forfeiture should that occur."

My hand sought the wadded cash in my pocket. "I'm here for the long haul, Mr. Pierce. I'm here to learn things no mortal man should know. I'm here to learn who shot Kennedy, to discover where Hoffa is buried, to finally understand the truth about President Clinton's underwear. Mold me, O Sensi."

Alton hooked his thumbs in his belt. He spit at my feet, rocked back and forth. "Miriam said you would be a handful."

"Miriam has no idea."

"We need to get something straight, Mr. Oliver. You will take this seriously, or I'll run you out of here on the next flight."

A breeze blew over the island and pushed the haze into the swamp. The buildings came into focus, and I watched a steady stream of people exit a classroom. They were too far away for me to guess their ages, appeared to be a mix of men and women. A guy in a wheelchair tipped over, landed on his knees. Amid laughs and snide comments, he righted the chair and continued rolling over the sidewalk.

"Your employees," Alton said, wryly.

"Mine?"

"They'll be working for you soon enough."

We retraced our steps, and I took a wide bend around the stove-pipe and its belching smoke. When Miriam said she was sending me to a seminary near Lake Okeechobee, I had expected clean air and blue sky, golf carts that puttered around on electricity, computers that hummed invitingly, sleek buildings and celestial sidewalks so white they blinded the eye, a welcoming committee several years removed from death. I had not expected Pentecostal Hell. Not that it mattered. The money more than compensated for the environment and my instructor's humorless personality. I wondered if he ever laughed. Probably not. And who could blame him? That cough of his looked like a symptom of lung disease, no doubt derivative of breathing this air for long periods. I decided to lay off the verbal jabs. It was no fun punching someone too sick to fight back.

The students lived in a dorm, and that's where I expected to sleep, but Alton led me to a house off by itself. The walls leaned to the left. Supported a roof that was ready to slide off at any moment. Gutter spouts swung off the corners and clanked in the breeze. Alton grabbed the closest spout and tucked it under its strap, issued an apologetic smile.

"When we heard you were coming we only had time to remodel the inside."

"If I'd known you had planned for my arrival, I would have draped myself in a robe and arrived on the back of an ass." I inspected him for a response, perhaps a twinkle in his eye or an air-starved chuckle that didn't escape his larynx. Nothing; not even a nod.

We went inside to the living room. The walls and ceilings had recently been painted and the smell still hung in the air. I took a big breath, hoped the chemicals would dilute the sulfur taste at the back of my throat. It didn't work. Alton walked me through the house, pointing out the bedroom and its king-sized mattress ordered especially for me. He opened the walk-in closet, and I moved the Prada suits and silk shirts around on their hangers. Slipped into a pair of Italian loafers. They hurt my toes, so I jammed my feet back into my boots.

"We'll fly in a larger size," Alton said. "And we'll get a tailor out here if the suits don't fit."

"I'm not wearing this crap."

"Suit yourself." Alton doubled over and coughed. The coughs were deep and moist and tore at his chest. We went to the kitchen and he showed me the newly installed disposal, told me it didn't take kindly to metal utensils.

In the dining room, on an oblong table, champagne beckoned from an ice-filled bucket. I popped the cork and poured Dom Perignon into two glasses, watched bubbles float like silvery beads to the surface.

"Caviar?" Alton said, and scooted a dish across the table.

I dipped a cracker. Nibbled. "A little salty."

"It's an acquired taste that I've apparently never developed."

"Where can a guy get a cigarette around here?"

Alton told me to check the pantry, so I went back to the kitchen and opened the side-by-side doors next to the refrigerator. On the shelves were enough Marlboro cartons to keep me in smokes for at least a year. I lit a cigarette, poked around for an ashtray, wound up using a saucer. We walked into the living room and I sank into the couch, blew smoke rings toward the ceiling. Alton pointed out the phone and told me to dial nine for room service.

"I just pick up this phone and order anything I want?" I said.

"I recommend the steak and lobster. The chef has a marinade sauce that's quite tasty."

"How about a case of beer?"

"There are three cases in the fridge," Alton said. "I assume Budweiser is your preferred brand."

"For real?"

"Mr. Oliver. I may not tell you everything but I will never lie to you."

I picked up the phone. "How do I get an outside line?"

"We are on an island in the middle of nowhere. There are no outside lines."

"Satellite uplink?" I said.

"A what?"

I suspected Alton had lived much of his life on this island, that technology had sprinted past him so fast he hadn't seen it come or go.

"I take it," I said, "that Miriam told you to treat me well."

"She did."

"The beer and cigarettes, all her idea."

"Bible Camp is not a monastery. She wants us to make you as comfortable as possible during your stay."

I took off my boots and tossed them on the carpet. "I promised to call my girlfriend when I got here."

"I've already explained—"

"I want you to get a message to her through Miriam. I want you to say everything is fine and I can't call her because I'm in the middle of a hellhole with no outside lines."

"I'll see what I can do." Alton excused himself and walked out of the house. I hoped he got that message out soon as possible. Rickie wasn't exactly known for her patience.

† † †

My training began on day three. I got up around ten and dressed in jeans, biker T-shirt, Harley bandanna, and my black boots. The boots were too hot for this island, but I was prepared if one of those snakes made it past the fence.

The environment had not changed, even a little. The air was still yellow, still smelled like crap. I walked into the classroom and took a seat in the rear. Four guys and one young woman sat in the desks up front. Alton came in wearing his cowboy hat, stepped to the blackboard, and started class one minute after eleven o'clock.

"What's the most important ingredient?" Alton said. "What's the thing that sells a cancer miracle above all others?"

The woman raised her hand and suggested making friends with members of the congregation prior to the healing was the most important part. She said every cancer victim had a story, and that story sold the miracle. Laney Bitternut had a bland face, almost featureless. Like her baby fat had failed to dissolve. She had blue eyes and brown hair and wore a baggy shirt and baggy jeans, the kind of woman who could slink anywhere and go unnoticed. She sat respectfully erect, as though she were in the presence of Aristotle himself.

Alton wrote "The Story" on a chalkboard and asked if anyone else had a suggestion. One of the guys spoke up and said visuals were most important. Chauncey Upton wore a Michigan State jersey. Like Laney, his face lacked distinction; a common nub of a nose, lips that formed a pleasant enough line but did not stand out in any appreciable way, a jaw that was neither large nor small. His hair was a different matter altogether. He had an Einstein frizz. A white man's 'Fro large enough to frustrate any brush.

"A cough," Chauncey said, "a raggedy, deep cough—"

"Not all cancers cause a cough," Laney said.

"Anyone else?" Alton stared me down, and I knew my high school act had come to an end. Scratching my armpit and fumbling answers were not going to satisfy this guy.

"Smell," I said. "A decaying smell is the secret ingredient to selling this miracle."

My classmates snickered.

"Care to explain how to pull that off?" said Alton.

"It's an elegant solution," I said. "You rub rotting meat on your jacket, then you take the jacket off and leave it onstage. After you get healed you walk among the congregation smell-free. It's an association game. Sick people smell like death, healed people don't. You no longer smell like roadkill, ergo God's hand performed its miraculous touch once again. Works every time."

Alton wrote "Decaying Smell" on the blackboard, and my classmates took turns sneaking glances in my direction. Laney looked longest and hardest. A buzzer went off twenty minutes later, and we all filed out. At least classes were short. Laney asked if I was hungry, and I said I could always eat.

The cafeteria had a serving line that curved around one wall and halfway down the other. I picked out a hamburger and baked beans, and she picked out a green salad and Thousand Island dressing. We carried our trays to a table and settled in across from each other. I dumped ketchup on my hamburger. Took a bite. Students sat at surrounding tables, and chatter filled the room. I decided not to call attention to the catering service out the back door, figured there was no reason to rub Laney's face in it. This island was too small for enemies.

On one of the walls hung a poster of a young man on a stage.

He wore a black shirt and black pants, and the camera had caught him in the middle of a backward fall. A preacher stood nearby, hand outstretched. Laney asked if I knew anything about the man in that photo.

"Which one?" I said.

She took a bite out of her salad, chewed, and swallowed. "That's a picture of Alton Pierce in his prime."

I saw no resemblance.

"He likes you," she said.

"Yeah?"

"He wouldn't give you the time of day if he didn't. That's how Alton is. He sees potential and he'll work with you. If you stink it up, he'll blow you off."

I ate a spoonful of baked beans, sipped iced tea. This room, like the classroom, was cool and sulfur-free, leading me to believe Bible Camp had supersized filters on its air conditioners. Overhead, ceiling fans moved enough air to produce additional cooling. Chauncey—he had a hot dog and bun on his plate—walked up and sat down. He extracted a pencil from behind his ear and tapped the eraser on the table. I studied his frizz. Wondered if he had anything else hidden up there.

"A resplendent and salient suggestion," Chauncey said. "Perspicacious and at the same time quixotic."

He had this strange way of staring at a spot on my face, like he was too nervous to meet my gaze. He zeroed in on my forehead.

"I never would have considered smell," he said. "In that milieu, as a redirection it should function every time."

"Where did you buy that vocabulary?" I said. "*Reader's Digest?*"

Laney snorted and dropped her fork on her plate. Chauncey

shot her a sneer, and his voice turned hard. "You will probably excel in this area of expertise. Ascend to the mountaintop, so to speak."

Laney snorted again.

"Why don't you tell him the truth?" she said to me. "Why don't you come out and say it?"

I kept quiet.

"Chauncey," she said, "you're talking to the next big faith healer, you dumbass."

His gaze brushed my eyes and settled on my chin.

I poured Sweet 'n Low into my tea. "What gave it away?"

Her cheeks turned pink, and she looked down at her salad.

"Really," I said. "Did Alton say something?"

"Look around," she said. "Do you see anyone who stands out in a crowd? Do you see anyone you would look twice at?"

I took a big bite of hamburger and spent a long time chewing. My classmates were forgettable, an important ingredient to miracle-faking. No one was too tall or too short or too ugly or too pretty. A little makeup, a change in hairstyle, and they could work in anonymity night after night. I glanced at Chauncey and wondered when he planned a trip to the barber, spotted the fabric at the temple. He was wearing a wig.

"You're a hot guy," she said. "Black hair, tall, got a smile that won't quit. You've got the 'it' factor."

Chauncey pushed away from the table and walked out of the room.

"Don't mind him," Laney said. "His ambition outweighs his talent and he knows it."

"And you?"

Laney ate half her salad before she replied. "I work hard and I don't mind long hours. Hire me and I'll be the best actor who ever walks on your stage."

I studied the picture on the wall, imagined that was me up there instead of that preacher, saw my hand come out and slap Alton on the head. A jittery feeling swept through me. I had lived my life avoiding responsibility, and now I was about to become a star. To survive in this milieu, as Chauncey suggested, I needed the loyalty of those working for me. And I knew just how to get it.

Wednesday, during Paraplegic class, I got the word out that I was having a Bible Camp bash. I asked Alton to hijack the helicopter next time it came in, wanted him to fly to a liquor store and get enough alcohol for twenty people.

"Twenty-two including you and me," I said. "Let's see. . . . We need some scotch, gin, champagne, and red wine for the ladies."

"You might want to alert the chef. He'll probably need to place a special order for the appetizers."

Thursday came and went. Friday arrived with a knock on my door. I followed Alton to the landing pad, where I picked up a crate of assorted liquor and carried it back to my house. Bible Camp seemed energized that day. My classmates smiled more readily, and the laughs seemed extra loud and long. I skipped Blind Man class, arranged bottles on the kitchen counter, thanked the cook when he brought the appetizer trays. The lights were too bright, so I backed off the dimmer switches until the edges in the room blurred and melded into each other. As an afterthought, I wrote a note and laid it on my pillow. ("No sex on my bed.") Last thing I wanted was to fall asleep in a nasty wet spot.

Laney was the first to arrive. She handed me a bottle of cheap wine, and I set it on the counter.

"We need some music," she said.

I pointed out the CD player and suggested I needed a DJ for the night. She punched the buttons, and Bob Marley rhythms vibrated the speakers. I poured a scotch on the rocks and watched her swivel her hips. She wore a sundress and purple flip-flops. Looked comfortable as hell. I moved the chairs and sofa to the walls, joined her with drink in hand. The music, the soft light, and the alcohol created an unexpected eroticism, and she moved into my arms and we danced that way until the doorbell rang. Chauncey, Dean Kirkridge, and Billy Brown came in, and I told them to help themselves to whatever they wanted. Alton arrived and sank into the couch. Latched onto a champagne bottle. The place filled, and Laney turned up the music. Stacy Ollinger pranced through the doorway wearing a toga, whooped it up, and danced with her arms over her head. Stacy loved to tell stories about how her pa on the farm back in Arkansas cut off pig testicles and poured motor oil over the wound to help it heal. I didn't know if she was a man-hater or what, only knew she was never getting near my balls.

I hunted up Alton and found him in the kitchen pouring drinks. His eyes were glazed, and he explained the ins and outs of miracle-faking to anyone who would listen. I said, "Praise the Lord," and someone in the crowd said, "Preach it, brother." Laney turned down the music, and I jumped up on a chair. Bright faces turned my way.

"We have come together," I said. "We have come together, my flock, to honor the Lord and to cherish our time at this holy place."

"Hallelujah," said Alton.

Big-haired Chauncey fell to the floor and writhed around and spoke in tongues. His voice was flat, an equal pause between words, a superb technique that reminded me of channeling. He kept it up for a full five minutes, finally stopping to catch his breath among a chorus of boos. Laney closed her eyes, extended her hands, and clutched my knee.

"What a big nose you have, Pastor Oliver," she said.

The boos stopped and roars of "Heal the blind woman" began.

"And Jesus said," I intoned. "Where one or two are gathered together, I shall appear."

"Praise the Lord," Alton said. "Praise God Almighty."

"In the name of the Holy Ghost and the Holy Spirit," I said. "In the name of all that is righteous, including Bible Camp and its esteemed professor, I command the devil to leave this woman."

I slapped Laney with both palms, and she laughed so loud and long she caught a case of the hiccups. My classmates formed a line, and in the ensuing hour I healed a cancer victim, someone with palsy, a humpback who stuffed a couch pillow under his shirt, and a paraplegic unceremoniously dumped on the carpet at my feet. Alton drank champagne and critiqued every attempt. The party lasted longer than I thought, and I drank more than I should have, once staggering into the bedroom and finding Laney naked and on top of Chauncey. So much for no sex on my bed. Although I suspected Chauncey was openly defying me, I shut the door and went back to the living room. I'd deal with Vocabulary Genius later.

Alton fell asleep on the couch, and the party wound down. I turned off the music and brightened the lights. Laney and Chauncey came out of the bedroom and said good night. Left holding hands. I helped Alton to the door, and he grabbed my collar.

"You will be the west who ever slived," he said.

I asked if he needed help, and he said he'd make it on his own. In the bedroom, I took off my clothes and thought about Rickie. She would have loved the expensive liquor, all these people dancing and having a good time. I sat on the bed, imagined her underneath me and fresh out of the shower. Hair wet and uncombed, skin smelling of strawberry body wash, that half smile she sometimes had when she looked at me. My hand slipped below my waist and I rolled onto my back, then rolled to the floor and wiped the wetness off my ass. Damn Laney and Chauncey. Next time I held a party I was locking the bedroom door.

I woke to a throbbing knot inside my skull, went to the kitchen and choked down a glass of tomato juice and vodka. My headache went away, and I looked around for the clock. Found it under a chair. Fifteen minutes past one, which meant I was late for Blind Man class. I think this was Alton's favorite miracle because he lit up when he talked about it. He knew it inside out, said one way to pull it off was to express yourself with hand movements that came a beat or two after you spoke. The time lapse between spoken word and physical demonstration created an oddity that satisfied the curious. You were blind, therefore you did strange things.

Alton was late, and Laney was for staying and waiting. Chauncey wanted to go. Everyone was hungover, and when one of the guys up front ran for the bathroom in the hall, the room cleared and everyone went their own way. I walked to the cafeteria, knocked on the back door, and talked to the chef. Royce Ashford had quit smoking years ago and dangled unlit stogies from his lips. He hadn't come to the party, had said if he started drinking again he'd wind up frying in the electric fence.

"Here," I said, and handed him a hundred-dollar bill. "A tip for the appetizers."

He stuck the bill in his pocket and went back inside. Royce didn't talk much.

Alton lived in a room attached to the cafeteria. I knocked and stood around outside his door. I tried the knob—it was unlocked—so I went inside and flicked the light switch, almost stumbled on the mattress on the floor. In the corner, on an end table, a single burner and a quart-sized pot occupied a metal tray. On a plate, crusted bread sprouted rainbow-colored mold.

Laney came in and said the actors were forming a search party. "Chauncey and I are starting with the dorms."

I told her I would check the perimeter and make sure he hadn't stumbled into the fence. She said we would have heard an explosion, but I was checking anyway. I walked outside, across the dirt, to the downslope that angled toward the snakes and alligators and whatever else swam those black waters.

In the swamp, on a log that angled into the water, a snake stretched out like a speckled belt. The snake had a bulge in its neck, and frog legs stuck out its mouth. Jaws convulsed, and a quarter inch of green sucked into the throat. The snake swallowed again and another quarter inch disappeared. Its windpipe stuck out the side of its jaw, and I thought about throwing dirt through the fence and plugging that air tube so the snake couldn't breathe and maybe he'd unswallow the frog, but the frog was already dead and well past rescuing, so what was the point? I watched until the webbed feet slid inward and disappeared, and the snake's mouth closed and the snake lay still.

I took a clockwise route around the island. Kept well away from the fence. The occasional mosquito braved the haze, and I killed it wherever it landed on my body, which was mostly on my arms. A small shape formed in the murk. I conjured up an image of Alton passed out on the dirt, mosquitoes on every exposed square inch, bleeding him until there was nothing but a cowboy hat and rotted lungs. A moan came from the shape, and I knew he wasn't dead, so I walked up and nudged his shoulder.

Alton's knees curled to his chest, and he was covered in sulfur dust, probably the only thing that kept the mosquitoes from sucking him dry. Bloody saliva trickled out of his mouth and pooled in the dirt. I shook his shoulder, and he opened his eyes. He stretched out his legs and rose to his feet, looked unsteady, so I stood between him and the fence. His hat lay in the dirt, and he made no move to pick it up.

"I was great," he said. "I was the best ever."

"I saw your picture in the cafeteria."

"I was young. I had moves you've never dreamed of."

His voice sounded dark and came from far away, a place I didn't want to go. "I heard about the tornado," he said. "I heard it dipped down and ripped up the tent. I heard they found the pulpit twenty miles to the east."

"We were lucky."

An alligator bellowed, an echo that died in the cypress. Sweat dripped down my neck and pooled between my shoulder blades. I was right about my boots. They were too hot for this island.

"That tornado was the hand of God," Alton said. "That was a direct sign."

"Think so?"

"One day we'll pay the piper." Alton picked up his hat, slapped it on his head. "One day we'll get what's coming to us."

I believed there was *a* God, but I didn't believe *in* God—and I didn't want to argue the point with someone who thought a supreme being sat up in heaven and hurled storms at deserving sinners. Religious faith aside, I refused to consider the rightness or wrongness of my actions, didn't want morals to get in the way. I was here, I was making two thousand a week, and if my future employment included fooling a few million people into giving up their paychecks, so be it. We were all fools. Some more than others.

I walked Alton to his room and helped him into bed. Brought him a glass of water and placed it on the floor next to the mattress. I wanted to tell him he wouldn't find redemption in self-flagellation, that a thousand miles of bloody knees and prostrate prayers were exactly that and nothing more.

"I have something you should know," he said.

"Can't this wait until tomorrow?"

He sipped from the glass and lay back on the pillow. "Rickie quit the carnival."

"She quit?"

"That's all Miriam said, 'Rickie quit the carnival.'"

"What do you mean that's all she said?"

Alton closed his eyes.

"I want to fly out of here today," I said. "I'm packing up and you get that helicopter out here."

"The helicopter is down for scheduled repairs; be down for seven days."

I turned toward the door, spun back around. "How do you get word to Miriam?"

"We exchange messages through the helicopter pilot."

"You knew about this when he flew in the liquor order?"

"I didn't want to ruin the party," he said.

Didn't want to ruin the party? I felt like throttling him.

Chapter 5

AFTER THAT FIRST APPEAL, which went as I expected—no new trial for Vernon L. Oliver—Sandoval visits once every three months. I stop work on my autobiography and watch a spider build a web in the corner of my room. The spider, not much bigger than a quarter, has a bluish tint on its back, tiny hairs that stand straight up and remind me of a punk rocker. I have been here two years, and this is the first being other than myself to enter this cell. This change stuns and excites me. I think about naming her Sting, decide that's too obvious and call her Intrepidus instead. She is a brave little spider, and I resolve to treat her well.

Monday afternoon, I sit at my desk and sift through a stack of letters I have allowed to accumulate. I open a small envelope from Kenya and flatten a folded page. The script is written in loopy letters, a woman's hand:

> Dear Preacher,
>   I pray for you to get out of prison and come to my village and heal my papa. We live in small village outside Nairobi. If you come we roast pig and have great feast and I give you necklace of lion claws. Please come and

we praise the God and we sing his song and you heal my papa. You great preacher, you talk to spirits and they listen, you speak to God and he bring down his mighty hand and you smite the spirits and they go from where they are hiding.

    Please come.

                        Sincerely,
                        Sister Amondi

Dredge taps the wall three times, which means someone on the block wants a private conversation. I stand on a chair, turn so my ear is against the air-conditioning vent. The vent is metal and cold, and attaches to the duct that branches between cells. A voice comes through the flowing air, a cordial hello, and I answer accordingly. Dredge has an idea he wants to share.

"I could always starve myself to death," he says. "I could flush the food down the toilet and give the guard an empty tray and in three weeks they wouldn't know what hit them. Or I could eat it and throw it up. Women kill themselves all the time doin' that."

Dredge is planning an escape, the death row euphemism for suicide.

"Or," he says, "I could slam my head into the wall. I'd turn my radio up real loud and shout to drown out the sound. If I did it three or four times, I'd crack my head open for sure."

Dredge's fascination for planning his death may be annoying, but I don't deny him his pleasure, knowing the more we talk about it the less likely conversation will take an uncomfortable turn. I do not want to hear how he purchased insulation from Home Depot and soundproofed his house. Nor do I want to hear the lilt in his voice when he describes the hunt for each boy he nailed to the door. Dredge, a selective predator, wanted only boys who had brown hair and freckles. I haven't asked why.

A voice comes from farther away, and I recognize a convict who lives across the hall. I cup my ear against the vent and listen hard. Jermaine Jenkins is this black guy from some farm in the northern part of the state, and he murdered his mother and grandmother for their welfare checks. Then he stole a car and drove to Atlanta, where the police caught him hugged up with two crack whores.

"You could hang yourself," Jermaine says.

Jermaine is racist, always talking about how the white man done him wrong, and how his brothers will rise up one day and take over this prison and "Where you honkies gonna be when that happens?" Other than that, he isn't a bad guy. He draws pictures and gives them to his attorney, who sells them on the outside. Jermaine makes so much money he needs an accountant, says if he ever gets out of here he's headed to some mountaintop somewhere and wants to be left alone. Says he'll shoot the first flour-skinned prick who sets foot on his property.

"You could tear your sheets into little strips," Jermaine says. "You could work them through this here vent and tie them around your neck. Kill you deader than a doornail, cracker."

"That's a good idea," Dredge says. "Hear that, Preacher? That nigger said I could hang myself no problem."

The vent goes silent, so I step off the chair and walk to the rear of my cell. If I didn't have this window, I don't know what I'd do. The sky is the color of dead fish, and rain spatters the puddles. It has stormed for five days, no sign of letting up, and the graveyard is a swamp. I conjure up an image of John T under the soil, water filtering down, trickles that seep into the coffin and drip on his body. I feel the water on my forehead, I swipe at my skin. I tell myself that is not me out there, that I am not dead, not in a coffin, not in that graveyard. But I feel moisture, I smell decay, I see darkness.

I turn from the window and sit at the desk. The Nairobi letter beckons, and I read it again and again. I tell myself I am not a door coming loose at the hinges, my head is screwed on tight. Dredge taps the wall and I have to go to the vent, otherwise he won't stop.

"What?" I say. "What do you want?"

"He had a mole below his right collarbone," Dredge says. "His name was Stevie and I caught him walkin' home from this pond. He had a fishin' pole over his shoulder, this real Andy of Mayberry moment."

When Dredge talks about his murders, he skips the sexual assaults. Stevie was Dredge's second victim. The boy had a mother and a father and two sisters and went to elementary school in a small town in the middle of the state. At the moment of abduction, the boy fought and lost his front teeth in the process.

"You should have seen those teeth," Dredge says. "They looked like bloody eggshells. If he had come quietly, he might not have got killed."

I have become Jailhouse Confessor, a position I didn't apply for and a position I don't want. And still I listen. I'm not sure why. Maybe I'm one of those rubberneckers who slows down his car and sticks his head out the window when he drives past accidents on the interstate. Or maybe I listen because these men are broken and I want to find out why. Maybe I want to blame their murders on a father who beat his son, a mother who refused to nurture her baby, an uncle who raped his nephew; maybe I want to make sense of chaos.

"Get right with the Lord," I say, "and he'll forgive your transgressions and take you into his fold."

Hope.

I've been selling that lie for years.

Lights may go out at ten, but the prison is a miniature city that never sleeps. Two convicts argue down the block, voices bold and penetrating. Footsteps echo in the hall, and from deep in the walls comes the scrape of metal doors opening and closing. We had meat loaf for supper and the smell, like a greasy fart, hangs in the air. I listen for feet thumping the wall in Dredge's cell, wonder if tonight will be the night. I doubt it. Thinking about suicide is one thing, pulling it off is another.

That thought brings me to my own life, takes me backward, mind floating freely, to a time when I stood in the grass near my sister's tombstone. Silvington had two cemeteries, one on the north side, where doctors and lawyers and rich farmers were buried, and one on the south side, where the less fortunate wound up. The south side had a white picket fence around the perimeter, and gravestones were modest pieces of granite. Here and there, wilted flowers drooped over vases and angled toward the grass. I had wanted Lucy buried on the north side, where the mausoleums reminded me of Stonehenge and seemed more respectful and more deserving of the dead. The north side had a full-time caretaker, and the flowers were always fresh.

I studied the dirt piled on top of Lucy's coffin, kicked at a beetle that scurried within range, sniffed fried smells escaping a nearby Burger Hut. Mom had this expression on her face, a rawness that suggested she was wounded in a way that would never heal. As we walked back to the car, I looked from marker to marker, names and dates a blur, trying to make sense of here today and gone tomorrow. The unfairness of it all hit me hard. Surely God knew an innocent had died.

That evening, as my parents entertained the neighbors, and pies, deep-dish pizza, and macaroni casseroles filled our kitchen counters, I stole a rope and a cinder block from a nearby yard. Then I rode my bicycle toward Zelldagger Creek, this twisty ribbon of water that bordered our trailer park. When I came to the last trailer on the street, I stopped and watched a man spray a white car and soap down the windshield. He wore shorts and appeared my father's age. A woman knelt on the grass and pulled weeds out of a flower bed, tossed them over her shoulder. Near her hip, a baby squirmed in a bassinet. I did not begrudge their happiness. Some people were destined to live happy lives, and some weren't.

On the bank, I knotted the rope around the block and knotted the other end around my neck. Spring rains had swelled the creek, and water licked at the plants on the shoreline. Lucy—I had called her Pepper because I sneezed if I was around her for any length of time—had had a rare blood disorder, a disease doctors gave up on soon as they made the diagnosis. No hope, no cure. That was the verdict. That was the fucking verdict.

I jumped off the bank and sank to the bottom, landed on my knees and settled to my heels, waited for the moment when I could no longer hold my breath and water rushed into my lungs. I opened my eyes, felt the cold current against my pupils, glared through the murkiness at the plants in the sand, watched a minnow dart into and out of the shadows. My lungs were scorched earth, a firestorm that threatened to suck me dry, and still I sat. And then, because I was a snot-nosed coward, my fingers sought the knot on the block, fumbled, worked at it . . . worked at it . . . worked at it . . .

Upward I kicked, toward the shimmering surface. I burst through and swam to the bank, crawled heaving into the bullrushes. I don't know what I expected; a bright light, a message from God, an invitation to the mother ship, but nothing happened. The water still ran westward, the sky was still blue, the clouds were still motionless. I was alive, and Lucy was still dead.

In the morning, I tell my brave little punk rocker hello. A ruckus down the block and someone shouts angry words. I tell her not to pay attention, that she is safe with me. She has a resigned expression, like she realizes she built her web on the wrong side of the tracks. I hop around and toss my head, tuck my hands under my armpits, and flap my elbows, anything to perk her up.

"Are you hungry?" I say. "Is that the problem?"

My food tray arrives, and I flick bacon onto her web. She walks in a circle, cutting silver strands until the crumb falls to the floor. I flush what's left of my food into the toilet, watch the eggs swirl downward. We are in this together, and if she's not eating I'm not eating.

Dredge bangs on my wall for hours, and I do not go to the vent. At six o'clock, my stomach has shrunk to the point of pain, and I conclude only a crazy person would go on a simpatico fast with a spider. I take off my shoe, raise it high, and bring it down hard. Intrepidus falls to the floor, legs curled inward, a spider whose life has ended.

I pick up my radio and throw it against the door. Convicts raise their voices until they are a full-throated roar. I hurl and slam and kick that radio into a trillion pieces.

The Dredges of the world, the John Ts, the Jermaines who killed their loved ones, deserve to be here. These are the scum of the earth and they should go willingly to the gurney. I am not like these people. I deserve to suffer, I surely do, but enough is enough.

Chapter 6

T HE HELICOPTER BANKED AWAY from Bible Camp and flew in an easterly direction. The cabin air, which smelled of axle grease and oil, was cooler than on the island, and I wished I had grabbed my jacket out of the closet. Alton sat next to the pilot, and his cowboy hat blocked my view. I pressed my forehead against the window, looked toward the tail rotor, watched the clouds redden as the sun fell behind them. On the island, the world had seemed claustrophobic, an environment that extended only a few feet beyond the electric fence. Down there, it had seemed easy to locate Rickie. Simple as flying to a phone, calling her cell, and saying hello. Up here, the horizon seemed impossibly far away, and the world felt huge, the task of finding her next to impossible.

The sky darkened and the stars came out and a half-moon appeared. Far below, headlights lit a road, a car traveling into the night, and soon a city took shape, a twinkling display of white, yellow, and red glows. We dropped in altitude, and skyscrapers loomed. Miami Beach, a pallid strip, appeared beneath the skids.

We flew over the water, and forty-five minutes later a scatter of lights appeared in the distance. The pilot turned on a tangent that took us along the shore of a narrow island, flying low, and soon the helicopter settled toward blinking orbs. The skids touched the ground, the blades slowed their rotation, and Alton and I got out. The Bahama air smelled salty and fresh. Felt balmy on my skin. The sidewalk led to a large house, where ten-foot ceramic flamingos stood on opposite sides of the door and peered down at all who entered. I stared up at eyes large as softballs, studied beaks long as samurai swords.

During one of Alton's more loquacious moods, he had filled me in on the history of the Double Flamingo, which had operated as a brothel from 1891 to 1957. The Double Flamingo advertised two orgasms for the price of one, an oddity in the prostitution world, where historically the goal is to get it up, get it in, and get it off. Patrons stayed from two hours to two days. The girls bragged each customer left with his organ at half-mast, a selling point for sailors who anchored boats offshore.

Alton invited me inside, to an expansive sitting room, which I suspected looked much as it had when the brothel was in full swing. Various arrangements crisscrossed the floor, a two-seater here, a five-seater there. I imagined the paleness of a gartered thigh against velvet upholstery, a breast exposed over by the wooden bar, an arm seductively draped over the back of a leather recliner. I walked across the room to a window that faced the ocean, listened to waves break over the shoreline. Wondered how many sailors had come ashore on this beach. Thousands? Tens of thousands?

Murmurs behind me, Miriam and Alton in low tones, and still I stayed at the window. Somewhere in the bushes, a cricket sang its night song, notes rising and falling, an unanswered invitation. The helicopter took off, and I knew Miriam and I were alone. Footsteps crossed the carpet, pads aimed in my direction, and I smelled her directly behind me. The luscious whiff of an intoxicating perfume.

"Welcome to Harbour Island," Miriam said.

I looked down at my hands and saw they were shaking.

"You have a beautiful back, Mr. Oliver," she said. "But I prefer talking face-to-face."

Giggles in the night, voices of a boy and a girl, drifted from the beach. Their bodies reflected moonlight, and their nakedness glowed against the ocean. They moved on, out of sight, chatter lost under the sound of breaking waves. I turned and looked down at Miriam, who gazed at me with raised eyes and a slight smile. She was dressed island-style, white shirt and white pants, and her toenails were a delicate pink. A bracelet glimmered around each ankle. She asked if I liked wine, I said sure, and she filled two glasses. We sat on a three-seater, and her leg settled against mine.

"I gave Rickie your message," Miriam said. "Told her you were in a place where communication was difficult. Next day, I looked out and her RV was gone, nothing but grass and tire ruts where she'd pulled in."

The wine went down easy, and she brought out a new bottle. We drank that bottle and she excused herself for a minute, returned holding a camera.

"Do you photograph all your guests?" I said.

"It's for the corporation designing the stage."

I scrubbed my fingernails over the bristles on my jaw. If I'd known about this I would have shaved before the flight. She lowered the camera, brought it back to her eye. "Take off your clothes."

"Are you sure you didn't hire a porn company?" I said, and unbuttoned my shirt. The clicking camera followed my movement, watched me unlace my boots and extricate my feet, adjusted itself to the slope of my legs as I pulled off my pants. I had never had a woman use this ploy to get me in bed, and I admit I was intrigued. The energy that had swirled between us back at the carnival, the night she made the job offer, overtook me, and her voice came quick and firm.

"This is business," she said. "The sooner we get this over with the better."

The storm below my waist subsided, and calm seas returned. I stood in the middle of the room, turned around when she asked, assumed various positions for minutes at a time. Eventually, I felt like a bored model in front of scrawling art students. After an hour or so, she told me to put my clothes back on.

"I should call Rickie," I said.

"Phone's in the den. You'll have to dial the operator, then give the number."

She bent over to pick up my pants and her top opened, exposing her breasts. She caught me looking and smiled the smile of a woman who knows what every man wants.

My boss, Miriam, forty-year-old tease.

Morning light came through the screen and warmed the guest bedroom. I stood at the window and watched the sand turn pink as the sun climbed above the sea. In the yard, a black man pushed a wheelbarrow over low-cut grass, picked up fallen palm fronds and stacked them high. He saw me and nodded his grayed head. I nodded back and headed for the phone, intent on calling Rickie for the twentieth time.

The den was in the rear of the house and was once a smoking room for brothel customers. On the wall, above a wide-armed chair, a painting hung on a golden nail. The mermaid was naked from the waist up, and her blond tassels discreetly wrapped around her neck and covered her breasts. The room had the scent of too many cigars smoked in a confined area.

I dialed the operator and offered Rickie's cell number. Static came over the line, followed by a computerized voice.

"... no longer in service."

I slammed down the phone and opened a new pack of cigarettes, twisted the plastic film into a crumpled ball. If I knew where her parents lived, I'd call and leave a message, but I didn't know where they lived, didn't even know their first names. Miriam came in and handed me a coffee and grilled cheese sandwich. She wore a halter top and black tights. Had painted her nails shiny red.

"No luck?" she said.

"Same recording every time."

She asked if I'd like to see the next island to the south, and I said sure. I ate the sandwich and drank the coffee and followed her to the garage, where an old pickup truck was parked among furniture odds and ends. The truck was a green 1957 Chevy, and a thatched roof perched where there should have been metal. There were no windows. She asked me to drive and suggested I wear the sunglasses hanging on the wheel to avoid getting an eye poked out.

"Grasshoppers are bad this time of year," she said.

Properly attired, I backed out and drove down a palm-tree-lined driveway. Following her direction, I maneuvered through town, a collage of clapboard New England and columned colonial architecture. A warehouse appeared on the right, and she asked me to back up to the doors. I did as she requested, and we waited as islanders loaded boxes into the bed.

A short time later, I drove out of town and crossed a bridge between islands. Miriam welcomed me to Eleuthera, told me the roof tended to come apart if the truck traveled more than thirty miles per hour, so I eased off the accelerator and cruised along. On the right, the Caribbean Sea sparkled shades of blue. The beaches were creamy in color and reminded me of buttermilk my mother fed me as a child. Naked black children stood on porch stoops in front of tin shacks and watched us drive down the road. I had no idea where we were headed, or when we would get there, but I wanted to know what was in those boxes. I hoped it was something besides drugs. I'd signed on as a preacher. Narcotic distribution was not in my job scope.

Miriam asked me to pull over and I swung the truck off the asphalt, jounced over a rut, and stopped beside a car so rusted it looked as if it might come apart in the wind. We watched an islander wade the shallows. Throw a cast net in perfect circles. He deposited fish, glittering and flopping, in a bucket that floated at his side. A pigtailed girl squatted in the sand and applauded each cast.

"Do you have any regrets?" Miriam said. "Have you ever done anything you wish you could take back?"

"I'm too young for regrets."

Her head moved side to side, like she shook off my words.

"I'm serious," she said. "Is there anything you wish you could take back?"

I did not want this conversation.

"I can see it on your face," Miriam said. "I can see you remembering."

I focused on the man, watched him throw that net, watched the caught fish flop into the bucket. "It's nothing; a few childhood memories is all."

She asked me to drive on, said there were people waiting, so I guided the truck onto the highway, and we rolled south at twenty miles per hour. Fronds crackled overhead. She was right about the grasshoppers. I wasn't driving fast enough to kill them, but the impact stunned them, and they staggered around the cab like besotted sailors. At the midway point of the island, Miriam began talking about herself in an urgent voice. I kept both hands on the wheel and did not interrupt.

Miriam MacKenzie had been born to Scottish parents, who, when they turned seventeen, took a ship across the ocean to seek fortune in the land of milk and plenty. Turns out, in Dremond, Wisconsin, the town where they ended up, there was milk and not much plenty. Miriam was raised on a dairy farm and started her days before the sun came up, when she helped her father milk the cows. Later, after she returned from school, she fed the chickens, mucked out stalls, and shoveled manure into the pit behind the barn.

"My parents had been raised next to the sea," she said. "They could look at the sky and tell you if there was a storm brewing, they knew the tides and where to string their nets, but they didn't know anything about farming. We weren't just poor, we were dirt poor. . . . I got a scholarship to the University of Wisconsin, left home, and never looked back."

She'd earned a business degree, worked as an accountant for a Chicago firm, saved her money, and invested in the first interesting proposition to come along. The canival was owned and run by an old man who died within days of her investment. She took over. Fired everyone who didn't want to work for a woman.

"I heard you had sex shows in the early days," I said. "Johnny Bentley said something about midgets—"

"Stephan and Pauline! Thinking about them does bring back

the memories. They were a married couple who put on a show for two hours a night, every night of the week. Hated every minute of it, as I recall."

I laughed.

"Seriously," she said. "They were like McDonald's employees eating free lunches. Eat hamburger every day, you wind up hating hamburger."

We drove up on a group of islanders in front of a row of weathered houses built against an outcropped rock. A palm tree bent in the breeze, which I surmised never stopped.

"We're here," Miriam said.

I parked in a dirt yard and turned off the motor. Men, women, and children surged forward. They wore ragged clothing over thin black bodies, had hungry eyes, the kind I'd seen on the homeless walking city streets back in the States. It dawned on me what was in the back of the truck, and I jumped into the bed and ripped open the boxes, handed out cereal, canned goods, rice sacks, macaroni and cheese, flour, salt, sugar, beans, and vitamins. Miriam patted a little girl who wandered past, said hello to a teenage boy missing his front teeth. I watched her out of the corner of my eye. I had never met someone so difficult to figure out. She planned to fleece millions, yet she gave to those in need. She seemed to want me sexually, yet wouldn't step over that line. She loved kids, although she never mentioned raising any of her own.

Supplies dwindled and eventually there was nothing left. The islanders moved off, carrying whatever they had grabbed, voices high-pitched and singsong. Miriam suggested it was time to go, so we got in the truck and drove toward Harbour Island. I glanced at her from time to time.

"What?" she said.

"What do you mean, 'what?'?"

"You're looking at me funny."

I stopped the truck and waited for goats to work their way across the road. They had a wet-hair smell, could crap and walk at the same time. A young girl, in a wraparound dress, raised a stick and prodded the slackers. Herded them over a rise in the land. On the dash a grasshopper recovered equilibrium and whirred toward parts unknown. Miriam looked at me, I mean really looked, like she was trying to see my soul.

"If you want, I'll help you find her," she said. "I'll direct some resources to it and we'll come up with something sooner or later."

"She might be back at her mother's, which I think is somewhere in Colorado."

"She's not at her mother's."

"She could be anywhere," I said. "But that's where I'd start looking."

Miriam got out a Kleenex and dabbed the welling wetness around her eyes. "She might be with the people who raised her, but she's not with her mother."

"What?"

"Do I have to spell it out for you?"

I drove down the road, tried to wrap my mind around Miriam's revelation, getting a glimpse, for the first time, of why she chose me as the star power for her new company. She had hoped my new financial standing would improve her daughter's life. I couldn't fault Miriam for that. What mother wouldn't want to help her child?

† † †

The helicopter was late, so Miriam and I went to a picnic table under the shade of a low-growing palm and drank margaritas in tall glasses. She opened a scrapbook to a photo of a baby girl in a playpen. The baby had brown hair and wore a pensive look.

"I never held her in my arms," Miriam said. "I gave her up, to a couple who lives in Boulder and raises foster children. They gave her their last name, but she was never officially adopted."

She handed me the book and I turned the pages, absorbed in the still-life progression of baby to woman. Rickie had made As in school, as her honor roll certificates noted. When she reached seventh grade she tried out for the drill team, and there were pictures of her in a green uniform holding two batons. In twelfth grade, she went to the prom with a boy who parted his hair in the middle and had pimples on his face. She wore a strapless black dress and a white corsage pinned above her breast. I felt envious of the boy in the photo.

"This picture," Miriam said, and pointed to Rickie atop a palomino, "was taken when she was thirteen. That's Seashore, a horse the Terrells gave her for her birthday."

Seashore. Even as a child Rickie had dreamed of the ocean.

"These pictures," I said.

"You're wondering how I got them?"

"Something like that."

"I paid for them," Miriam said. "I sent the Terrells a monthly stipend in exchange for my secretly watching my daughter grow up. I bought the pony, I paid for the prom dress, I paid for everything she was ever given."

In every photo, Rickie stared at the camera without a smile. My girlfriend, despite the amenities, had endured a miserable childhood.

On the beach, a tern skittered toward a receding wave, dipped its beak in the sand, retreated to high ground as the next wave approached. The air smelled especially salty this afternoon. Rickie would love it here, and I pictured her lying on the sand atop a white towel, tanned body soaking in the sun.

"I wanted to concentrate on my career," Miriam said. "I wanted to live the *Cosmopolitan* dream."

I flipped to a graduation photo of Rickie in cap and gown. Traced the flow of her shoulder. Lingered on her slender hands. Irritation crept over me, and I wanted to strike out at Miriam, to hurt her somehow.

"She never talked about you," I said.

Miriam's eyes were partially closed as if she were remembering something, perhaps trying to turn back time. She seemed fragile, only for a moment, then the Miriam I knew returned.

"She knocked on the Airstream and asked for a job," she said. "Didn't even tell me she was my daughter."

"That's crazy."

"She acted like we were strangers."

"You probably were," I said.

Miriam shook her head. "She knew who I was. I could see it in her eyes. She was expecting a mystical experience, like I would recognize a daughter I hadn't seen in eighteen years out of the clear blue."

I finished my drink and poured another.

"I didn't know which made me more upset," Miriam said. "The fact that she had invaded my privacy without calling or the fact that she didn't say she was my daughter when she saw me. I offered her a job, which to my surprise she accepted, then felt like I've been taking a test ever since. Like I have to summit this motherhood pinnacle before she'll claim me."

The chop of the helicopter sounded, and a black period against the clouds transformed into an oblong body. I watched it curve toward the ocean and level off low enough for the down force to ripple waves. The helicopter swept toward us, its shadow a specter on the sea. Miriam said something I didn't quite hear, and I asked her to say it again.

"I need your help," she said, ". . . with Rickie."

I suspected Miriam had manipulated the conversation to put me squarely in the middle of the rift between her and her daughter. I'd do what I could, but if Miriam wanted me to side with her she was wasting her time. Rickie had my loyalty and that would never change.

The helicopter settled onto the landing pad, and the noise wound down. I looked away and tried to ignore the fact that my taxi had arrived. I did not want to exchange the fresh air on this island for the pollution at Bible Camp.

"You have less than ten weeks left," Miriam said, as though she read my mind. "You go on back and I'll track down Rickie."

"I'd rather stay."

"We're on a tight schedule, Mr. Oliver. Very tight."

"It's like living in the Dark Ages," I said.

"That's the way Alton likes it. The less interference from the outside world the better he can do his job."

I agreed to go, on one condition. Each time the helicopter landed at Bible Camp I would receive updates on the search. Miriam and I had different motivations, but we had the same goal. I made a logical decision to trust her. One I hoped I wouldn't regret.

Chapter 7

TWO DAYS AFTER LEAVING Harbour Island, I perched on a
stool in a velvet-lined room and concentrated on my elocu-
tion lesson. Mrs. Tamarack, Bible Camp bookkeeper, paced on
the other side of a window and listened through a headset. Her
hair was tied in a knob atop her scalp, and she had an intense gaze.
When I said something that came out wrong, she blinked and
threw back her head like I'd hit her. Mrs. Tamarack had taught
most of the big-name televangelists, worked with a high-up politician or two. She ate caramels like they were the only food in
existence, and plastic wrappers cluttered the sound board.

"Do you know what a syllable is?" she said. "Do you even
understand the basic structure of the English language?"

"I—"

"You must learn to speak with distinction, Mr. Oliver. This
corn-fed act isn't going to work on the airwaves."

I admit Mrs. Tamarack intimidated me. In her presence, I
became a meek seven-year-old who could barely say the alphabet.

"Words are composed of discrete sounds," she said, "and the
sooner you learn that the sooner I'll be out of your hair."

"Yes, ma'am."

"Say 'God.'"

"God."

She unwrapped a caramel, popped it in her mouth, turned buttons on the console. "How many syllables does *God* have?"

"I think he owns them all." I laughed at my own joke.

"For our purposes, Mr. Oliver, occasionally *God* has two syllables, with the stress on the front."

"God," I said.

"GA-odd."

"GA-odd," I said.

"Again."

"GA-odd."

"Good," she said, chewing her candy. "You're getting the hang of it."

"Pop a pebble in my mouth and call me Demosthenes."

"Don't get too proud. You have a long way to go."

"Yes, ma'am."

That evening I walked the perimeter and preached to the snakes and gators and white herons. Said *God* so many times my jaw hurt. Switching gears, I worked on testimony, stressed the front end so much it came out as two words. *TEST imony.* Alton appeared in the murk and nodded approvingly. He handed me my weekly pay in a white envelope, suggested I not spend it all in one place. Alton had a wry humor he rarely showed. The only money I'd spent on the island was the tip I gave to the cook for the job he did on my party. Soon, I'd be able to afford any stock hog on the market. I wanted a big bike, lots of chrome.

I swatted a mosquito on my arm, smeared blood and guts in a circle. Alton said something about needing to shovel more sulfur and invited me to the boiler. He wanted to talk about my relationship with my employees, which until now I thought was perfectly fine.

He opened a door in the rear of one of the classrooms, and we descended into the gloom. At the base of the stairs, a tunnel led to a cavern, where in the center of the concrete floor a furnace heated a metal vat. Bubbles emerged from a malevolent liquid and burst their skin, hissing and spitting, a myriad of volcanic explosions spewing yellow fumes into an exhaust vent connected to the pipe that branched throughout the island. The air was thick and hot. There was a heaviness in my lungs.

Alton took off his hat and shirt, shoveled sulfur into the vat. A sheen broke out on his skin and slicked his shoulders. I started sweating and couldn't stop, looked around for a water fountain, something cold to drink. There was nothing but the vat and boiling liquid and heat and Alton toiling away. I asked if he wanted help, and he shook his head.

"We all have our penance," he said.

He took a big breath, doubled over, and coughed toward the floor. A bloody thread settled on his jaw.

"Listen," he said. "While you were away, Chauncey asked if he could compete for your job, claimed you were inexperienced with the intricacies of handling actors. He cited his directing experience, several plays in his hometown theater—"

"Jesus Christ, the guy thinks he's Francis Ford Coppola."

"He's talking about leading the actors on strike if he doesn't get a fair shot."

"Let him," I said. "I'll fire every last one of them and hire twenty more."

Alton propped the shovel against the wall. "You fire them and they might go to the press about the inner workings of this organization."

I regretted talking without thinking things through. Alton was right, of course. I asked him to send the malcontent to my house sometime this evening, and we walked down the tunnel, up the stairs, into the open. The haze had thickened. A fog ascending from Alton's personal hell. He wiped his lips, and his fingers came away red.

"You should get that cough checked out," I said.

He laughed. I swear to God he laughed.

If Chauncey hadn't been wearing his Michigan State jersey, I wouldn't have recognized him. He tottered in front of me, shifting weight foot to foot, hands trembling, hunched over as though carrying a load. The Einstein 'Fro was gone, and in its place was a forest of stubby white hair. His face was wrinkled, his lips turned toward the jawline in a perpetual old-man frown. The wattles under his neck were the coup de grâce. Magnificent fleshy growths, they were enough to make any centenarian proud. I had to hand it to him. Young Chauncey looked like he had fallen asleep at the base of a tree and woken up sixty years later.

"The vacuum is in the closet," I said, intent on teaching him a lesson. Chauncey worked for me and the sooner he realized it the better.

His voice had that rasp of a lifetime of lozenges, cigarettes, and gallons of Listerine. "Excuse me?"

"So are the garbage bags," I said. "And while you're at it, wash my dishes, dry them off, and put them away. I hate a dirty house, don't you?"

In our previous interactions, he'd had this odd way of looking everywhere on my face but my eyes. Now, he looked at me dead center, a stare that spoke of rising hatred.

"Don't forget to clean my toilet," I said. "There's Comet and a brush on the bathroom sink."

Chauncey turned on the vacuum, a dusty clatter, and walked behind it in steps so slow he seemed not to move blink to blink. The cord wasn't long enough to reach the bedroom, so he unplugged and soon the vacuum started again. I hollered at him to make up my bed, and he fluffed my pillows, smoothed the quilt. After that he washed dishes, wiped down counters, dragged three garbage bags to the door. He stayed in character the whole time, a petulant, recalcitrant old man resigned to his punishment. I'd seen the hacks at Tabernacle Carnival, three church plays, drama class in high school, had never seen a character absorb a person like this old man absorbed Chauncey. If the guy had leading-man looks, he would have already made millions on the big screen.

"The toilet?" I said.

He headed for the bathroom, and I turned on the CD player and listened to a mariachi band blow their trumpets and shake their tambourines. Chauncey came out brush in hand.

"I . . . I . . . Listen," he said.

He pointed the brush at me, and I turned up the volume. When the song was over, I went to the kitchen to get a beer. Didn't offer him one.

"I am not a maid," he said.

I motioned to the couch, and he declined the invitation.

"I didn't bring you here to clean my house." I'd pushed him far enough. It was time for the dictator to show benevolence.

"You could have fooled me."

"You know more about acting and actors than I ever will."

He straightened, and for the first time I sensed the young man inside the makeup.

"I want you to become my eyes and ears," I said.

"You want me to infiltrate my fellow thespians?" His gaze settled on my upper lip, as though he studied snot that had traveled south and taken up residence. I swiped at the scrutinized area and came away with nothing.

"Allow me to shape it another way." I tapped my cigarette on the ashtray, knocked grayness off the end. "I'm willing to pay an extra thousand a week to help manage my people."

Grudging appreciation appeared in his eyes. And why not? Money talked in this world. He asked to be excused, carried out the bags, shut the door. I went to the refrigerator and got out the rest of the six-pack. The house was clean, I was catching a buzz, and Chauncey had been put in his place. Life was good in Pentecostal Hell.

The following day, the helicopter flew in and I received my first letter from Miriam. Discovered she had hired a people finder located in Houston. She said they were the best in the world, and if anyone could find her daughter it was this agency. A private investigator used Rickie's credit card number to track her on a journey that took her south, reported she checked into a Gulf-side park down in Louisiana. I smiled when I read the part about the credit card. Rickie was smart as they come. If she was making it this easy, she wanted to be found.

The investigator had questioned the elderly couple in the space next to hers, and they said she was a very nice young woman who came over one night and ate steak and potatoes and a side of creamed corn, talked about her boyfriend and how she hated him, although you could see in her eyes that she didn't mean it. I slowed toward the end, reading each word aloud.

> *The investigator is concentrating on RV parks along the beach. Keep your fingers crossed.*
>   *Love,*
>   *Miriam*
> *P. S. I'm working with a publicity firm for your coming-out party. The buzz will be terrific!*

I folded the letter and dropped it in my dresser drawer. *Boyfriend.*

At least Rickie still considered us a couple. But even *boyfriend* was a fragile word. Preface it with *ex-* and the definition became something altogether different.

At the top of the tunnel steps, I met Alton, making his way one clomp at a time. He was sweaty, hatless, and his hair lay like rotted seaweed on his forehead. He leaned against the wall.

"Once," he said, "this was back when I was twenty-two and working for Pastor Dix down in Texas, I told a man in the congregation I had an inside track to getting the sick onstage and the man offered me a thousand dollars if I'd get his boy up there. Sammy Franklin was the boy's name, and he had a disease that made him old and short. I'd never seen anything like it. He looked like one of those Ethiopians, the way his skin was stretched over his face, only he was white and not black."

Alton slapped dust off his jeans, and sulfur settled at our feet.

"I took the guy's money," he said. "I took the guy's thousand dollars and told him I'd get his boy up in front of Pastor Dix come hell or high water."

"I'll bet Dix was pissed."

"I said I took the money, I didn't say I did it."

Heat rose from the cavern, and the air became stifling and sticky hot. Alton didn't move. Neither did I. I suspected he had something to get off his chest, and the sooner the better.

"What would happen," I said, "if someone threw a stick of dynamite down in that boiler?"

"What?"

"Nothing," I said. "I'm just talking."

"Mrs. Tamarack tells me you're working on a sermon. She says you can't make up your mind between 'I Saw the Light' or 'Hellfire and Brimstone.' Personally, I'd choose 'I Saw the Light.' Those folks likely to show have already been saved."

"I can't believe you took a thousand dollars off that man."

"He was only the first. Once I got that grand in my pocket it was like a dam busted loose and I worked the congregation on every stop, took their money and moved on to the next town. There's lots of needy people in this world."

Alton slumped and cupped his chin with both hands. "I started seeing them at night. I'd be asleep and they'd appear one at a time, come right out of the pearly gates and drift over me like they were ghosts or something. They didn't do anything but hang in the air and look down at me, but those eyes. . . . They drove me nuts and I got off the circuit and came here, started training actors to take my place. I started working in that boiler room and the ghosts stopped coming. It's like they never existed."

Alton's head came up. Like whatever he had to say, he had said and was glad of it. I didn't know what he wanted out of me. Absolution? Soothing words that confirmed he'd rightly chosen one hell over the other? I nodded sympathetically and laid my hand on his shoulder. Said I'd looked him up because I wanted to talk to him about something.

"I want you to see about getting my people a raise," I said.

Alton snorted.

"I'm serious," I said. "My employees must make a living wage. Raise them to seven hundred a week and promise them a four-thousand-dollar bonus after they graduate. And make sure they know it came from me."

"I'll see what I can do."

"That's not good enough," I said.

Alton's eyes opened wide, and a respect I hadn't seen crept into his gaze.

The investigator located Rickie in a Mississippi campground, followed her to a riverboat casino, attached a homing device to the undercarriage of her RV while she played blackjack. I tried to imagine what Rickie looked like sitting at the casino table, if she had her hair in a ponytail or if she allowed it to fall to her shoulders. I missed her, especially that warm lithe body next to mine. But my yearn was more than physical. I wanted to know why she would search out her real mother and not introduce herself. Rickie might have set up some weird motherhood test, as Miriam suggested, but I suspected there was something more at play. Rickie demanded loyalty—would not tolerate betrayal of any sort—and I could think of no bigger betrayal than a mother giving up her child. I suspected my girlfriend wanted her mother to suffer.

Two more letters came that week. The investigator had followed Rickie into the admissions office at Florida State in downtown Tallahassee. From there she drove up the eastern seaboard, stopped and walked campuses of colleges and universities along the way. She ended up in Vermont, where she stayed in a park overlooking Lake Champlain. After that, the letters arrived about once every ten days.

> Dear Vernon,
>
> Our girl worked for three days as a security guard at a Barenaked Ladies concert, then rode the cog railway up to the top of Mount Washington. She appears to have chosen to attend Dartmouth College in the spring. (It's in Hanover, New Hampshire.)
>
> Love,
> Miriam

> Dear Vernon,
>
> Rickie worked for a week at Grape Growers, an organic farm in southern Maine. She made two hundred and twenty dollars, which she spent on clothes in a thrift shop in Bangor. Did you know she prefers to eat lobster without the melted butter?
>
> Love,
> Miriam

> Dear Vernon,
>
> Alton tells me you're still not wearing the clothes I purchased especially for you. Pentecostals love to see their preachers well-heeled; believe the more you succeed finan-

cially, the closer you are to God. It's all part of the illusion.
Please pick out a suitable suit for your first sermon.

Love,
Miriam

The letters ended with the shortest note yet.

Dear Vernon,
  It's time to go to work.
  Pack your bags and let's get you off that island.

Love,
Miriam

On the last Friday of my third month at Bible Camp, the helicopter ferried my actors to Miami, where a bus awaited to transport them to a location Miriam had not revealed. Alton and I shook hands and I headed for the helicopter. Left him in the yellow haze. I climbed aboard, and the helicopter swept into sky so blindingly blue I covered my eyes. I didn't look down, and I didn't look back. If I never saw that island again, it would be okay by me.

Chapter 8

WALKED INTO A HARLEY shop in Fort Lauderdale two days after leaving Bible Camp, paid cash for a Dyna Super Glide on the show floor. The bike had a black gas tank, and painted flames flowed toward the seat. I straddled the hog, boots planted on the floor, and wondered what it would feel like with Rickie on the rear, her body against mine.

After signing the papers, I drove off the parking lot onto the street, aware of pavement rushing beneath my heels. The ride out of Florida, across Georgia, Tennessee, and Kentucky, into Indiana, had a bittersweet feel. The sensation of riding a Harley, the responsiveness of the throttle, the throb of the big engine between my legs, the blurred land flowing so close it felt like I could reach out and touch it, was like nothing I'd experienced. I felt full and empty at the same time. Living a dream was one thing. Living it without Rickie was another.

Four days into my trip, I throttled down and turned into fifty acres of scraggy mobile homes on the outskirts of Silvington, Indiana. Next to a beaten-down mailbox, a woman in dreadlocks held a radio and tapped barefoot to a song I couldn't hear. Isabella Singleton, Izzy for short, worked the streets. The year I turned twelve, she took on the Silvington High basketball team for two hundred dollars and a sack of Idaho potatoes. Among trailer park inhabitants, there was common belief the team overpaid. Izzy would do anything for ten bucks and a pack of Kools. I looked away when I drove past. When she wasn't wearing her glasses, she had a reputation for mixing up signals, and a glance in her direction was enough to bring a hopeful knock on a trailer door.

Farther down, next to a rusted swing set, a boy in shorts, no shirt, jammed his finger up his nose. He had a pimpled face, and his gaze was hard as concrete. I knew that look from inside out. The ferocity needed to survive this slum.

I could not drive these streets without thinking about Lucy, how I had wheeled her around after she became too sick to walk. When kids tossed rude comments in her direction, she raised her haughty blond head and spit words that backed offenders to the curb. "Fuckwad" was her favorite comeback; "Dickbreath" came in a close second. I had no idea who taught her to cuss. Knew if I used those words and our parents found out, I was in for a whipping. Dad had coarse hands, strengthened from shoveling asphalt onto Indiana roads, and when he swung his fist the impact left a bruise that lasted for weeks.

Cerulean Avenue beckoned and I took a right-hand turn, arrived at a crusted single-wide with a picnic table near the front door. I remembered the table for its lopsidedness, a malady Dad cured when he nailed a board on one of the legs and balanced everything out. Dad fixed broken skateboards, blown bike tires, leaky faucets, and shattered windows. If it was broke, Dad could fix it.

I turned off the bike, forced the kickstand into the gravel, and took off my helmet. Glanced at the left-hand mirror. Since last seeing my parents, my jaw had firmed into a straight line, and the

eyes under the black lashes seemed worldly and wise. My hair was
in a ponytail, which made my forehead seem extra large. I took
out the tie and shook my head, a shaggy dog coming home after
wandering the country.

Mom stepped outside. She wore spandex pants too small for
her hips, had knotted her shirt at the waist. Her rust-colored
hair was tangled, as though she'd been lying down, heard someone drive into the yard, and hadn't had time to brush. I'd never
seen her mad, not even when Lucy was dying. Shaking Mom's
faith was impossible. She was a "dyed in the wool" Christian and
believed if God wanted to take her daughter he must have had
a reason. She walked uncertainly my way, as if she couldn't put
together the motorcycle with the boy who had left home.

"Mom," I said.

She hugged me, and I hugged her back.

"Dad is working on a bridge up near Indianapolis," she blurted.
"He won't return till the weekend."

I followed her inside and took my customary spot at the table.
During our nightly prayer meetings, Lucy had sat across from me,
propped with pillows when she could no longer sit up on her own.
My parents believed God would send an answer, Express Mail, if
they prayed hard enough, and their daughter would regain her
health overnight. Dad had honed his skills as deacon of Silvington
Baptist Church, and he prayed loudest and longest. Mom prayed
with quiet resolution, face so still her lips hardly moved. When it
was my turn, I mimicked magnificent soliloquies I'd heard on the
religious station. Lucy never prayed, accepting early on she was
predestined to die young and no amount of talking to God would
change a thing.

Mom asked if I was hungry.

"I could eat."

She made a bologna sandwich and brought over a glass of milk. Her feet scraped across the floor, like it was all she could do to pick them up and put them down. Years had passed since Lucy's death, and Mom still reminded me of an airplane running out of fuel and no place to land. Sooner or later she would crash in a time and place not of her choosing.

I ate the sandwich, drank the milk, wiped my mouth on a napkin. Mom touched my hand.

"It's such a shock to see you," she said.

"I'm on my way to Chicago."

"Chicago?"

"I'm a preacher," I said. "Pentecostal."

Mom and Dad were Baptist through and through, which meant they believed everyone else—and that included Pentecostals, Lutherans, Jews, Mormons, Catholics, Hindus, Buddhists, and Muslims—were going to hell. She washed my dishes, wrung out a dish towel, and sang a soft tune. Mom had a pure soprano voice and was a member of the church choir. She was best known for a soaring solo in the annual Christmas concert, but away from church mostly sang her Barry Manilow repertoire.

"I saw Kimberly the other day," she said. "She had one in the stroller, another on the way."

Kimberly Appleton was a high-school girlfriend who helped out when Lucy was at her sickest. Kimberly was Catholic and preferred giving blow jobs to being penetrated. Wore sexual guilt like a heavy overcoat. Evidently, she'd worn out that coat or had gotten married.

"I have a girlfriend," I said. "Her name's Rickie Terrell—"

"The day you left, you hardly even said good-bye, just threw some clothes in that old duffel bag of yours and walked out the door."

"Mom."

"We thought you were dead. . . . You never called, you never wrote, you never even picked up your last check from Steakhouse."

"I'm sorry, Mom."

"Pentecostal is the devil's own religion, all that singing and dancing around, those false healings and sinful preachers."

I got up and gave her another hug.

"I'll pray for you to see the light," she said. "I'll pray for you to take Jesus into your heart and wash away your sins so you can receive eternal life. John 3:16, amen."

We both knew I wasn't staying, so there was no need to offer. I walked outside and shut the door. A neighborhood kid ran on long tan legs across the street, ducked behind a storage shed. I sat for a long time without starting the Harley. I might have come into a little money, but I could not, would not, deny my past. I was the preacher who had a story to share. That sounded so corny I had to stop laughing to buckle my helmet. Hopefully, there were enough suckers to make this venture worthwhile.

On the way to Chicago, bike twisting and turning over back roads, I got a call on my newly activated cell. I parked under an oak and dug a flask from my jacket pocket. Listened to Miriam lay out my itinerary for the next three days.

"Day one," she said, "that would be tomorrow. Day one, you meet with a religious editorial writer out of the *Chicago Tribune*. He appreciates the new Cadillac in his driveway, so no worries about tough questions. Day two, we give the show a dry run. Day three, you get up on that stage and earn your keep."

I swallowed whiskey, capped the flask, tucked it back in my jacket. On both sides of the road, cornfields ticked in the breeze. Silos rose from the earth like red thumbs, presumably housing feed for a nearby pig farm that produced a sour odor when the wind switched direction. The connection picked up static, cleared, and Miriam said something about the investigator approaching Rickie outside a restaurant in Hanover. She was wearing a waitress uniform and had her hair in a braid that fell down her neck to her back. In his report, two detailed pages he'd faxed Miriam, Rickie had seemed interested when he talked about my debut and my wish for her to appear, but she turned down the offered plane ticket because it was her first week at her new job, and she didn't feel right about asking for time off.

"What's that?" I said. "What did you say?"

"She's not coming."

Miriam was silent for a long time, and I thought we'd lost each other.

"Are you ready for this?" she said.

The sermon I knew by heart. Had worked on delivery until my throat ached. Rickie turning down an offer to see me was another thing altogether. I revved the engine and drove down the road, wound out the big bike until I was doing a hundred and twenty. Fields blurred, and I blinked to stay focused. If this was it between me and Rickie, I didn't plan on looking back.

I was that kind of guy.

† † †

Lights were off in the auditorium, a basketball gymnasium on the outer edge of west Chicago, and sun coming through the windows lit the congregation. The air was much cooler than in the tent where I had worked months earlier. Smells were the same, and the odor of rotted flesh, urine, and feces floated on the air-conditioned breeze. My flock was ten thousand strong, according to Miriam, who stated this was the largest gathering recorded for a first sermon. She pinned the success on yesterday's article in the *Trib*.

The interview had gone well. I told the reporter, a short man who wore red suspenders and smoked a pipe, that I had not chosen this life, that it had chosen me, and as God's vessel I was only doing his will to promote peace and harmony in the universe. Feeling like Namath predicting victory before the Super Bowl, I guaranteed a miracle that science could not dispute. He called me a "man of powerful faith"; wrote that I was "wise beyond my years." The photo, a profile showing my hair down to my shoulders, ran on page one of the religious section. Miriam thought the picture was a bonus because I looked seriously spiritual.

"Every little bit helps," she said.

"Praise the Lord."

"You are so bad," she said.

"Devil don't got nuthin' on me, sister."

We waited in a hallway at the far end of the gymnasium, listening to a band sing a nasal adaptation of "Jesus Loves Me," and I had just snorted two lines of coke I'd purchased off a guy working a street corner. To my surprise, Miriam had given up on me wearing fancy clothes, saying I needed to set myself apart, and if I thought the Harley motif would do the trick, that was good enough for her. I studied the stage through the window in the door. The band had a lead guitarist, bass guitarist, drummer, and lead singer. The Manhattan Maniacs were from New York City, and they made a living off gutter bars and wedding parties. Miriam liked their fusion of blues and heavy metal, gave them a tryout, hired them on the spot. The band was so surprised they shaved their heads, and the lead guitarist ate meat for the first time in years.

They occupied the rear of the stage and above their gleaming pates a curtain shrouded what Miriam said was one of the largest LCD screens in the world. I could not validate that boast. Only knew the screen was fifty feet high and thirty feet wide. The stage was made of metal, and a handrail fenced the perimeter. There was a single microphone up front, no pulpit. During yesterday's run-through, the tech company turned off the controlling computer, and I was left standing in front of a mike with a hairless band behind me. I would have preferred to see the bells and whistles ahead of time, but Miriam wanted to surprise everyone and that included me.

"Stay at least five feet from the front corners," Miriam said.

"You're telling me this now?"

"And walk extra hard. Stomp around when you're up there."

"Got it," I said. "Stay away from the corners and stomp extra hard."

I zipped my jacket to the throat. Glanced down at my boots. I had decided on the unlaced look, hoping the recklessness I exuded would work in my favor. I wanted the crowd balanced on a razor, I wanted to cut them into thin slices and leave them bleeding. Holy shit, I was high off this coke. A last-minute inspiration, and I went out the rear entrance and ran to my bike. I cranked that bitch wide open, settled down, and cruised to the front entrance, where two of my actors wore badges and worked security.

"I'm going in," I said.

Stacy opened the door and stepped back. I revved the engine, and people in the bleachers looked around and cupped their hands over their eyes. The sun settled behind me, and I knew all they could see was a silhouette in an orange glow. I began a slow ride through the gym, stopped in front of the stage, and slammed my boots on the floor. I sat tall in the saddle, gripped the front brake, gunned the motor. The rear tire spun, squealed, and smoke boiled upward. My mouth gaped and I screamed, not knowing what I was saying, only knew that I had the attention of every last man, woman, and child in those seats. I threw back my head and laughed. Tossed a crazy look at an openmouthed woman who cradled a baby in a front row seat. The woman extended her arms, a human offering, and that settled me, made me remember I had a sermon to give.

I throttled down, and the band began a jungle drumbeat that increased tempo when I stepped onstage. I raised my hands to the heavens and howled. Someone in the band shook a tambourine, adding the higher pitch to the bass. Vapor seeped out of a grate near my feet, and fog swept above my head and folded in on itself. The coke was in full bloom, rocking me hard, and my eyes were so wide open I felt like my lids were welded into place.

"JEE-sus," I said. "I am here to TEST-ify in his name."

The curtain fell from the screen, a synthetic collapse that created a breeze and blew the fog upward and outward. A murmur swept over the congregation, and I sensed massive leaning forward. I turned and saw myself on display, every bit of forty feet high. A frontal pose with my face turned upward. Digitalized blood dripped out of a gash in my chest and pooled discreetly over my pelvic region, ran in rivulets down both legs, and puddled at the bottom of the screen. My big toes, large as bread loaves, framed the band.

I stomped to my right, and starbursts exploded above my giant shoulders. I stomped to my left. More starbursts. Impressed, I wondered if I stood on the first stage to interface vibration and computer graphics.

I turned to my flock, to the people in their seats with prayer on their mouths and money in their bank accounts; felt the beginnings of an energy I hadn't experienced when I worked for Yost. I had never been the focus. The focus. The focus. A spotlight lit a bright circle, teasing, never settling in one spot. The music reached a crescendo, and I lowered my head, closed my eyes, and raised my arms. The spotlight settled on me, and the hot glare warmed my forehead.

For the first time in my life, my memory failed. I could not recall a word from my sermon, could not remember a single Bible verse, had lost my cue to start Chauncey on his mission to seek out the embedded actor. The only thing I could think of was Lucy, and how her skin changed color before she died, how her fingernails loosened and fell off, how her gums bled onto her chin. I wanted to speak to these people about life and death. I wanted to shake them up and turn them inside out. I began in a halting voice, conscious of television cameras on all sides, of wheelchairs in the aisles, of casts and bloody bandages, of people holding white canes and petting Seeing Eye dogs.

"Let me tell you a story," I said. "Let me tell you a story about a little girl who died when she was seven. Let me tell you of doctor visits and hospital visits, of a family so devastated they almost didn't survive, of a boy who drank and smoked marijuana to ease the pain. Let me tell you of a boy who consorted with the whores and the drug dealers, who left home for the streets of New York, where he robbed old women of their purses and committed crimes in darkened back alleys. Let me tell you of a boy destined for hell, a boy who turned his back on God, a boy who would rather run with the devil than sit in a church pew."

I'd never slept with a whore, never been in New York, never robbed an old woman, and never committed a crime in a darkened back alley, but I was so carried away my lies thundered across the auditorium with the same conviction as the truth. I had my congregation by the throat, and I could squeeze the life out of them.

"I, Vernon L. Oliver, was that boy. I was the sinner in the devil's evil clutches. I was the boy who prayed so hard to God to heal his sister that my throat hurt and my eyes burned from lack of sleep. I was the one who turned his back on all that was good and precious in this world. I was the one who quit reading my Bible and quit tithing my ten percent to my church every Sunday. I was the one who didn't realize that all prayers are answered, that sometimes that answer is no. I was the one who didn't realize his sister's death was part of a larger plan for his life.

"But then"—and I raised my voice, a suddenness that forced my congregation backward—"I found GAAA-odd."

An actor halfway up the bleachers spoke in tongues, and the congregation swayed as one. Shouts of "Washed in the blood" issued forth. To my right, slots opened in the stage floor and silver mirrors appeared. A bluish light shaped itself into a cube that expanded until it was eight feet high. A life-sized form appeared inside the cube, and I almost swallowed my tongue. No wonder Miriam wanted to keep her stage a secret. I watched the hologram materialize, watched Jesus, in a white loincloth, hang from the cross. It was a vaporous image, constituting and reconstituting in the fog, high-tech snatches of a two-thousand-year-old murder.

To my left, on the opposite corner, a second hologram formed, this one a greenish light that showed a boy kneeling in front of Jesus. The boy had a deformed leg, and Jesus placed a green hand on a green forehead, and the leg grew into something good and wholesome. Another image formed, this one of Jesus turning one fish into five hundred. On the big screen, my chest opened, revealing my heart beating rhythmically, a red fist in a hollow cavity. I watched myself raise my arms and form a cross, slowly turn my back to the audience. Blood ran down my spine and covered my nether region. The band, no doubt relieved they weren't performing under a gigantic anus, sucked down their rum and Cokes—compliments of Miriam—and the bass guitarist went off on a thumping riff that lasted all of two minutes. I faced my audience.

"I found GAAA-odd," I said. "Like Paul on his way to Damascus, GAAA-odd came to me in a white light. Like Paul I fell on my knees, like Paul I felt the Holy Spirit enter my body and lift me on high. Like Paul I felt JEEE-sus wash my sins away, felt him wash them right down the drain . . . where they belong."

I had woven back to my memorized sermon, and "down the drain" was Chauncey's cue to work the crowd. He pushed Laney up the wheelchair ramp and stood behind her while I held two Bibles at my sides. Silence settled over the auditorium. I raised the Bibles high and slammed them on each side of her head, a double slap so loud my flock gasped and moaned. Laney collapsed to the floor, and I launched the wheelchair into the air. It landed on the foul line, wheels broken and spinning, of no further use to anyone.

"Go for it," she said. "Rock their world."

I grabbed her feet and slid her over that stage like I was dragging out the trash.

"In the name of GAAA-odd," I said.

I brought back a boot and kicked her legs. The band went crazy, drums loud and hard, cymbals darting in and out, a crashing that added an odd syncopation to the cacophony. I stomped on Laney's arm. I kicked her in the head. Her eyes begged for it, desiring abuse sweet as cotton candy.

"In the name of the Holy Spirit," I said. "In the name of Jesus, who died on the cross so we might seek eternal life, I command you, devil, I COMMAND you to leave this woman."

Laney's head jerked backward, and her torso arched upward. The speaking in tongues reached a crescendo and stomping on the bleachers began. Noise that grew louder as cheers swamped the stage. I spoke in Laney's ear.

"I think we just scored the winning basket."

"Please don't make me laugh." She prodded her legs, like she felt them for the first time. Chauncey slipped his arms under her, but she shook him off and came erect on her own. Now was the time to pass the offering plates, but there were no plates to pass. Miriam had decided the begging would be dubbed in afterward, a 1-800 number and a voice-over that pleaded for money for Pastor Oliver's ministry. Light exploded in the holograms, and Jesus's face morphed into mine. The symbolism was obvious. I wasn't just another preacher coming up in the Pentecostal world. I was something special. Someone who had a direct pipeline to God. Hell, I *was* God.

Chauncey stepped off the stage and stood in front of my bike. A woman wearing a flower-print dress got up from her seat and dragged a boy who had a flipper instead of a left arm. Chauncey turned them around, intercepted a legless man in a wheelchair. The man had gargantuan biceps, and he muttered to himself as he tried to wheel around my front man. The sick and the maimed began to advance from all sides, too many for Chauncey to handle, and I decided it was time to wind up the service.

"I have looked the Father, the Son, and the Holy Ghost straight in the eye," I said, ad-libbing now, "and they have commanded me to preach the word, to set you sinners straight, to maim and torture and kill the devil wherever I find him. I am the Biker Preacher, rescued from hell and set on a righteous path."

I jumped down from the stage, cranked the bike, and drove out the way I'd come. The parking lot was full of cars, and stark buildings rose against a sky so clear it was like God himself had orchestrated my exit. I drove around town, stop-and-go traffic, for a good two hours before I headed toward the Hilton for the afterparty. On a street corner, I purchased another gram from this black guy who looked at my hog like he wanted it bad. I snorted a line and howled at a car traveling past. Fuck! I could get used to this kind of life.

The party was held in adjoining suites on the top floor of the Hilton. Laney had a cut on her ear, and her back was so sore she could hardly move. She jokingly said that if this kept up she'd have to ask for more money. All twenty of my actors were there, and everyone agreed it was a magnificent job of improvising on her part.

Miriam entered with her cell phone to her ear. She was in a strapless evening gown, and her stiletto heels accentuated her calves with each elegant step across the carpet. Every head turned her way. She made a show of handing five thousand dollars to Laney.

"A bonus," Miriam said. "For a job well done."

Laney thanked her and dropped the bills in her purse. Chauncey was on the couch and Laney was in his lap, and he had his arms around her. Everyone had satisfied looks, and I suspected the actors who worked background were salivating about that bonus and couldn't wait for me to sling them around. Miriam dropped her cell in her purse and told me calls were already coming in, that David Letterman wanted the Biker Preacher and the holograms the first night we were available. Oprah called and offered an hour the following week. Said to bring the bike and show up in all leather. She wanted me to bring along the woman I had healed, asked if I could produce medical documents proving a miracle. Miriam, who had bribed a doctor at the Johns Hopkins Hospital, told me that wouldn't be a problem. She had thought of everything, down to the sandwiches circulating the room.

Someone cranked up a stereo, and the actors danced and drank and speculated about the next meeting. Miriam and I walked to her room and sat on a long white couch. The sophistication I'd seen at the afterparty disappeared, and she seemed overcome with sadness. I felt it, too, an emptiness so intense it seemed destined to last forever. We small-talked about the stage and the holograms and me nearly naked up on the screen and if the audience liked it and how it would come across in television land. Conversation dwindled and we were quiet for a long time, both avoiding what was really on our minds. Miriam brought it up first.

"I can't believe she didn't come," she said.

She turned down the lights and we drank our drinks until they were empty, refilled and started all over again. Adrenaline left my body one heartbeat at a time, and my eyelids grew heavy.

I didn't remember crawling into bed. Only knew I woke with her body curled into mine. She turned toward me and I knew she was awake and I knew what she wanted. I pressed my flesh against hers, wanting the hollowness to go away.

We woke to a ringing cell, and Miriam stirred from under my arm. She looked like I felt, hungover and apprehensive about last night's coupling. I wasn't sure where we went from here, if it was back to the boss/employee relationship or if we had begun an affair. I tickled her ribs, and she pushed my hand away. Said it was the investigator and asked me to hush. A tremor worked up her arm to her jaw. She listened for another couple minutes, dropped the phone, stepped into her panties.

"The homing device went out on the RV late yesterday morning." Miriam shook so hard she couldn't grab her dress off the back of the chair. "He said it went out while she was on the Ohio interstate, said she must have changed her mind about coming to the service and was driving nonstop from New Hampshire to Chicago to make it on time."

"What?"

"There's been an accident, Vernon."

I began to pray, shut it down soon as I started. God had not answered my prayers for Lucy, he sure wasn't going to answer them for Rickie.

Chapter 9

PASSING TIME IN PRISON is all about mind control and sleep. Convicts who sleep eighteen hours a day spend three-quarters of their captivity in relative freedom. I'm not one of the lucky ones. I sleep six hours a night, spend the bulk of my day thinking, eating, reading, and working on my book.

Four o'clock in the morning, I wake and stare into darkness. Planning in captivity sounds easy to the uninitiated, but complications arise because I shuffle activities. For instance, on some days I brush my teeth after breakfast and other days I wait an hour. The question then becomes what to do while I wait that hour. I could wash my cell window, scrub the Plexiglas behind the bars until it sparkles, but the window is small and takes twenty minutes to clean. I could read the other forty minutes, a process of closing my eyes and calling up any book from my past, but I don't like starting a book and stopping a short time later. Instead of cleaning the window and reading, I could sit and think for that hour, but normally I reserve my thinking for the hours between lunch and supper.

When I first arrived, I lived my day according to whim, which meant if I felt like working on my manuscript, I worked on my manuscript. If I felt like taking a dump at six o'clock in the morning, I took a dump at six o'clock in the morning. If I felt like reading my favorite passage in *Cold Mountain* or *The Shipping News*, I read my favorite passage in *Cold Mountain* or *The Shipping News*.

Now, I dole my life out in distinct increments, arrange them differently day by day to offset boredom. What I crave most is change, and that thought alone sends an earthquake through my belly, for the biggest change is coming for me soon enough.

Dredge, neighbor and boy rapist/killer, says he heard John T cried his last minutes on this earth. Dredge says John T pissed on himself when he saw the needle, says he was still bitching about beef ribs instead of pork. I have no idea if any of it is true, but it makes me wonder how I will react when the time comes. Will I offer impassioned last words or will I glare at my accusers without speaking? Will I listen for the phone to ring, the last-minute reprieve, or will I draw so far inward sounds lose their meaning? I have no idea, and because I don't like thinking about these things, I force them from my mind. I can do that, I can control my mind like people control their pets. I tell myself when and what to think, can transport in a microsecond to scenes so far removed it's like prison never existed.

Occasionally, I think about the good times with Lucy, like when I stole our parents' car, and she and I rode around the countryside. We slept in the open and cuddled under a scratchy wool blanket, ate baked beans for breakfast, farted the rest of the day away. On the third morning, she shrugged into her Mickey Mouse shirt—her favorite cartoon character—and asked what happens when we die.

"You go to Jelly Bean World," I said. "All you can eat."

Lucy curled her bottom lip inward, released it a little at a time. Maybe I should have said I had no idea, that she might go to heaven or she might go to hell or she might be dead and gone and that's all there was to it. She looked at me for several minutes, eyes steady as lily pads on a still pond. Then she giggled, high-pitched bubbles that dissipated into the surrounding field.

"Jelly Bean World," she said. "All you can eat."

At that moment, I was not sure who was taking care of whom, only knew my heart swelled so much it pounded my sternum. We left shortly after that, made a swing to the trailer, where I took my beating from Dad and a plea from Mom to never run off with her daughter again. Lucy came to me that night, slept with her head against my shoulder. I tricked myself into thinking if I didn't move she wouldn't die, and I spent the night motionless as a mummy. I knew it wouldn't work. I was fourteen and cynical beyond reason. She was five and believed in Jelly Bean World to comfort her brother. What was there to say?

Four years into my sentence, change comes to the block in the form of a new guard, a woman who wears her uniform tucked tightly into her waistline. The buttons that line her shirt remind me of polished cat's-eyes. Her name is Carleen Kathleen Stuttgart, and she goes by Carly. She wears her hair short, and her blue eyes speak of kindness and honesty. Carly is the first guard to consistently break the "no communication" rule and says hello when she hands me a food tray. The first time it happened I was so surprised I didn't say anything back. Now, we regularly exchange pleasantries.

She walks down the hall, headed my way with the mail run. I know it's her because the footsteps are light and quick, a purposeful woman in hard-bottomed shoes. I accept my letters, one from a believer in South Africa, another from a witch doctor in Jamaica. The witch doctor started sending me mail early in my career, mostly crude drawings of me with a knife in my chest. In this most recent picture, I am kneeling and have my head on a wooden block. A meat cleaver hangs in the air above my neck and pins protrude from my arms, legs, and buttocks. I have no idea why he singled me out, consider it the price of fame. Once you're on that mountaintop, even a witch doctor from Jamaica will try to knock you off. I am annoyed. Playing King of the Hill is one thing, kicking a man when he is down is another.

"Thank you," I say, and hold up the letters.

"You're welcome, Vern."

Carly truncates my name, another unexpected display of intimacy. She reaches inside the slot and pats me on the arm. I sense her pity and try to put myself in her place, see her as the girl who works at the Humane Society, feeding the animals one day at a time, waiting for death sentences to be carried out.

"You don't remember me, do you?" she says.

I study her face.

"September 27, 1997 . . . in the Astrodome?" she says. "I brought my little girl to one of your services and sat in the front row next to the wheelchair ramp. You looked right at me when you were preaching, like you wanted to gobble me up."

"I'm sorry—"

"Her name was Pauline Noel Stuttgart and I was turned away. I held my girl in my arms and I was turned away. I'd sent you part of my salary every week for a year and I was turned away."

Her hand slips from mine.

"How is she?" I say. "Your little girl."

"She's dead, died of complications shortly after."

I cannot look her in the eyes.

"I'm sorry," I say. "I don't remember much from those days."

If I coax my mind to that point in time, I would remember everything about it, including her. But why should I? Life is painful enough without having my sins thrown in my face.

"Is it true you murdered those people?" she says. "Is it true you blindfolded them, then held the pistol barrel to their heads and pulled the trigger? Is it true you burned them in a fire and drove white crosses into their graves?"

I come fully erect, a tall, long-haired man, a Samson with no pillars to topple. Is this woman my Delilah? Will she ask me to cut my hair? I speak, and my voice rumbles thunderous as a storm over the hills. "I am a man who has felt the hand of God, I am a man who has made the crippled to walk and the blind to see, I am a man who cured cancer and heart disease, I am a man who is unjustly accused and I stand in this cell innocent as a newborn."

A weak smile comes over her face. "And those miracles?"

"A gift. . . . One I did not ask for and one—"

"I have ovarian cancer," she says. "The doctors keep cutting me but they can't seem to get it all."

Her purpose becomes clear. Carly wants me to do for her what I didn't for her daughter.

On the day Lucy was scheduled to return home from her seventeenth hospital visit, Dad screwed together a bed in the living room. The bed had handrails, but couldn't tilt up and down because that kind of bed was too expensive for a family that survived off construction paychecks. I watched him smooth the sheets, balance a stuffed bear on the pillow. He worked in silence, which did not surprise me. Dad had not talked to me in over a year, least not in the way he had before Lucy got really sick. I did not hold it against him. He worked, he prayed, he helped Mom. There was no time for motorcycles, baseball, or girls. I placed the television on a table at the end of the bed, inserted the plug in the wall socket.

"So she can watch cartoons," I said.

Mom carried in a crate of lettuce and carrots. She'd read a book that stated nutrition was the answer to everything, and she was determined to go down fighting. She peeled carrots and cleaned lettuce, ran huge handfuls through a juicer she'd bought at a yard sale.

"Taste this," she said, and handed me a glass.

I sipped and tried not to gag.

"Delicious," I said. "Best thing since sliced butter."

Mom cut me a look, which meant I'd better shut my mouth while Dad was around. She might have been the fighter, but Dad was the enforcer and it didn't pay to make him mad. I wasn't worried. These days Dad lacked the energy to punch anyone.

Mom sipped and wrinkled her nose, mumbled something about vitamins and minerals and how specific combinations worked to combat infection, heal organs, things like that. She had never been to college, and I often wondered where her life would have led under different circumstances. She might have been a physician or an attorney, a CEO or a professor. Instead, she was stuck in Silvington, Indiana, married to a construction worker, and trying anything she could think of to save her child.

The ambulance brought Lucy home that evening. I stood in the snow and watched the rear doors open. The air felt cold, and the trailer had a bluish tint. I breathed in and out, cloud crystals forming inches from my nose. Two attendants eased the stretcher into the yard, and I stepped back so they would have clear passage. Lucy waved at me when she went past. I waved back and followed the procession inside.

Later, as she sipped her vegetable drink, I brought in a box and told her I had a surprise. I'd saved two hundred dollars from my dishwasher job, had purchased a VCR and a box of videos. I set up the VCR and pushed in a Bugs Bunny tape. She fell asleep and woke up, fell asleep and woke up, fell asleep and woke up. Mom said it was time for a bath, and Lucy said she wanted me to do it.

She felt light in my arms, a cloud threatening to blow to the horizon. I ran a washcloth over her body, over the shrunken skin, the ribs now so prominent. She stared straight ahead, limp under my touch. I held her on the edge of the tub and dried her off, dressed her in panties and one of my pullover shirts. The shirt came to her knees, and she liked to sleep in it because it kept her warm.

"I know what's going to happen," she said.

Lucy had grown-up eyes—dying will do that to a child—and I couldn't look away. She extended a crooked pinkie, and I did the same.

"I want you to do something," she said. "I want you to swear."

In Lucy's world, pinkie oaths carried more weight than the average child's. The average child swore an oath and the next day forgot it while she hung upside down on the monkey bars. Lucy never forgot an oath. In the gravitas of her world, she demanded that those around her keep their word.

"If it hurts so much I can't stand it," she said, "I want you to end it."

Those were her exact words. She wanted me to end it.

"I want you to hold a pillow over my face," she said. "I won't struggle. When it's time, you go ahead and do it and get it over with."

We hooked fingers, and my heart felt like someone had stabbed it with an adrenaline needle.

"Swear," she said.

"I swear."

I carried her back to bed, and we watched Road Runner until she fell asleep and stayed asleep. Mom, Dad, and I had our nightly prayer meeting, said good night, went to bed. Mom got up every hour and walked into the living room. Dad didn't snore, which meant he never fell asleep.

When the pain started, it came in waves. Lucy described it as glass running through her veins. On the days when the pain was particularly bad, I stayed home from school and turned the TV up full blast. Mom made vegetable drinks, and Dad went to work, came home too tired to eat. Men and women from church visited us, read the Bible, and prayed. They offered words of wisdom and words of praise and words of hope.

"God will heal her," they said.

The doctor prescribed morphine, and Mom learned how to administer it through an IV attached to Lucy's arm. The drug worked for several weeks, then the pain became too strong and Lucy moaned through a drug-induced haze. On a Wednesday morning, we gathered around the bed before Dad went to work and offered up thanks for our daughter, our sister, and if God saw fit would he please send a miraculous healing our way. I prayed in terse words, praising him for his wisdom, while fantasizing shoving a knife into his chest, slowly exploring that cavity for his heart. I doubted I would find one.

That was the day I picked up a pillow and stood next to her bed. I stood there for hours. I had every intention of keeping my word, yet each time Mom left the room and I tried to force the pillow up and over my sister's head, my hand would not move.

In the ensuing weeks, I tried again and again to honor my vow. As the pain grew, her moans turned into screams and I spent more time outside. Her screams followed me through the trailer park, to the reeds along the creek where I lay on my back and looked at the sky. I never brought my hands to my ears, not once. I might not have been able to kill my sister, but I would never deny her existence.

Then she died.

I doubted she was alert enough toward the end to know that I had failed her. It didn't matter.

I knew.

After supper, I hand my tray to the guard, then work on my autobiography. Pages are piling up, something that delights my attorney. Whenever he visits, I see greed in his eyes, the prospect of a seven-figure contract, a way to recoup fees and then some. I do not know why he complains about my bill. My trial made him famous. If it weren't for me, he'd still be in a little office in a little building on the poor side of town. He'd still be making dimes and nickels off slips and falls, still be wondering how to pay his electric bill, still be wearing the same frayed suit he wore the day we met. Now he drives a Porsche and lives in Beverly Hills. He wears Armani and works high-profile cases. He goes to parties with starlets and movie executives. Five nights a week, he opines on the *Nancy Grace* show.

Sandoval insists he has a movie deal, but the more I think about it, the more I question if I want to see an actor portray me on the big screen. What if he gets it wrong? I have a good side, I truly do.

From seven to eight, I write steadily, resting occasionally so my hand doesn't cramp. A tap on the wall between my cell and Dredge's, and I step onto the chair and turn my ear to the vent. His voice is hoarse, like there's a noose around his neck.

"I got a letter from a woman who wants to marry me," Dredge says. "She loves me and can't do without, says she can't sleep at night without fingerin' her clit and thinkin' of me."

"She must have a grudge against her pussy."

Dredge's voice is full of wonder. "I don't even *know* her."

I don't bother to tell him the woman is after money, that when he dies in that gurney his suitor hopes she will receive a Social Security check for the rest of her life. It is false hope. The State of Florida does not allow death row inmates to marry.

"Does she have a name?" I say.

"What kind of question is that?"

It's summertime, and the vent blows cool air across my forehead. Words drift from far down the black hole. Convicts on the end of the block are holding a conversation.

"She's probably a blow-up doll," I say. "You got a letter from a no-name blow-up doll."

"She's not a blow-up doll, she's flesh and blood and she wants to get married."

"She's probably got the clap." I move so close to the vent my lips brush metal. "She's probably a harlot working on the street and sucking her pimp's dick every night."

Dredge says her name is Miss Dorothy Haslett. She wears

pink panties and rides a ten-speed for exercise. Sleeps under a crystal to bring her power. He says she's into *Star Trek* and wears Spock ears to conventions.

"She doesn't care what I did," Dredge says. "She believes there's good in all of us."

Heavy footsteps down the hall, and I step off the chair. I suspect the great State of Florida knows their convicts communicate through the vents, suspect even more strongly the cells are bugged to catch us talking about missing victims. Which, in my case, is not applicable. The bodies were right where I left them.

The guard walks past, and I go to the desk and try to recapture the feelings I had on the flight on my way to the hospital where Rickie lay injured. I remember drinking Jack Daniels and looking at Miriam. We were back in the clothes we'd taken off each other only hours earlier. I watched her torso tilt toward the front of the plane like she willed it to go faster. Smooth away her furtive gaze, and the time we'd spent in bed seemed so far away it might never had existed at all.

Chapter 10

THE HOSPITAL CHAPEL WAS on the ground floor. There were eleven cushioned pews, and along the walls statues in recessed cubicles stared at those who came to pray. There was Jesus on the cross, Mary Magdalene, a copper Buddha, God on a throne, and others I didn't recognize. I'd been in numerous hospital chapels, and they fell into two categories—the politically neutral, which had zero religious symbols, and the politically correct, which tried to cover all bases. The staff had tried to cover all bases. A natural act for a hospital located in a baseball town. Rickie had been airlifted to Cleveland General's emergency room three days ago, after she ran the RV off the interstate and rolled in a soybean field. She had been in and out of surgery since admission, was too doped up to speak.

A man came through the door and sat at the end of my pew. He carried a Bible and wore a preacher's collar, had black eyes and a nose that flattened above a mustache. I watched him bow his head and not move for the next twenty minutes. He looked up and caught me staring.

"A believer?" he said.

The man had a smugness about him, like he'd been graced with a direct pipeline to a higher power and the rest of us were damned without his guidance. His question annoyed me. A believer in what?

"I lost my faith when I was a kid."

"A skeptic?" he said.

"You could say that."

"And yet here you sit."

I shifted in my seat, leather pants scraping where my legs rubbed together. My tobacco intake had zoomed to three and a half packs a day, and I needed a smoke. I was here, in this chapel, in this pew, for no other reason than this is where people go when their loved ones are seriously injured and in the hospital. I had wanted quiet time and wound up with jibber-jabber.

"I'll pray for you," he said.

"You don't even know my name."

"I'll pray for the man I met in the chapel today," he said. "God will put two and two together and realize it's you."

"I didn't realize God was a mathematician."

"He knows all things."

I didn't hold the preacher's proselytizing against him. He was ginning up business, the mark of a good salesman. Still, enough was enough. He seemed to sense he had worn out his welcome, because he opened his Bible and began to silently read. I looked straight ahead and tried to empty my mind of all thoughts, a trick that relaxed me when I became wound too tight. The harder I tried, the more I failed. Guilt gripped my heart in its rough hand. It was a physical sensation and one that hurt my chest each time I inhaled. Rickie balanced on the rail between life and death, and all because we were playing a stupid lover's game. I should have put an end to it and gone to her soon as I left Bible Camp.

The rear door opened, a burst of noise from the hallway, and Miriam stepped inside. The door closed, and the chapel quieted. She glanced at the preacher, then turned her focus on me.

"You should go to the hotel and get some sleep," she said. "I'll call you if there's any change."

We had not had time to pack before the flight out, were in need of a shower and a change of clothes. She had rented rooms in a nearby Sheraton, but neither of us had left the hospital.

"I'm not leaving," I said.

"You can't do anything." Miriam's gaze held an abrasive glitter, pain she couldn't hide behind her smile. I also sensed relief. She confronted the ultimate motherhood test and so far had met the challenge.

"Go," she said.

The irony did not escape me. Vernon L. Oliver, he who had recently healed a paraplegic in front of ten thousand witnesses, could not heal his own girlfriend. I got up and walked down the aisle, stopped in front of the cubicle where a thoughtful God commanded his throne, fought the urge to spit in his direction.

Miriam was right, there wasn't a damn thing I could do.

Outside the hospital, I caught a cab and rode to a department store, where I purchased jeans and a pullover shirt, Jockey underwear, and two pairs of socks. At the Sheraton, I stripped and stepped into the shower. The hot water felt good on my shoulders, and I leaned against the wall and closed my eyes. Steam rose around my feet and floated upward. I soaped a washcloth and scrubbed clean, then repeated the process.

My cell rang, so I got out and fumbled around, raised the phone to my ear. Miriam told me to turn to channel 79. I flicked on the TV and watched a tape of the Chicago revival. A phone number for believers who wanted to help this fledgling ministry streamed across the bottom. Every so often, the camera cut away to where Yost worked a room filled with people sitting at desks and answering phones. Yost carried himself like the old man Chauncey had played the night he cleaned my house at Bible Camp. Hunched over. Defeated. His *60 Minutes* dream blown away like a leaf in an ill-timed wind.

When the camera panned the audience, I leaned forward, water dripping off my hair to my thighs, watched the congregation raise their hands, listened to the hallelujahs, marveled at our connection. Through it all, the hog gleamed in front of the stage. The show ended and Miriam gave me another call, asked me to guess how much money those phones had taken in from credit card numbers. I had no idea, and she told me the show was airing three times a day and so far we had cleared $7.4 million.

"How is she?" I said. "Has she said anything?"

"Get some sleep, Vernon. I'll call you if I need you."

Downstairs, in the hotel lounge, I smoked a pack of cigarettes, drank Budweiser on draft for the next two hours, started in on tequila shots with these hairdressers who had come from all over the country to attend a convention. I learned right away Cleveland was one of the hairdressing capitals of the world. A big-boned woman bought my drinks. Confided in my ear she was a lesbian and if I took her to my room she would let me lick her pussy. She was named after Marlo Thomas, the first woman to go without a bra on TV. Marlo had a tattoo on her neck, a fishhook in her eyebrow. She liked my long hair and said there were about a million things she could do with it if I gave her the chance.

"I'm not really a diehard lesbian," Marlo said. "If you take me up to your room I'd probably let you stick it in."

"My girlfriend is in the hospital," I said to no one in particular.

I got up from the table and plopped in a dark booth in the corner. The band began a rock-and-roll beat, and couples moved to the dance floor. I called Miriam and didn't get an answer. Called her again, no answer. I ran out of cigarettes and asked the waitress to bring me two more packs and a double rum and Coke. Marlo wobbled over and wanted to dance, and I followed her to the floor. Took a right and walked outside. Called Miriam again.

No answer.

A cab drove past and I hailed it, told the gray-haired Armenian behind the wheel I needed a driver for the night and he was it. He drove me down the street and dropped me at a bar. I walked in and ordered a drink, watched a guy feed a jukebox a dollar's worth of quarters. A girl, or maybe a guy, walked over. Offered a blow job for twenty dollars. He/she had pouty lips, high cheekbones, an Adam's apple. I declined and drank my tequila, listened to a band I didn't recognize hammer out a song I couldn't understand. The room was smoky and small, and each time the door to the restroom opened a urine stench settled over me. In the corner, a guy in a black shirt lay facedown on the table, and his exhales blew ripples across what I could only assume was vomit. I drank three more drinks and smoked my way through another pack. When I got up, he/she ducked under my arm and said they were going my way. I tossed them to the side and walked into the night.

The taxi was still there, driver fending off potential customers, so I got in and he drove down the block. The night was cool and cars cruised both directions, drivers exchanging looks with prostitutes who congregated under the streetlights. Every so often the taxi turned a corner, and the wind pushed like an invisible hand against the window. Styrofoam cups blew into the air and settled downward, only to be picked up and swirled along the sidewalks. The driver dropped me at Lucky's Tavern, and I drank two more drinks. At closing time, I left and caught a ride back to the hotel. Paid the driver an extra five hundred for his trouble.

In the parking lot, a cop pulled up in a squad car and flashed his lights. I staggered toward him and what happened next was a blur that ended with me in handcuffs on the way to jail.

I always suspected I'd wind up there sooner or later.

The next morning, Miriam and I left the courthouse and climbed into the rear seat of a taxi. The sun was dead ahead and low in the sky, and I blinked against the light. My head pounded, my stomach knotted from the alcohol. Miriam had made a few phone calls, gotten my charge reduced from resisting arrest to disorderly conduct, had paid the ticket on the way out the door. I expected a lecture. At least something about how it didn't look right for a televangelist to piss on a cop car while shouting "Fuck you, God."

"You don't have to say it," I said. "I know I'm an asshole."

Miriam faced me for the first and only time during the ride. There were no words, just an empty look, like someone had unscrewed a plug in her psyche and her fortitude had drained away.

We passed a bar, and I almost asked the driver to let me out. It's not like I could sink any lower in my employer's eyes.

Nurse Barlow had on a green uniform, and she wore her hair in a loose ponytail. Her voice had the tone of a professional distancing herself from the horrors of her job. I didn't blame her, figured dissociating herself during the day was the only way she could sleep at night. She told me the doctor thought it was a good idea if Rickie was surrounded by loved ones when she regained consciousness. Loved ones meant Miriam and me. Rickie's foster parents had failed to show. Obviously, they'd only raised her for the money Miriam sent their way.

I had not seen Rickie since coming to the hospital, could not produce an ID that showed she and I were related. Miriam had bluffed her way in from the onset and had been allowed to sit in the corner of the ICU.

I thanked Nurse Barlow for making an exception to their rules. "Not a problem," she said.

I followed her swaying hips down the hall, stepped to the side to make room for an orderly who pushed a man on a gurney. A sheet covered the man from toes to neck. He had a big head, full of unruly hair, and he gazed at a woman who walked at his side. I could not tell if they were saying hello or good-bye, only knew he was in the hospital, on a gurney, under a sheet, and none of those things added up to anything good.

Cleveland General, like all hospitals, had an astringent smell that turned my stomach. I breathed through my mouth, tried to control my nausea. Nurses padded the halls in rubber-soled shoes. Walked into and out of rooms. When I looked to my right or left, I glimpsed tubes running out of machines and connecting to various body parts. A priest administered last rites in one of the rooms, in another the preacher I'd met in the chapel read the Bible to a woman who closed her eyes and placed her hands in a prayerful pose. I wondered how many patients got religion at the last moment, a frantic effort to sail into eternity unscathed. I despised their hypocrisy. Man should die as he lived.

"Will she recognize me?" I said.

Nurse Barlow shook her head. "We won't know anything for the next couple of hours."

I shoved open the door and stepped inside. Miriam rose from a chair in the corner and grasped my hand. She had combed her hair and applied makeup, still wore the same wrinkled dress. Rickie's head was shaved, and her ears, eyes, nose, and mouth reminded me of slits in a pale pumpkin. The side of her head was bruised, skin an ugly purple, and her arms, crossed on her chest, were bandaged from cuts she'd suffered going through the windshield. For a wild moment, a careen down a fantasy sidewalk, I allowed myself to believe someone else's girlfriend lay there, only I knew that wasn't true, that Miriam had Rickie's purse and the ID in it said loud as anything this was Rickie Terrell and no other.

She was lucky to be alive. If the RV had rolled on top of her, the driver who saw the accident—he had slammed on the brakes, pulled off the interstate, and run into the field—would have come upon a crushed, deader-than-hell young woman. A state trooper arrived next, and he scooped dirt away from her mouth so she could breathe. I could only imagine her unconscious and lying in a soybean row, bleeding, eyes open and seeing nothing.

Now, she lay motionless, machines taking her pulse, breathing in metallic gasps. On the windowsill flower arrangements added color to the drabness of the room. Red, yellow, pink, green, it was all there. Nurses flitted in and out, offered encouraging words and recorded stats on a chart at the end of the bed. Miriam twisted tissue into little balls and piled them on her lap. I sat next to her and remained silent.

Eventually, I turned on the television and watched the religious channel run advertisements about the Biker Preacher's television show. The first time the show came on, I didn't watch it; the second time I left it on. The near nudity, my forty-foot body on the LCD screen, was so eye-catching I wondered if it was a distraction. The band had played well and I planned to keep them, although I wanted louder cymbals during the healing. Most of all, I wanted to descend from on high, made a mental note to talk to Miriam about building a platform strong enough to support and lower a two-hundred-pound man and a full-grown Harley.

Noise from the head of the bed and the slit in the bottom half of Rickie's face moved ever so slightly. Miriam nodded encouragement, and I heard something that sounded like a cough. Again, clearer this time. I got up and leaned over my girlfriend.

"Teddy bear in the round," Rickie said. "Street bobble into glorious uplifting."

"She's not making sense," I said.

I had not allowed myself to consider the possibility Rickie might leave the hospital a vegetable. Now it seemed a reality, and the thought of it twisted my insides. I resolved to take care of her, didn't matter how long. If that meant feeding her and wheeling her around in a wheelchair, so be it. Miriam sobbed and wiped her eyes with a tissue. The slit moved again.

"Nice-looking Harley," Rickie whispered.

"What?"

"I said, 'Nice-looking Harley.'"

I steadied myself on the handrail.

"You look ill," she said.

"The way you were . . ."

"You thought I had lost my marbles?" she said.

"The doctor, he, we, I thought you might be a vegetable or something."

"Payback's a bitch," she said. "You left me, you bastard."

I tried to laugh but it came out all choked up, so I squeezed her fingers and she squeezed back. I told her I was sorry I hadn't come for her, and she said all guys are idiots. Miriam looked down at her daughter and whispered words of thanks. Rickie spoke so low only I could hear.

"That cunt gave up her right to be here."

The slit closed, but her hand was still squeezing mine and I wasn't about to move. I asked Miriam to leave, and she grudgingly walked out the door. I had something to say. Didn't know how to say it without coming straight out.

"I want us to get married," I said. "I'll buy you a beach house anywhere in the world. I'll buy you as many houses as you want, I'll—"

"Okay."

"Okay?"

"Jesus Christ," Rickie said. "You'd think you were the one with the head injury."

Nurse Barlow came in and suggested we had talked enough.

"Seriously," she said, "you need to come back in five or six hours after she's had a rest."

I said good-bye and walked into the hall, where people jostled ten deep. Miriam had not wasted time spreading the news, and whispers of "That's the preacher who brought his dead girlfriend back to life" threaded the crowd. A woman in a pink frock fingered my sleeve and asked me to room 205, told me her father wasn't doing well.

"I saw you on television," she said. "I saw you make that woman walk."

She handed me a hundred-dollar bill, and I handed it back.

"I'm sorry; I have prior obligations."

I was thinking of the ring I was going to buy, of where we might hold the wedding. Miriam's Harbour Island house was the perfect place. I wanted all my actors there, along with Alton, maybe my parents, but I doubted they'd come. An intimate wedding in the Caribbean. If that didn't make Rickie happy, nothing would.

Chapter 11

"GOD HATH FORSAKEN ME," I say to Carleen Kathleen Stuttgart. "He's locked me into a box and thrown away the key."

Carly's arm extends through the slot into my cell, her hand on mine, something she has begun doing every time she serves me food. I study the crook on the inside of her elbow, where the uniform bunches into a blue fold, and wonder if she knows how easily I can break her arm. I suspect she has weighed this possibility, but the cancer rotting her ovaries makes the chance worth taking. Her hair has fallen out, thanks to the latest chemotherapy treatments, and a strawberry blond wig sits on her scalp. Wispy ends dangle to her shoulders. Her face has thinned, and her once pretty cheeks are now so hollow they sink into her jawline. During my services, I'd seen thousands who were withering away, but their anonymity created enough distance so their afflictions hadn't seemed real. This is different. I *know* this woman. I have a hard time looking at her, I truly do.

"I brought you something," she says, and offers a chunk of hard candy. "Watermelon flavor. I thought you might like it."

I toss the candy in my mouth, and my knees weaken as the flavor wraps around my tongue.

"I think I love you," I say, and we both know I'm kidding.

"Tomorrow, I'll bring you an orange flavor or maybe a strawberry." She withdraws and pats down her uniform, self-conscious of the weight she has lost. Carly has told me about herself, five-minute snippets that create a picture of someone who has had bad luck in life. Raised in New Orleans, she wound up in Florida because she fell in love with a traveling computer salesman who got her pregnant and didn't love her back. The birth was the highlight of her life, even after the baby became sick and doctor bills got so large she had to go on public assistance, something she hated, having come from a family that never took anything for free. She applied for the prison job after her daughter died, asked to be transferred to my block when she learned she was ill and not getting better. She was Pentecostal—washed in the blood of the lamb—and read her Bible daily. She believed she was on a nonstop ride to heaven.

"What do the doctors tell you?" I ask. "Any good news?"

Silvery wetness forms around her eyes. "I wish we could hold a revival, with the music and the dancing and the motorcycle, and you could call down the Holy Spirit and cast out this cancer demon, cast him right out and back to hell."

"Amen."

"Amen," she says.

I suck on the candy and study her face. "God spoke to me in a dream last night."

She can't hide the excitement in her voice. "About me?"

I get out my pad and scrawl seven words, afraid to say them out loud. I bring my finger to my lips, turn the pad so she can see it.

God wants you to help me escape.

Carly grips the metal slot, and her knuckles whiten.

God said I must have my freedom to heal you. I must be outside these walls. Help me and you help yourself.

She nods, a confirmation we both know is ironclad as any contract ever drawn.

I listen to conversation in the vent. Jermaine Jenkins, the black artist who hates white people, will be set free this afternoon, compliments of a DNA testing program the State of Florida instituted after Virginia executed an innocent man. Apparently, some other drug addict killed Jermaine's mother and grandmother. His voice comes through the vent and everyone shuts up.

"The black man done been wronged and I been wronged more than most," Jermaine says, and rambles on about honkies and how the white man controls everything. They'll have to kill him before he goes to prison again.

"That's right," someone farther down says. Dredge starts hollering Jermaine is one lucky nigger. Jermaine agrees and talks about what he's gonna do first thing, a desire that surprises me.

"If I were you," Dredge says, "I'd find some pussy, somethin' to take the edge off bein' in here so long."

"Pussy'll come later," Jermaine says. "First thing I'm doing when I get out of here is ordering five Big Macs and two large fries. I'm gonna sit at a booth and eat them like a free man."

Dredge is incredulous. "Leavin' death row and first thing he's goin' to McDonald's and eat hamburgers and fries. Hell, we got hamburgers and fries here."

Another convict speaks. "We ain't got McDonald's hamburgers and fries."

The block quiets, and I suspect every convict has envy in his heart. I sit on the floor and cross my legs. It is two o'clock and my time to think. It hurts too much to think about Rickie, to yearn for a touch I will never feel, so I try not to dwell on my past. I decide to think about Carly, and I wonder why she has not responded to my proposition. Surely she weighed the possibilities. She can die of ovarian cancer, or she can help me escape and claim she was seduced by my charm, and spend a few years in prison. Choosing incarceration and a potential long life over certain death is a no-brainer.

A guard walks down the block, and I hear a metallic groan as Jermaine's cell door opens. He walks past, a black man with darker-than-average skin. His head is bald, and the faint outline of a tattoo shadows his scalp.

"Good luck," I say.

"Preacher," he says over his shoulder. "You need a haircut."

Later that afternoon, I request a haircut and sit on the floor while a trustee, a model prisoner from the minimum security cell block, sticks his arms through the slot and runs clippers over my skull. I have not had my hair cut since I was a child, and locks gather around me like a hirsute history of my life. At six, Carly brings my dinner tray and tells me to look under the roll. She mentions my new look, and I tell her I made the change to symbolize a new start.

"New starts are good," she says.

I move the roll and pick up a folded paper. Carly reaches in and touches my hand, and I look at her arm wondering how loud she would scream. I entwine my fingers in hers, and she watches me curiously. This is the first time I have touched her back.

"I've lost forty pounds," she says. "I'm all skin and bones."

"You are a beautiful angel sent from on high. My harbor in a rocky sea."

"Pray for me," she says, and walks down the block.

I open the note and read the tiny words at a feverish pace.

> *Dearest Vern,*
>
> *Do you have any money? If not, I'll take out a second mortgage on my house, as the escape will require bribing several trustees and a laundry truck driver. Unfortunately (and I use that word because you've only shown yourself to me as a loving and peaceful man), you must perform a violent act to put things in motion. You must harm a guard, Vern. You must be thrown in the hole.*
>
> *Praise God on high, may he forgive us our sins.*
>
> *Love,*
>
> *Carly*
>
> *P.S. Please destroy this letter.*

That evening, I glance from my clock to the slot in the door, clock to slot, clock to slot, clock to slot, clock to slot. I hear footsteps, heavy and plodding, a man who has walked this walk many times. I do not know his name, only know when his face appears the skin is liver-spotted around his temples, and he will look through the window as he inserts my tray through the slot and he will see but not see, see but not see, see but not see, and then he is here and the hand is on the edge of the tray, an expectant clutch of skin, bone, and veins wanting me to reciprocate so he can be on his way.

My fingers close around his wrist, I yank, and his hand and arm come through the slot into my cell. He twists and reaches for the pepper spray on his waist. I hold him, not having thought past this moment, believing instinct would guide me, but it fails when I need it most and I must decide between biting and breaking, and then I realize I have a third choice, to bite and break, and I lower my mouth to his fingers and grind teeth against bone. Warm blood spatters and outside the door he sinks to his knees, mouth open in a scream. I scream back at him that the Lord forgives because they know not what they do, yank the arm in the direction it does not bend. Muscles, tendons, and ligaments give, and his elbow pops. I let go and his arm dangles like the deadweight that it is. Blood drips to the floor and his face turns white. He falls backward. Guards run up in bunches, a flurry of shouts and blue uniforms outside my cell, an order to turn around and insert my hands into the slot, to cuff up because they intend to transport me to the hole.

"Bastards," I say. "You're nothing but a bunch of whiners who couldn't make it in a cop uniform so you wind up here. You lie with your sisters and consort with the devil. The Holy Ghost has risen and smited you with one blow. Confess your sins, confess them or face eternal damnation."

They come for me, officers in riot gear, faces grim for the challenge ahead. Pepper spray hits me in the face, blinds me, and I stand erect and howl toward the door. I do not need to see clearly to navigate my cell; this is my home, my domain, and let those fuckers enter at their peril. They spring upon me like jackals, nightsticks raised, huffed beer breaths in my face. I feel the weight of them and recede to a corner, swing out through the blur, catch a guard on his jaw with a crack that sends teeth against the wall. I revel in the texture—the cussing, the smells, the feel of my fingers as they claw against a bared throat—but as suddenly as it begins, it is over. The weight of them is too much for me, there are too many arms and legs pounding my body, too many nightsticks beating my head. I am bloody and breathing hard, I am the lamb at the slaughter, I am leaving this cell. I force myself to stay conscious as they hoist me upward and drag me into the hall, and it is only now I hear convicts cheering in loud voices. The guard with the broken arm and gnawed fingers is gone, and we follow his blood spatters on the floor. My leg drags behind me, sharp pain at the knee, and the skin around my right eye swells until I can only see out of my left. My tongue probes the inside of my mouth, and I discover a guard isn't the only one to lose teeth in the scuffle. Two molars are missing on the right side of my jaw.

A guard punches me in the stomach and another takes a shot that lands on the side of my head. I lose consciousness, wake in a room on a yellowed mattress. I am spreadeagled, Jesus on a horizontal cross, and my hands and legs are cuffed to the edge of the bed. A warmness soaks my crotch, and now I am the drunken old man who spent too long at the bar.

A doctor in a white coat prods my knee, says I'm in the prison hospital and the best he can do is an Ace bandage and a couple days of pain pills. I open my cracked and bloodied lips. Carly's plan is under way.

I am dragged into the hall two days later and told I am headed for the hole. On my way, a stumble through poorly lit halls, I look for anything that suggests escape is possible. All I see is guards and walls and metal doors. We enter another hallway and I note the concrete is darker, understand immediately my escape will begin where the prison is most vulnerable, a block built in an era before motion sensors and electronic door locks and security cameras.

We come to a rusted door, and I am cast inside a cell like a sack of dirty laundry. My leg twists under me and I cry out. The door slams and light from the hallway disappears. The air turns muddy and humid. There is no bed, nothing between me and the floor, no vent to stabilize the temperature at 72 degrees. In the corner, sewer stench flows from a black hole. I lie on my back and try to sleep, wonder when my angel will come for me.

Three weeks later, time that went by without me seeing Carly, Sandoval visits and rambles on about how he still has some tricks up his sleeve. We are nearing the midway point in the appeal's process, and he desperately needs to find new evidence to set me free. Valid evidence, that is. My followers send him fraudulent conversations on tape, doctored pictures, affidavits swearing I was elsewhere at the time. We don't discuss the futility of his efforts. Clients who sign confessions don't get second chances in the court, and Sandoval is destined to fail. He knows this and still remains upbeat. It is a brave front.

Today, he sweats profusely, and his tennis whites are stained under the arms. I am naked, clothes balled in a corner where I use them for a pillow.

"I bribed a guard for your manuscript," Sandoval says. "I spent the last couple of nights reading, then photocopied it and sent it off to the screenwriter."

Writing an autobiography is one thing, someone reading it is another. I feel exposed, vulnerable, and take a moment to slip into my underwear, climb into my overalls.

"I haven't finished it," I say.

"I know."

"I'm writing in my head," I say. "I don't need pencil and paper."

"The screenwriter has read it."

"I breathlessly await his verdict."

"He doesn't have to like it," Sandoval says. "He's paid to transform one genre to another."

"A literary whore—"

"He said it's quite good."

I can't hide my smile.

Sandoval rubs his chin and clears his throat. "I have several literary agents calling the office. Cathy Paulson, Kat Knickers, Larry Wadsworth to name a few."

I stretch out on the floor, ignore the ache in my knee. "How do you like my new accommodations? I call the decor Spartan Chic—it's sparse but the lack of furniture increases floor space."

"Are you all right?" Sandoval says. "Are you holding up all right?"

I snicker at the inaneness of his words.

"Sandoval," I say. "I've never been better."

Light footsteps down the block, and for a moment I am insanely happy, only to realize whoever approaches walks much slower than Carly, much less deliberate. A guard shows up holding my supper tray. A short man who thrusts his chest out, he's trying to appear bigger than he is. His voice comes loud and stern. "Step away from the door, Mr. Oliver."

"I thought you were Ms. Stuttgart," I say.

"Mr. Oliver, if you want to eat, I advise you to step away from the door."

I step backward.

"Move to the rear of your cell, Mr. Oliver."

I step all the way back, lean against the wall.

"How is she?" I say. "Is she doing all right?"

He balances the tray on the metal slot, retreats into the middle of the hall. I cannot read his eyes or facial expression.

"Come get your tray, Mr. Oliver. Then back away from the door."

I do as he requests and the slot closes and he walks down the hall. I have no window to look out of, no Dredge to placate, no spiders to kill. My only hope is a woman dying of cancer. I laugh at the ludicrousness of the situation, laugh so loud and long my throat hurts.

Chapter 12

A MONTH AFTER RETURNING TO Harbour Island, I had my hog shipped via cargo boat. Rickie and I rode south the morning of the wedding, took the bridge to Eleuthera, slowing down whenever I spotted grazing goats on the side of the road. We wore helmets, black leather, and new boots. She liked how mine looked unlaced and wore hers the same. I had discovered a sandy two-track during my travels, and I turned off the asphalt and we rode up a hill that overlooked a secluded inlet. Talking Rickie into holding the ceremony at her mother's house had proved harder than I expected. My bride had relented, on one condition. The family photograph taken on these occasions was a no-go. I hadn't argued the point. I had not forgotten my silent pledge to help bring Miriam and Rickie closer together, and giving up a photograph to get the two in the same zip code seemed like a fair trade.

We dismounted and took off our helmets. High up, gulls wheeled across a turquoise sky. Sea oats rattled on the slopes, the updraft bringing a salty ocean smell. I ran my fingertips over Rickie's face, paused on her temples, on the veins so precariously close to the surface. Her hair was fuzzy and short as a newborn chick's. The swelling had gone down and her wounds had healed.

She watched me with those big eyes, jammed her hands on my chest and pushed me away.

"It's beautiful," she said.

"It would be a nice spot to build."

"Too bad Miriam lives close by."

I looked away to hide my disappointment.

"She's trying," I said.

"Did I ever tell you my earliest memories?" Rickie scooped sand and sifted it through her fingers. "Did I ever tell you what it was like growing up?"

Shifting breeze tore at her words.

"Do you know what it's like to grow up unloved?" she said. "Untouched? Do you know what it's like to want a mother's beating heart only to be pushed away? Do you know what it's like to be treated as a commodity?"

I'd brought her here to tell her something important, had chosen this grandiose setting to match the conversation.

Things were not going as planned.

"That bitch gave me up," she said.

"That 'bitch' has offered us forty-nine percent of Miracles, Inc., which, at the moment, is worth around fourteen million."

The conversation was finally going my direction. I straddled the bike, and Rickie made no move to get on.

"She's quite the businesswoman," she said.

"Yes, she is."

"She thinks she can buy my love."

"Yes, she does," I said.

"Seven million is a good start."

I told her to please get her pretty ass on the bike, that we were rich and let's forget the bad and remember the good. Rickie walked off into the sea oats, hunched slightly at the shoulders, stood for a long time without moving. She seemed shut down, like her brain needed quiet time to continue its repair. Eventually, she came out of it, walked my way, and quoted the first stanza of a favorite poem.

> *It was many and many a year ago,*
> *In a kingdom by the sea,*
> *That a maiden there lived whom you may know*
> *By the name of Annabel Lee:*
> *And this maiden she lived with no other thought*
> *Than to love and be loved by me.*

I remembered the poem from a collection in a book back in the RV. Edgar Allan Poe was the author, and he was writing about doomed lovers. I thought it was an odd reflection on our wedding day, and told her so.

"Life is not a bowl of cherries," she said.

On the way back, Rickie clung to me and said forty miles per hour was her favorite speed, that the bike was better than any vibrator she'd had between her legs. I slowed until her thighs tightened, and she moaned. Maintained forty all the way to Miriam's house, figuring, if I was going to spoil my wife, I might as well get started.

I wore a white shirt, beige slacks—creases so sharp I felt like I was in the military—and a pair of Birkenstock sandals. I'd left the shirt open at the throat, anticipating the 90-degree heat on the beach. Miriam, in a front row seat, adjusted the flower in her hair.

Poked the shell earrings in her lobes. Her dress was form-fitting and long, and I could not look at her without remembering her touch.

Rose-covered trellises created an archway over the sidewalk. The house had been newly painted, and the Double Flamingo sparkled pink in the afternoon sunlight. Actors in costume—1930s lingerie for women, sailor garb for men—mingled on the lawn and drank ale amid bawdy toasts and sexual barter. Laney had on a bodice partially ripped down the front, and every so often a nipple peeked from around the lace. She waved at me and plucked the garter on her leg, went back to talking to Chauncey, who had a stuffed parakeet glued to his shoulder. Mrs. Yost, who could not be talked into wearing a nightie, adjusted her fruit hat, and smoothed the lapel on her blouse. Mr. Yost, in suit and tie, scowled in my direction.

My mother had written a letter suggesting she and my father failed me, and if I would only give up the Pentecostal ministry and return to my Baptist roots, she was certain the family would meet in its entirety in heaven. Apparently, because the first-class tickets were not in the envelope, they had cashed them and applied the money toward bills. Relieved she wasn't here preaching to the sinners, I did not hold their decision against them.

Everyone was hot and sweating, and I suggested we get this show on the road. Walked up to a black man Miriam had hired to perform the ceremony. The sea captain, dressed in a World War II uniform bursting at his belly, had a white burr head and his breath smelled like he'd begun celebrating early. A photographer, beret over his stringy hair, stepped out of the background and held a camera to his eye. Clicked away.

What came next was mostly a blur—the tranquillity of waves

on the beach, rows of faces in the seats, Miriam dabbing at her eyes, and Rickie gliding forward, white-gloved hand nestled in the crook of Alton's arm. She had on a veil and was dressed in flowing white and behind her two little black girls held her train off the ground. Alton smiled and Rickie smiled and Mrs. Yost played and Miriam sniffled and I stood there with my hand clenched, holding a ring I hoped I wouldn't drop and lose in the sand. The sea captain spoke a few words and I remember saying "I do" and Rickie saying "I do" and me sliding a ring on her finger and her sliding a ring on my finger, then kissing her in front of sand and sea, in front of everyone who cared to be there.

To love, honor, cherish, and protect.

I had given my word, once again, to someone I loved. I had failed the first time, did not intend to fail again.

The reception was held on the front lawn, where the Manhattan Maniacs jammed under palm trees. They wore black caps over their bald heads, took requests, and played "Margaritaville" with a bluesy beat. Rickie, who snuggled beside me on a love seat positioned under one of the mammoth flamingos, had gone off into a daze. I prodded and massaged her neck, but she never blinked. Laney came up and held out a gift. I opened the box, which held a silver pot and an assortment of exotic teas.

"I heard Rickie likes the sea so the teas all come from the islands," Laney said, and pointed out Jamaica Tropical Fruit and Caribbean Mango Blend. She was wearing a diamond ring she had purchased out of her bonus money, and she and Chauncey planned on marrying in the next couple of years.

Miriam brought out a gold-plated tray holding a contract and two pens in polished inkwells. She positioned the tray in front of me, and my wife blinked herself to consciousness. My wife. She was finally mine. No more running off in an RV, no more struggling to pay bills, no more missing her in the middle of the night. Miriam spoke in an official voice that tapered affectionately the more she went on.

"We are gathered today to celebrate the union of my daughter and a young man I have grown to also love. To honor and support them, I am giving them part ownership of Miracles, Inc. I offer them my love and devotion and fervently hope they sign as soon as possible so we can get on with this party."

Rickie paused before writing her last name. We had not discussed if she would take mine, keep hers, or form a hyphenated combination, and she seemed to decide at the last minute she would go with Oliver. Which was fine with me. Rickie Oliver. It had a nice ring to it.

I signed, and Rickie and I became instant millionaires. Miriam extended her arms, and I met her halfway. After a reciprocated hug, Miriam opened her arms again, and Rickie stepped into the embrace. Miriam's shoulders shook, and I knew she was trying to heal through Rickie's touch. But Rickie was no Pentecostal preacher and Miriam was no actor, and when they separated they were the same as before.

The photographer, who held his camera at his side, glanced at me and I shook my head. Miriam had laid herself at the feet of an unforgiving God. There was no point in asking Rickie if she had changed her mind about the photograph.

Mrs. Yost tottered over. Gave me a sloppy kiss on the cheek. Mr. Yost was in a rear bedroom nursing a headache, and I guess she was cutting loose. The bananas glued on her hat looked real enough to eat. She handed me a card holding a hundred-dollar check, and Rickie and I said we would use the money for something good. Mrs. Yost tottered off and began a rickety tango with Chauncey.

I asked my wife if she wanted to walk back to the beach and she said sure, so that's where we headed. The sky turned deep blue, almost black to the east, but to the west the sun was still above the ocean and violet threaded the clouds down low. The air cooled and the breeze lessened and the waves kept their timeless rhythm. We settled onto the sand, side by side, and she built a sand castle, fingers working at the shape until it formed a pyramid.

"I think I'm crazy," she said.

I unbuttoned the top of her dress. Her hands followed mine, redoing what I'd undone.

"I'm trying to talk to you," she said. "I'm trying to tell you something."

"I'm listening."

"Sometimes I go off to this bad place." She drove her palm into the pyramid and smashed it flat, wiped grit off her hands. "I think terrible things."

Rickie built another pyramid closer to the water, and the waves ebbed around the base, eroding her efforts. She started talking about Seashore, about the horse she'd had as a child, said it was the only thing back then that loved her.

"Do you know what I did?" she said. "Do you know how I reciprocated?"

I watched the waves level her castle, watched the sand liquefy and absorb into itself.

"I stopped feeding it, Vernon. . . . Do you understand? I stopped feeding it and it got sick and died."

"You were a teenager, for Christ's—"

"I thought those kinds of thoughts were gone," she said. "I thought I had submerged them so deep they'd never come back. . . ."

She stared out into the ocean.

"Things changed after the accident," she said. "It's like something cracked inside my brain and let my demons back out."

The neurologist had suggested Rickie might exhibit eccentricity, so I was not altogether unprepared for the bizarreness of this conversation. Instead of feeding her fantasy world, I changed course.

"Why don't you go back to college?" I said. "That'll take your mind off things."

She gave me an exasperated look and said college was an impossibility now, then said she was tired of talking. Suggested we head back to the reception and act like a normal bride and groom. Normal sounded like a wonderful idea to me, so we got up and walked the way we'd come. Miriam was slow dancing with Alton, and they looked so comfortable I wondered if that was the first time those bodies had been so close together. Rickie and I drank and danced, opened gifts for the next hour. I discovered a card we had missed in the seam of the couch. Opened the envelope, scanned the inscription. I looked around, studied every face but Rickie's, a silent accusation she recognized because she asked what was wrong. After assuring her everything was all right, I walked to the bathroom, locked the door, reread the card.

Dear Vernon Oliver,

If you do not deposit $5,000 a week in this offshore account, I will go to the media and expose your opera-

tion. That's $260,000 a year out of millions. Consider
this extortion the cost of doing business and move on with
your life. I expect the first payment within seven days.

The letter had an account number for a bank in the Cayman
Islands. The envelope wasn't postmarked, which meant someone
in the house had placed it on the couch. All signs pointed toward
Mr. Yost, who had not talked to me since the night the tornado
hit the carnival. Chauncey was also a possibility. Hell, it could be
any of the actors. Rickie knocked on the door. I came out and her
gaze searched my face.

"Tell me," she said.

I picked her up and carried her to the bedroom.

"It's nothing," I said.

"You sure?"

"I'm sure," I said, although I was anything but. My gut told me
this was only the beginning, that extortion led to other crimes and
if we weren't careful we'd all wind up dead or in prison.

Chapter 13

"I don't give a crap about artistic license," I say. "I have never been in a car chase."

Sandoval stuffs the screenplay in his briefcase, and the gold ring on his finger reflects the murky light. He has a pinched look, like he holds his breath. I don't blame him. I've been breathing sewer stench for five months and have not grown accustomed to the smell. I close my eyes and open them and he is still there, in the concrete hall, in a chair, sweaty shirt stuck to his chest. He hates visiting me in the hole, and I suspect if it weren't for the chapters in my head, he would abandon me altogether. Today, he read me the screenplay's opening pages, which begin with the time Lucy and I went joyriding in our parents' car. There was no car chase. We didn't see a cop car on those country roads.

"We're trying to get Danny Schofield for the lead," Sandoval said. "You know, that actor who came out of professional wrestling? His people are interested."

"If I wanted a steroid freak to play me on the big screen I would have suggested Stan Hammel."

"Our budget can't afford Hammel."

Sounds—doors opening and closing—emanate from another part of the prison. The noise is garbled and hollow, as though I'm underwater. The irony amuses me. Carly's escape plan requires I crawl deep into the whale's belly. I am Jonah in an orange jumpsuit, and I await my deliverer. She has not visited, and I believe she has had trouble transferring to this part of the prison. Sandoval drones in that boring voice of his, says starting a movie with a car chase grabs a viewer's attention. Film studies back up the theory.

"Short attention spans," he says. "It's a problem in the theater these days."

Moviegoers aren't the only people with short attention spans. Solitary confinement has had an unusual effect on my brain. Before entering this cell, I could concentrate for long periods. If I had a problem, I grabbed hold of it until I worked it out. Now, my mind reminds me of an impatient finger on a remote, switching from channel to channel, rarely focusing on anything long enough to understand its meaning.

I tell Sandoval I am making great progress writing in my head, but truthfully I only work in fits and starts.

Car chase. I can't believe the movie will open with a car chase.

Seven months come and go, and still no Carly. I do not inquire about her. I'm here, I'm in the hole. It's not like I'm going anywhere. When she's ready, I'll be ready. To prepare myself, I do sit-ups and push-ups for two hours a day. Least I think it's two hours. For all I know it might be four hours or ten minutes. To track the days, the months, the change of seasons, I keep a mental count of the breakfasts that enter my cell. Winter turns into spring and spring turns into summer and the air turns hot. On the worst days, I stretch out on the concrete and absorb its coolness. Sweat oozes from my skin and my mouth turns cottony; my tongue becomes too lazy to work. I drink water but cannot get enough of it, and my urine turns brown as cider. I mumble out loud on the worst days, tell myself this must eventually end, that Carly is coming for me and I will flee this hole, but my words are the speech of someone who has lived in the whale's belly for too long, the beseechings of a forsaken man.

Sandoval visits frequently, and it takes me a while to understand why. He thinks I might die without finishing my book. On some days I don't respond to his questions, on others I'm talkative and don't want him to leave. Months turn into a year, one year into two, two years into three. My existence turns foggy and I sit cross-legged on the floor, in a gray haze that numbs my body and makes it difficult to move. I eat and drink enough to stay alive, scrape my nails on the concrete when they grow long, practice what I'll say when Carly opens that door. Instead of berating her for taking so long, I will welcome her into my abode, shake her hand, and suggest we be on our way. We'll walk out of here arm in arm, two old friends rejoicing in their reunion.

One day, Sandoval strides down the hall with more passion than usual. I know his footsteps, how his right foot walks heel to toe and his left comes down squarely, a thud only he makes, and I wonder why he comes so quickly, realize he has news to share. He arrives and paces back and forth. His tie is askew, like he didn't take the usual time to dress himself, and his shirt is open at the belly. Skin peeks out, a tan rim above his belt. Punditry has been good to my friend.

"Damn." His tone is anything but boring.

This is the first time I have heard him cuss. He repeats himself, an attorney who needs his needle lifted and dropped on a different track. I lie on my back and study the bulb overhead. The light never goes out, a dim sun lit for eternity.

"Vernon," he says, "we lost another appeal."

I sit up and crook my finger. I tap the tip to my palm. Sandoval moves close, and I whisper in his ear.

"Carly Stuttgart promised to help me escape."

His teeth form perfect squares in a pink gum line. His breath smells like he ate scallops for lunch. "She passed away, Vernon."

"Carly passed away?"

"She died shortly after she provided me with your autobiography. I think she had some sort of cancer."

I try to conjure up a kernel of emotion, try to feel something, anything that suggests I'm still a functioning human. After a time, I crab into a corner, where I watch my attorney watch me. He asks if I will dictate into a tape recorder, and I tell him no. I see the anger in the squint of his eyes, the twitch of his lip, the flush around his collar.

"They plan to kill you," Sandoval says. "They have a syringe with your name on it."

He wants to hurt me, but I can't be hurt. I am the lighthouse that withstood years of sea and sand, I am the—

Sandoval says good-bye and walks down the hall. He stops several times, once starting back toward me, but in the end, he continues on. I shout after him, a growl that comes from deep inside.

"You don't understand and you never will."

Guards shackle my hands and feet, walk me to death row, deposit me in my original cell. Bloodstains on the floor are gone, and the walls have been painted light brown. Fresh sheets sit in a pile on the bed. The toilet gleams, and I wonder if it's possible to forget a concrete sewer after breathing the stench every day for four full years. Decide it's something I will remember for the rest of my life. Such as it is.

The sky through the window has a tint that reminds me of cotton socks fresh from the dryer. Wind blows, a whisper I can't hear through the thick pane, but I know it's happening because weeds along the far fence bend toward the ground. A grave has been dug, a brown rectangle surrounded by green grass, and a marker has been added.

I place my chair under the vent, climb aboard, knock on the cell wall. No answer.

I knock louder.

"Dredge," I say. "Answer your doorbell."

A voice comes from far down the vent, and I ask whoever it is to repeat himself.

"Dredge had a heart attack about two weeks ago," the voice says.

The air blowing through the vent feels cool on my eyelids, a delicious feeling I will remember forever.

"He's dead?"

"Naw," the voice says. "That punk in that grave got shanked on cell block E. Dredge is in the prison hospital."

The irony does not escape me. The great State of Florida, Lady Justice herself, will spend time and money to fix a heart it wants to stop. I ask the voice for a name and he tells me he's Zach Handover, that he murdered five people inside a Wendy's in Orlando.

"Least I ain't never raped a woman," he says. "Least I ain't never stuck my dick up a boy's ass. If they'd put that cocksucker in this cell, he wouldn't have needed surgery."

I climb down and sit at my desk, rummage through letters that arrived while I was in the hole. There must be a thousand or more. I read a note from a boy in Australia. He'd tried to send a full-sized Harley poster, only to have it returned because the State does not allow convicts this luxury. Determined, he chopped the poster into squares and writes he will send them one at a time. I open his letters and piece the poster together. The road takes shape, then the bike, then the background of snowcapped mountains. The poster—another of Miriam's moneymaking schemes—is a picture of me on a pass in the High Sierra. My hair streams in the wind, and I have this smile, like I'm so happy I can't stand it. High up, on a trail that overlooks the pass, hikers wearing bright backpacks wave as I rumble past. I close my eyes and feel the heat of the big engine, I smell that cool mountain air. God, I lived a life.

Footsteps in the hall, and I scoop up the poster pieces and stash them under my pillow. A guard walks past, a glimpse of a pressed uniform. I stand at the window and study the graveyard. Raise my hand as though to ward off an invisible threat, understanding, for the first time, what it feels like to be truly afraid.

After a while, I sit at my desk and pick up the pencil and doodle on the pad. I draw big circles and small circles and in-between circles. I fill up a page and start another. It feels settling to have pencil in hand. I will begin with my wedding anniversary, in a place as wild as any on earth.

Chapter 14

LION ROARS FLOATED ON the night air. In the distance, the drum of hooves on the Kenyan savanna faded away and the whir of insects filled the vacuum. Dust settled over the Land Rover, and the air became thick and dry. Rickie, who had taken a pee break outside the passenger door, climbed back in and unscrewed a thermos. I started the engine, and we drove over a two-track so dim it barely showed under the headlight glare. The caravan, five vehicles in all, followed close behind. I glanced at my wife, whose skin had a green tint from the dashboard lights. Rickie had a solemnness I understood completely. There was something about poverty and disease that wore on the soul. She poured a cup of coffee and handed it to me.

We'd been married for three years. I had hoped to fly to Paris or Rome for a candlelight dinner, but Miriam wanted to complete a documentary before *60 Minutes* aired its piece on Miracles, Inc. She wanted the world to know we'd built eight clinics and nine schools across Africa, that we were heading to Central America in the fall, where contractors had scheduled a groundbreaking in Guatemala. Neither Rickie nor I argued with Miriam. My wife and I made $5 million apiece per year, and we accepted the inconvenience—driving over bumpy roads, dining with natives who preferred gazelles to Ho Hos, and taking bathroom breaks that didn't include running water—as sacrifices worth the effort. I thought we'd gone overboard with charity work, that one or two clinics were enough of a smokescreen, but Miriam continued to spend more and more, claiming it was good business. She didn't fool me; my mother-in-law *liked* helping the less fortunate. Sometimes, I wondered if that hadn't been her motivation all along.

The dashboard radio crackled, and Miriam asked if we'd like to camp or continue to the village. She was in a Land Rover in the middle of the caravan, behind the camera crew truck.

"Mommy Dearest wants a powwow," Rickie said. "I guess her bony ass is tired of riding the seat."

I keyed the mike and suggested there was no sense stopping when we had so little ground to cover. Miriam consented, and the caravan rolled over the savanna.

Two hours later, we arrived at a village and parked in front of a pale building that rose in ghostly testament to our charity. A generator hummed, and moths flitted around lights mounted under eaves. The outlines of thatched huts broke up the shadows. Embers glowed in circular fireplaces, and the scent of burned wood drifted into the cab. We were accustomed to raucous greetings, replete with loud drumming and colorfully dressed natives, were surprised when no one appeared. We got out, and I unrolled our tent in dry crackling grass. Miriam appeared out of the darkness.

"I wonder where everyone is," I said.

My mother-in-law had a knack for looking composed in all environments. She took off her safari hat, tied back her hair. "Isn't this the village that has the snake problem?"

I instinctively looked at the ground.

"Pythons," she said. "They tend to eat at night."

Rickie and I took sleeping pills to calm the coffee jitters, crawled under the mosquito netting and reclined on our air mattress. We'd been in Africa long enough to know pythons preferred smaller prey, so any concerns we had faded away. She lit a candle and I handed her a diamond bracelet, told her "Happy Anniversary." She gave me keys to a Harley custom designed for my long legs, lay in my arms, and I rubbed a sore spot on her shoulder. We were quiet, unafraid of the silent moments in our relationship.

I closed my eyes, opened them sometime later when animals lumbered past the village. Rickie wouldn't wake up, so I walked outside the tent by myself, to the nearby Land Rover, where I switched on the spotlight and swept the beam over gray backs and swaying trunks. Ears flapped and swatted against ancient skin. I turned off the light and watched the movement of the herd block stars low in the sky, breathed the muskiness that followed them on their journey. I'd seen enough impalas, water buffaloes, and lions to fill a football stadium, never grew tired of the elephants. Elephants did what they wanted when they wanted, and there wasn't an animal their equal on earth.

A rustle to my right, and I swiveled the beam, cut a swath through the darkness. Yellow eyes, low to the ground, reflected the light. I couldn't make out the animal, hyena maybe, could have been a warthog. It moved away, and I headed back to the tent.

"Elephants," I said, and closed the flap behind me.

Rickie's jaw twitched, and she rolled her head to the side. My fingertips sought the pulse in her neck. The thump picked up speed, stayed that way for a minute or so, and settled down. A scary dream, no doubt. I tucked the blanket under her neck and eased myself down to the mattress. The sting of her abandonment had not lessened through the years, and I suspected it would never go away. Occasionally, I could see agony in her eyes, the shadows that flickered in the background. If I could, I'd take her pain and make it my own. I'd swallow it like a bitter pill and live with the consequences.

In the morning, I made coffee and stood around while the land brightened under the emerging sun. Far off, snow-mantled Kilimanjaro rose from the earth. To the east, where the land flattened, the savanna had a grayish tint that turned blue where it merged with the sky. Closer, not more than a hundred yards from the village, trees grew along a meandering river.

A squat black man walked out of a hut and bent over a cooking pit. He piled on kindling, blew on the coals, and soon smoke curled upward and drifted over the village. Rickie came outside, Miriam joined us, and we ate cheesy burritos the camp cook made over a Coleman stove.

"Change of plans," Miriam said. "We're turning around and heading back to Nairobi this afternoon."

I set my coffee cup on the Land Rover's hood. We had not filmed the clinics to the south and whatever prompted this change had to be important. Rickie handed me a napkin, and I wiped my mouth. My wife wore a white shirt and white pants, sandals brown as the earth. She had not combed her hair, and a stray lock fell over her temple and down her cheek. A camcorder case dangled from her neck. She was filming our journey, creating a private record of our travels.

"I received a call from *60 Minutes* last night," Miriam said, and

held up her cell by way of explanation. "They offered, in the interest of balanced programming, to interview someone from our
organization."

"They're out for blood."

"Tell me about it."

I saw concern in her eyes, and I know she saw the same in
mine. Miracles, Inc., had created powerful enemies in the Pentecostal world, and it had only been a matter of time before they
took their smear campaign to the airwaves.

The sign over the hospital door spelled the name of the local witch
doctor, THOMAS RADIMA, who no doubt profited from the publicity. Miriam didn't like these boneshakers and neither did I, but
villagers were more accepting of modern medicine if it involved
chanting, dead animals, and mysterious herbs. Hence, the Mr.
Radimas of the world were free to roam our facilities.

Miriam, Rickie, and I entered the building, and a doctor walked
up and introduced himself. The color of Raj's turban matched his
white teeth, white lab coat, and white shoes. He bowed and shook
Miriam's hand, led us down the hallway to a cavernous room
where children occupied nine of fourteen beds. I walked down the
aisle, followed by the sound guy, who held a mike over my head.
The camera guy, a heavyset man who constantly mopped sweat off
his forehead, shot me from different angles. Rickie stayed in the
background, arm crooked, camcorder to her eye.

Raj's wife walked into the room and handed the children pills
in blue cups. Her skin was coppery and smooth, and her black
eyes were alert and businesslike. She wore a sari the same color
as her husband's coat. Color-coordinated his and hers, the perfect

husband/wife, doctor/nurse combination. Anyone who saw our documentary would think this couple had chosen to practice in Kenya for humanitarian reasons. I knew better. Raj and Raj's wife were mercenary as they come. They were here because Miriam had paid off their student loans in exchange for five years' work in the bush, a welcome trade for a young doctor and a young nurse hip-deep in debt. They planned to open a practice in Los Angeles soon enough, where they would gut their share of bank accounts for nose jobs, liposuctions, and breast enhancements.

My crew and I walked up to a baby, and I patted her bony arm. Wanjiru was nine months old, and her mother had passed along her AIDS virus. No one knew how the disease arrived, but one day it did and now over half the village was infected. This was the mother's third child, the last two dead from the same fate. I stepped back and Raj went on camera, explained how Miracles, Inc., was helping children all across the continent.

A loud knock shook the main entrance. Raj excused himself and I followed him down the hall, through the open door, into sunlight. Villagers milled around a weeping woman. She dug her fingernails into her arm, and blood ran over the charcoal skin.

Her boy was missing.

Miriam took me to the side and in low tones suggested we not begin our return journey until this afternoon. Rickie and I went to our tent, waited to hear word from the searching villagers. She opened a package of saltine crackers, nibbled, and wouldn't look my way. I ate one of her crackers and slapped at the largest grasshopper I'd ever seen. Add a grub to the meal and we'd have a Kenyan dinner for two.

"Ginormous bugs," I said.

"Do we have any weed left?"

The only way that Rickie and I could handle the decimation of this trip was to be stoned throughout the whole time. I got out a pipe, and we smoked the rest of our stash. A sweet, earthy odor filled the tent. I thought about taking her for a ride in the Land Rover, far enough away so we could have a private moment, but I was tired of the shifter jamming my leg and suspected she was tired of her butt sliding around on vinyl seats. She stripped and asked me for a back rub. I kneaded her shoulders, and I could tell from the way her hips moved that she wanted more. I kissed my way down her spine, and she rolled over and looked me in the eyes. We were too far into it to stop, and our movement and our moans became louder than the tent could hold. She came and I came, and we lay with arms entwined, sweat dripping off our bodies.

"You are such a prick," she said.

I rolled off her.

"I saw you ogling that nurse," she said. "You couldn't take your eyes off her."

I picked up the pipe, toked, and nothing came out. She'd drop it soon enough; she always did. Shouts ripped through the air, and we hurriedly dressed. I went outside, Rickie close behind, and we jogged toward villagers milling in the long grass next to the river. A shot rang out, and shouts turned into wails. We came up on an engorged python, caught in an orgy of moaning men, women, and children. The snake had been shot in the head and still writhed and twitched like snakes do after they've been killed. Mr. Radima, dressed in a burlap sack, chanted and turned slow circles. The witch doctor wore beads in his ears and had calculating eyes, and I could not look at him without thinking about miracles I'd pulled off in my services.

A villager slit the snake's throat and worked the knife tip toward the lump, exposing the stomach one inch at a time.

"Let's go," I said. "I don't want to see this."

Rickie stayed where she was, camcorder to her eye, a tree instantaneously rooted. The blade ripped closer to the lump and the villagers quieted, leaving Radima to chant in what appeared to be increasing desperation. Raj whispered villagers believed the witch doctor had the power to exchange one form with another, and if the boy was in the python's belly, he would escape and reappear. I knew Kenyans believed a witch doctor could remove boils and influence soccer matches, but had no idea they took faith to this extreme.

Two feet appeared, cloven hoofs that brought relieved sighs from me, Rickie, and Raj. I looked around for Miriam, who stood next to the doctor's wife. The knife slit onward, and python skin fell away from the gelatinous lump. The knife curved again, a bloody flash that exposed impala horns jutting from a furry scalp. Joyous shouts rose above the savanna, and only then did I realize the villagers had waited to see if the witch doctor had performed his magic in its entirety. Even Radima had his skeptics.

As if on cue, a boy in frayed shorts stepped out of the brush and ran toward us. His mother hugged him, clutched Radima's feet, bowed her head. I was impressed and wanted to congratulate his two actors for timing and passion, resigned myself to a respectful nod. I wondered how the witch doctor had pulled this off, suspected he'd found the swollen snake the day before, counted the villagers and deduced they were all alive, which meant there was an animal and not a human in the snake's belly. Radima had staked his reputation on a sure thing, a wise move in the miracle healing world. Rickie knelt and touched the horns.

"It's dead," she said. "It was alive one minute and the next it's dead."

Miriam suggested it was time to leave Africa, so we walked back to camp and took down the tents. I didn't complain. I'd seen enough deprivation, snakes, and witch doctors to last a lifetime.

Chapter 15

You've become the figurehead of a multimillion-dollar industry," Ed Bradley said. "You live in a mansion in Sarasota, Florida. You fly from service to service in your personal jet."

Ed Bradley and I faced off on neutral ground, a St. Petersburg penthouse Miriam had rented for the interview, so high up bathers looked like insects on a tablecloth. Wind gusted over the Gulf, and breakers splashing the beach were silver as my inquisitor's hair. I'd dressed in leather chaps over leather pants, wore a chopper T-shirt. Mostly chrome, the bike stood out against the black background. Harley logos adorned my sleeves. The company paid me a million a year to market their brand, and, like a good little whore, I accommodated their wishes.

I sat behind a walnut desk that provided welcome distance between me and my interviewer. Cameras rolled, a microphone hovered near the ceiling. I cocked my head, attempting to exude the very picture of amiability. Ed Bradley smiled that disarming smile of his. This guy was good, I had to give him that.

"The rumors swirling around your ministry," Mr. Bradley said, "around Miracles, Inc. They are unfounded?"

"Of course."

"The miracle faking, bilking your congregation out of eight hundred million dollars, all lies?"

Ed had his numbers wrong. Miracles, Inc., had grossed $450 million since its inception. I lowered my voice and smiled my most accommodating smile. "Mr. Bradley, when you reach the top of your profession, the critics take aim, something I'm sure you can understand."

I had deflected and complimented him in a single sentence. Admiration came over his face, then disappeared. "Please, if you don't mind, I'll read a quote from an interview published in the *New York Times*."

I had read the piece a couple months back. Nick Wheaton, slicked-down talking head of Godliness Cathedral, a sanctuary large enough to house a Boeing 357, had accused me of heresy, said I'd had affairs with prostitutes who would testify to my sexual appetites.

"And I quote," Ed Bradley said. "'Miracles, Inc., and its idolatrous figure, one Vernon Oliver, who thinks he's the Second Coming of Lord Jesus himself, is an organization of that red-eared Satan. This is the devil's work and I'm insulted you've asked me about it.'"

Nick Wheaton's accusations hadn't surprised me. There were only so many suckers, and the money we made at Miracles, Inc., hurt his own bottom line. Ed Bradley rolled up the paper, tapped it in his palm. One, two, three, four, five, six . . . seven, eight, nine, ten, eleven, twelve, thirteen, fourteen, fifteen.

"Do you have anything to say to this?"

I rested my hands palm up on the desk. "Would the devil build schools and clinics in Africa, Mr. Bradley? Would the devil give fifty million dollars to feed the hungry right here in America?"

We had given $45 million to various charities, United Way the biggest recipient, but $50 million was a nice round number and sounded more impressive. I was glad Miriam had a big heart. Without these figures, Ed Bradley would have the ammunition to cut me into little pieces.

"Yes," Mr. Bradley said, "but—"

"Would the devil purchase Bibles for those who can't afford the Good Word? Would the devil—"

"He goes on to say that you don't have a sanctuary, that your office address is a mail drop in the Bahamas."

I turned toward the camera.

"If you're a true believer, if you feel God is talking to you at this very moment, please know there are millions of children who don't have your advantages, who grow up in slums and eat scraps for breakfast, lunch, and dinner. These silent voices are crying out for help," I said. "If you hear them, please visit SaveYourSoulTo-day.com. For only sixty-four cents a day you can feed an orphaned child in the poorest parts—"

"Yes, but about this mail drop—"

"Mr. Bradley," I said. "I normally don't trade tit for tat, but Mr. Wheaton's sanctuary cost $70 million, and that's a whole lot of children going hungry."

"Are you suggesting Pastor Wheaton—"

"I'm only stating the obvious, Mr. Bradley. The smaller the overhead, the more a church can do for the rest of the world. Our lack of a physical sanctuary means we can spend our money helping people."

"But the jet and the houses?"

"The Lord rewards those who perform works in his name. I make no apologies for accepting my Savior's blessings. We work hard to make life better for the less fortunate, we strive to make this a better world. At Miracles, Inc., we pray daily that God will guide us—"

"So the miracle faking, the affairs, all unfounded?" Bradley said.

"The ramblings of a paranoid schizophrenic, Ed."

The interview ended and Ed Bradley shook my hand, said I was a good sport and he would send a check for the kids.

I thanked him and left the room. I was not dissatisfied with how things had gone.

I took a taxi from the airport, spent the ride listening to the Jamaican driver describe how they roasted pig in his homeland. He told me about digging holes, building fires, and making sure the meat was done—"You know, mon, you cannot eat the pig raw!"—a description that filled most of the forty-five minutes. I gave him a twenty-dollar tip, punched the security code, and walked through the gate into my front yard.

We'd purchased in an area filled with million-dollar homes, and ours was no exception. A stone fence surrounded five acres that stretched toward the Gulf of Mexico. To my right, Rickie's RV huddled under a live oak that spread its branches over the caved-in roof like a protective umbrella. I preferred to get rid of the monstrosity, but she wanted to keep it to remind us of our past. She won, of course.

The driveway circled past a two-story house with a terra-cotta roof. Thick white pillars supported the overhang above the front door. The four-car garage housed my motorcycle collection, sixteen in all, including the bike Nicholson rode in *Easy Rider*.

I walked up the driveway and hollered Rickie's name, wanting to tell her about Miriam pushing up the groundbreaking at the Guatemalan clinic, and her desire that we fly out soon as possible. I had not left my wife for more than a day or two, and I wasn't about to start now. I called her name again.

She often wandered in search of shells, walked adjacent private property like she owned it. I entered the foyer, footsteps echoing off the floor. We'd used a local designer/contractor to furnish the house, and his firm had installed marble tile throughout the seventeen rooms. He'd opted for an open look, which meant mirrored walls and sparse furniture. I fired him after sitting in a driftwood chair that had enough knots to bruise even the hardest ass. Rickie said this guy had the best reputation on the coast, and we should approach his sensibility with an open mind. I hired him back, on one condition. That he provide a comfortable seat in the living room. Against his better judgment, a fact he repeated with much wrist waving and eye rolling, he purchased an Ethan Allen sofa and positioned it against the wall.

"Hey!" I said, to what was apparently an empty house.

I walked out to the backyard, angled toward a metal storage shed next to the stone wall. Prior to our Kenya trip, Rickie spent hours peering through the window in the shed door. I hadn't bugged her about this odd behavior, hoped it was like a splinter working itself out on its own. Now, as I pressed my nose against the pane and focused on cluttered shelves and cardboard boxes, the scent of strawberry body wash wafted on the breeze and I knew she was behind me. I inhaled, allowing the sweetness to fill my nostrils. Vernon L. Oliver could close his eyes and pick his wife out of a crowd. I wondered if it was like that for all husbands.

"There's a cat in there," Rickie said.

I turned and took in the new haircut, the spikes that jutted into the air. She wore a collar around her neck, another first, and studs glinted in the sunlight. Her nipple-to-belly-button chain dripped out of her halter top and shimmered against her skin.

"I think it got hit by a car," she said. "It was all cut up and looked like it had a broken hind leg."

She pressed her face to the glass and pursed her lips.

"We should leave the door open," I said. "It'll come out eventually."

Her fingers went to the collar, and she spun the strap around and around. "If you ever wanted to kill me, you could grab this collar and choke me to death."

"What the hell, Rickie?"

She stared at the window. "It took a long time to die."

"You should have taken it to the vet," I said. "Or at least let it out."

In Guatemala, we broke ground for three clinics and one school, shook hands with politicians, and talked into cameras. The president's spokesman requested the gold-plated shovel, and we handed it over. On a Sunday afternoon, Miracles, Inc., held a revival in the soccer stadium outside the capital, Guatemala City. I sat on my new Harley, perched a hundred feet above the stage, on a platform that overlooked the stadium. Rickie's anniversary gift was a chopper with ape hanger handlebars, and she had paid extra for the throwback suicide clutch next to my left leg.

People streamed through the entrances and filtered into the seats. The stadium filled up fast, close to a hundred thousand strong. We'd installed speakers and big-screen televisions on the exterior, for those who couldn't fit inside. All told, Miriam estimated close to two hundred fifty thousand people were attending. Most of them were Catholics, but Catholics loved a good miracle and didn't allow my denomination to deny them the privilege of believing. Beneath me, the Manhattan Maniacs shook tambourines and blew trumpets and beat bongo drums. Their sombreros bobbed in time to the music.

Miriam's voice sounded in my headset. She and Rickie were in the control room, a trailer behind the stage.

"The actors have been detained," she said.

"Detained?"

"Laney said they're sitting in their car in front of the hotel while police search their vehicle."

"Jesus Fucking Christ. Call her back and tell her to pay them off." That was how it worked down there. Cops, looking for bribes, cruised the streets and blue-lighted foreigners. Rickie and I had been pulled over seven times, and I always kept a fistful of money handy.

"She's trying," Miriam said. "It appears half the police force has their hand out."

Murmurs, a ripple of upturned faces, and I sensed the crowd was restless. Which took some doing. In my travels, I'd discovered cultures closer to the Equator moved slower and had more patience than those farther away. The band looked up at me, offered a collective shrug, and broke into a Ricky Martin song. The lead singer, his voice more suited for screaming, stumbled over the lyrics and the jeers began. I swung the mike closer to my mouth.

"I'm dying out here," I said.

The speaker hissed and crackled. "She says they're moving

again but the streets are so clogged they aren't going anywhere fast. They're on foot."

"They're walking?"

"Apparently," Miriam said. "They estimated it will take a little over an hour to get here."

"Shit."

Sparklers on the platform corners shot above my head, and a gunpowder scent was suspended in the air. I cranked the Harley and leaned on the brake, throttled wide open. The tire squealed, and smoke blocked my view. Adrenaline rocketed through my body, like it always did at this point in the service. The ride down was slow and the Harley was loud and sombreros bobbed beneath. The holograms had been moved above the corners and now perched on their own platforms. I thought about asking Rickie to serve as an actor but she wasn't in makeup and anyone closely scrutinizing the service would recognize her for sure.

"Do you want me to send out a stagehand?" Miriam said. "We have one who acted in a junior high play."

"Spare me." That's all I could think to say. God, it was hot this close to the Equator. I made a mental note to request electric fans if we ever traveled here again. I throttled down on the bike, told Miriam I was going it alone. We had discontinued the LCD screen to the rear, had decided the holograms served the same purpose. I applauded the decision, had never grown accustomed to seeing my own mostly naked body onscreen.

I faced the crowd, bent down and grabbed a Bible at my feet, heaved the book overhead. Since we'd been in business, our competitor's Bibles had grown progressively larger and Miriam had put an end to the nonsense. Ours weighed close to a hundred pounds and could crush a small child. I brandished the Bible

and screamed nonsense words. The band played and the inter-
preter on my right screamed along with me and his voice instead
of mine came out of the speakers. Julio talked with his hands;
his sequined vest flashed with his movement. We used him for
Spanish-speaking audiences and he was particularly proud of his
hair, which was black and curly and hung over his ears. Julio was
one charismatic guy. If we ever franchised this business, I wanted
Miriam to give him a shot.

"Hello, Guatemala City," I said, and lowered the Bible to
approval screams. I was already beginning to feel the connection, that bond between myself and my audience, knew my words
through Julio's voice would entrance them soon enough. The feeling always began in my core and worked its way outward until
it flowed from my fingertips. Tonight was no exception. God,
the Holy Spirit, and Pastor Vernon Oliver had come to visit. An
unholy trinity wrapped up inside one big lie.

The next half hour, I cajoled and moaned, I groaned, I spoke
righteous words that lifted the spirits of everyone watching. In the
front row, a man slumped to the earth and talked in tongues. I did
a double take and decided he wasn't one of ours, raised my arms,
and cried out in his Holy Name. I spoke into the headset and told
Miriam to send that stagehand out, that I was ready to begin healing and I needed him to run interference.

"They aren't here yet," Miriam said. "They're still twenty minutes away."

"Send him out."

The stagehand walked to the front of the stage and rolled up
his sleeves like he was getting ready for a fight. I motioned him
over.

"No blind, no sores, no broken limbs, no disfigurements," I said.

Miriam spoke in my ear.

"Don't do this," she said. "Wait a little while—"

"The healing has begun!"

I lifted the Bible and dropped it to the stage. The thud was so loud it threw off the drummer, but he recovered and the band segued into the Jaws' sound track. That's how I felt, like I could eat my flock and swallow them whole. Julio jumped around and gesticulated wildly, talked when I didn't and I had no idea what he was saying, had never felt so strong a bond to the audience. We had become one organism, and I was the puppetmaster. I shouted, and they shook their rosaries. I crooned, and they crossed themselves and brought their fingers to their lips. I shot words across the stadium, an M1 on full automatic, and the ones who could stand rose and lifted their chins to the heavens. My newly promoted assistant guided a bent-over woman to the stage. She wore a dress down to her ankles, and her feet were brown and small.

"Here we go," Miriam said.

I brought back my hand like it was some miracle drug the FDA had not yet approved and I smacked that woman on the head. I felt the power inside me go through my hand and settle in her mind. I wasn't drunk or stoned, or anything of the sort. This was real as it gets. She bounced backward like I'd hit her, landed on her rear, and relaxed to her back. The stagehand, Julio, the band, and I stared down at her.

"Rise and walk!" I said.

Julio repeated my words, and the woman got to her feet. She had a strange look, like she was in a trance, and then she did what I and the rest of my crew thought was impossible. She straightened up and strutted that stage like she owned it. I mumbled, "Son of a bitch, would you look at that," and Julio repeated my words in English before he could stop himself. I felt so good, I healed four more people in succession. Between healings I spoke into my headset.

"What's my name?" I said.

"God," said Miriam.

"What's my name?" I said.

"Jesus."

"What's my name?" I said.

"The Holy Spirit."

She broke in and told me the actors were here, but I was winding down, listening to Julio lead the crowd in a Spanish version of "Jesus Loves Me." Onstage, we had a cancer victim, a bad-back victim, a child in leg braces, a woman with a mysterious ailment, and someone with arthritis, all claiming to be healed. The music stopped, the crowd began filing out, and the euphoria died, an abruptness that emptied my body of all its strength. I'd seen other Pentecostal ministers use mass hysteria to mind-control victims, had no idea how it felt before now. It was better than any coke I'd ever done, better than any sex I'd ever had, better than any bike I'd ever ridden. There was only one problem. None of those ministers had ever proved a miracle: no healed cancer, no blind who could see, no paraplegic who could walk, no arteries scrubbed so clean they were like new. Mass-hysteria healing didn't stick, and it was only a matter of time before its victims reverted to what they were before.

When the bad-back woman grabbed at her spine, I jumped off the stage and headed to the trailer. Miriam met me at the door, and she, Rickie, and I fast-walked to a waiting car. Miriam and Rickie didn't need to say what we all knew.

I should have waited for the actors.

We left the hot air and short brown people an hour later, settled into the air-conditioned cabin for the trip back to the States. G-forces pressed me into my seat, and I stayed that way until the Lear leveled at thirty-seven thousand feet. I was shaky but recovering quickly. We took off our seat belts, and Miriam mixed a drink. We went over what went wrong, resolved to travel with the actors to the service from here on out. Rickie opened the cover on a Styrofoam plate, cut up spaghetti and meatballs. I had my own dinner in the microwave—Alaskan king crab legs and melted butter—waited for *60 Minutes* to air before I ate. I turned toward the flat screen on the cabin wall.

The show opened with a hooker.

Shasta Underwood, who wore a red blouse and a cross that nestled in the valley between her breasts, claimed she could describe my penis. The camera cut to Ed Bradley in a brown jacket and brown pants. The bland signature of a man who would never hurt anyone. He nodded encouragement, and Shasta Underwood went on to say I paid her to watch while I made love to various men and women.

Miriam, expressionless, sipped her drink and crossed her legs. I'll say one thing about my mother-in-law, she was cool under fire. I'd been called a philanderer and a faggot in front of millions of people. Allegations like these had brought down more than one Pentecostal minister.

The camera cut to a "victim" who claimed I paid him to fake a healing. Kirk Poussin had green eyes and orange hair, and he said his liver cancer was bad as ever. Ed Bradley handed the guy a tissue, and he wiped his eyes. Miriam asked if I'd ever seen Poussin, and I shook my head no.

"So Miracles, Inc., is a fake?" Ed Bradley said.

"It's the devil's playground. It's Lucifer and all his demons mixed up into one big rock show."

"And you have how long to live?" Ed Bradley said.

"I'll be looking into Jesus's eyes inside of three months. Hallelujah."

Miriam and I watched the rest of the show, which ended with the interview in the office. Rickie never looked up.

"Well," Miriam said. "At least they left in the part about the charities."

I hunted around for my cigarettes, got out my lighter. "There is that."

"Americans love a good apology," Miriam said. "I'll set up a news conference and you can stand in front of the mikes and beg for forgiveness."

Rickie brought back her arm, plate balanced in her palm, and I knew what was coming. Didn't have time to duck. The plate hit me in the chest, and spaghetti sauce soaked into my shirt.

Miriam turned toward the window.

I picked noodles off my lap, dropped them in the plate. I wanted to shake Rickie and tell her I wasn't the one who left her, that I was in her life to stay, but I knew that conversation would hurt Miriam's feelings. So I kept quiet. There was no point in having both of them mad at me.

Asking forgiveness for something I didn't do galled me, and the more I hung my head and the more I wiped my eyes, the more my belly embers glowed.

"Pastor Oliver, is it true that you've had homosexual affairs? Is it true you sleep with men? And how does the Bible look upon those who do?" The reporter who asked the question wore a tweed jacket, patches at the elbows, no doubt a bitter aspiring editor stuck on the journalism beat.

I stood under a flowering dogwood tree, on the lawn of a church Miriam had rented for this event. The wind blew, branches bucked, and petals fell on my shoulders like fibrous snow. We were in New Leaf, Kansas, a town she had chosen for its name.

"Pastor Oliver." This from a skinny woman who worked for ABC. "Pastor Oliver, we have reports you embezzled millions from Miracles, Inc. Is this true, or are you simply running a fake faith-healing organization?"

Satellite vans clogged the street, and curious townsfolk gathered on porches. The limo, rear window cracked, idled in the parking lot. Miriam was in the backseat. Rickie had stayed home, saying she wasn't a politician's wife and therefore couldn't be expected to stand next to me and smile rapturously while I confessed to extramarital affairs. I studied the reporters, took in their predatory body language.

The ember in my belly turned into a five-alarm fire, and I made a snap decision to go against Miriam's instincts. No groveling for me, no water carrying, no boot strapping, no getting down on my knees before Genghis Kahn and his instant feeds. On the street, a kid rode past on a bicycle, rang the bell on the handlebars. *Braaang.* The wind shifted and I smelled grilled sausages, imagined friends gathered in a backyard, sharing good times.

"To the Nick Wheatons of the world," I said. "To the preachers so full of ego they cannot allow it within themselves to accept a fellow minister, I forgive you. To the prostitutes and everyone else who told lies about me and my ministry, I forgive you. To the reporters who stand before me today with these heinous allegations, I forgive you."

A rancorous onslaught babbled forth, and I asked for the questions to come one at a time.

"Is it true you live in a hundred-million-dollar mansion?" a reporter shouted.

"I am the way," I said. "I am the way, the truth, and the life; no one comes to the Father but by me."

"Did you really lay your hand on your wife's head and bring her out of a coma?" said a reporter.

"I am Jehovah," I said. "I am the Second Coming."

"So, you're saying you are Jesus Christ?" This aging reporter had an NBC emblem on his shoulder; no doubt his TV anchor aspirations had expired long ago. His barbarous gaze bore into me, and he repeated his question.

"I am Jesus," I said. "Sent here to right wrongs and heal the sick. I am the Cherokee healer, the shaman; I am the Buddha, and the Muhammad. I am Gandhi and Mother Teresa; I am here to unite the religions of this world. Visit me at SaveYourSoulToday. com if you'd like to contribute to the betterment of humanity."

I stepped from the microphones and walked to the limo. Slid in across from Miriam.

"It's like you got started and couldn't stop," she said. "It's like you were driving down a mountain and your brakes failed."

"Out of control."

"Even bad publicity is good publicity."

By the time I made it back to Sarasota, the "Jesus Interview" had aired on all major networks and was running a continuous loop on Fox News. In the airport, reporters shouted questions and snapped pictures, followed me through the terminal like I was meat and they were starved dogs. I paused at a window that overlooked the tarmac, watched our jet climb into the sky. Miriam was headed for Harbour Island, where she planned to spend a couple weeks away from the grind. I didn't blame her. She wasn't the only one who was burned out.

I ducked into a taxi and we drove out of the airport onto the highway, where cameramen hung out of SUV windows and shot our exit. The driver accepted two hundred dollars to go faster and opened the throttle until the speedometer reached 100. The SUVs broke off the chase. It's not like the reporters were going to lose me. I was plainly headed home.

The driver wheeled into the cul de sac and slowed the taxi to a crawl. RVs, cars, and trucks lined the road. On one side, men, women, and children held signs that deemed me a heretic and on the other the crowd sang "He Has Risen." I got out and ran for the gate, punched in the code, slipped inside. Peeked through a slit into the street, watched two women in burkas unroll their prayer mats, kneel, and bow in my direction. Behind them, a heavy-jowled woman fingered a rosary and chanted the Hail Mary.

A limo drove down the road, parked, and Pastor Nick Wheaton clambered out. He had pussy written all over him, from the fastidiously combed hair to the pink suit and slip-on shoes. In one hand he held a Bible, in the other a megaphone.

"Burn in hell," he boomed.

The crowd picked up the chant and he stood in their middle and raised the Bible, a black anvil ready to descend and smack the devil between the eyes. I looked back toward the house, wondering if the water hose would reach this far, and I saw Rickie pouring liquid on what looked like my clothes. I walked past the crushed RV, down the driveway, to the sidewalk, where I watched her screw the cap on the lighter fluid container, then toss it to the side.

"Hey," I said.

Rickie, wearing a red bra and panties, kissed me on the cheek. Told me to step back. She lit a match, dropped it on the pile, and flame shot upward. I smelled burning rubber, no doubt the soles of my spare boots melting somewhere in the pile.

"Jesus," she said. "I want a divorce."

That evening, we sat on stools at the kitchen counter and drank French wine. The wine cost five hundred dollars a bottle, didn't taste any better than the cheap stuff from California. We had the lights off and it was so dark I couldn't read her eyes, the turn of her lips, the slope of her shoulders. All I had to go on was her voice, which stayed an even tone throughout most of the conversation. I lit a cigarette and tried to see her face in the crimson flare-up. Dark irises stared my way.

I got a handful of strawberries out of the fridge, rinsed them under the faucet. The berries were ripe and sweet and tasted good with the wine. Every so often protest shouts and siren wails intruded on our discussion.

"You burned my Harley vest," I said.

"You care more about your goddamn clothes than you do your own wife."

I couldn't believe Rickie had brought up the D-word. Now that it was out there, our relationship seemed more precarious than ever.

"How come you never talk about your sister?" Rickie said.

She laid her hand on mine, and her fingers pressured ever so slightly.

"I won't judge you," she said.

"Talk won't bring her back."

"Did she suffer?"

I grabbed the bottle and walked out of the kitchen.

"Don't you do that," she said. "Don't you walk away from me."

Outside, the moon was up, and waves had a yellow sheen. I stepped into the night air, strode across the yard, to the beach. Fish darted close to the surface, leaving phosphorous streaks that lit the water like aquatic lightning bugs. Wind blew from offshore, and the air had a salty scent to it. Rickie's voice came through the darkness.

"I hired an attorney," she said.

I could not keep the disgust out of my voice. "Yeah?"

"He put a private investigator on retainer," she said. "He discovered the weekly payments to the Caribbean account."

"What?"

"I know about your mistress," she said. "I know about Susan Ivy."

I hurled the bottle at the stone wall. A crash, and the bottle smashed to smithereens. I had never heard of Susan Ivy, suspected it was the alias my blackmailer used on his account.

"It's not what you think," I said.

"Are you denying that she is your mistress?"

I grabbed Rickie's arm, turned from a punch that landed on my shoulder.

"You bitch," I said. "I'm tired of this shit."

"Cheater."

"That money pays off an extortionist. We'd lose this business if—"

"I don't believe you."

I let her go and into the darkness she walked, footsteps growing dimmer with each pissed-off stride. At that moment, as I settled onto the sand, as waves rolled in and fish swam beneath the surface, I was as angry as I'd ever been. Susan Ivy, or whoever she was, had miscalculated. She was correct in thinking I wouldn't come after her for five thousand a week. What she hadn't counted on was wrecking my marriage.

Hours later, I went back inside. Rickie had the projector turned on and pointed toward the living room wall, watched the python writhe on the ground. Focus wobbled in and out, and at times the image was so blurred I couldn't distinguish head from tail.

"You should upgrade to a CD camcorder," I said.

"Fuck you."

There was no sense talking to Rickie when she wasn't in a listening mood.

Chapter 16

THE GUY BEHIND THE Beretta counter was not what I envisioned when I attended Orlando's annual gun show. I had expected behemoths in trench coats booming proclamations across the expansive auditorium, a sales force as threatening as the weapons they sold. Steve, horn-rimmed glasses on a long nose, had a limp handshake and a Mike Tyson voice. Behind him, a black mannequin dressed in thug jeans cradled a television under his right arm. Steve picked up a 9mm pistol from the counter, ran off stats about bullet speed, caliber, recoil, and knockdown power.

"You'll want hollow points," he said. "They expand upon impact; leave a nasty hole."

We were in a center aisle, under American flags dangling from rafters. Patriotic country music pounded out of wall speakers. Families sauntered past, kids eating cotton candy and drinking Pepsi, adults waving NRA banners. The air smelled like cologne and gun oil. Steve handed me the pistol, and I stared at it as if a strange appendage had attached itself to my fingers.

"Shoot him," Steve said.

"Excuse me?"

"That thief is stealing your television," he said. "Shoot him before he gets away."

I pointed the Beretta at the mannequin's chest, squinted, lined up the sights. A shot rang out, the chest ruptured, and I almost had a heart attack until I realized the sound came out of speakers next to the mannequin and the explosion was a special effect triggered by the remote in Steve's hand. He removed the core and replaced it with a new one.

"That's one dead bad guy," he said.

The pistol held seventeen rounds, came with two clips and the ability to make its owner ten feet tall. Families headed toward the Beretta counter en masse. On the other end of the auditorium came another shot, a second exploding mannequin—a brown man holding a CD player—and half the crowd headed in the other direction. An aisle over, a blond woman, dress slit to her waist, extolled the virtues of a Mossberg shotgun. All businesses had their hooks. Mine was hope, and the gun industry's was sex, explosions, and patriotism.

The salesman handed me a form, mumbled something about the Brady Law and how it was hard to make a living, asked me to move to the side so he could handle his next customer. I scratched out the appropriate information—no, I had never been convicted of a felony, and yes, I agreed to wait five days before I received ownership of my new toy—then handed Steve four hundred and fifty dollars. He asked if I wanted the hollow points, and I said sure. Figuring I might as well look the part, I purchased a shoulder holster like the one Marsellus Wallace wore in *Pulp Fiction*.

The Beretta arrived at my home via Federal Express six days later. I unwrapped the package, strapped on the holster, adjusted it so it didn't ride into my armpit. The pistol smelled oily and the holster smelled leathery, and I felt tall enough to dunk a basketball without leaving the ground. I pointed the pistol at the grinning long-haired preacher in the mirror, then headed toward the kitchen to see Rickie.

At the counter, she sorted through worms she'd dug out of the flower garden. Picked out the smallest ones and deposited them on a plate next to a shoe box. Inside, a baby robin huddled on a blue washcloth. Rickie dangled a worm in front of the beak, tapped the bird on its head, spoke in a soothing voice.

The bird had fallen from a nest in one of the trees in the backyard, and she had named it J. Alfred Prufrock, after a character in a T. S. Eliot poem. J. Alfred Prufrock peeped and craned his neck but never opened his mouth wide enough to swallow a worm. I got a beer out of the fridge, popped the top, and held the can over the sink until the fizzing stopped.

I was glad things had quieted down on the home front. Rickie hadn't mentioned the divorce in several days, something I put to her preoccupation with the baby bird. The Jesus news had run its cycle, and Nick Wheaton had left the cul de sac. Miracles, Inc., had had a banner month—doubling our usual income—and proving Miriam's words prophetic. Bad publicity really is good publicity.

"You going to keep that thing in here forever?" I said.

I shifted my stance, so the pistol was in full view. Rickie didn't look up, kept talking to the bird. She wore tights and a white blouse, and her ass had a nice curve to it when she leaned over the counter. I opened and slammed a cupboard, grumbled about nothing to eat, and she told me to order a pizza.

"I'm thinking about cutting my hair short as yours," I said, attempting to get a rise out of her.

Rickie cut a worm in half, held it next to the beak.

"Right down to the scalp," I said. "A military buzz cut."

"Mmmmm."

"J. Alfred Prufrock must have lockjaw," I said.

"Birds don't get lockjaw."

"I was kidding." I unsnapped the holster, a metallic click. She looked up, and her gaze went to the pistol.

She extended her hand. "Let me see it."

"You need training to handle this—"

"Let me see it."

"It's not loaded, nothing in the clip or the chamber." I slid the Beretta into the open, handed it to her.

She hefted it up and down. "It's heavier than I thought."

"It's a semiautomatic."

"That makes it heavy?"

I answered her with a yes. I had no clue.

She wanted to hear about my trip to the gun show, and I told her about standing in the Orlando auditorium and watching the mannequin chest explode.

"That little slide is the safety," I said. "You move this here, then you pull this back, and it's ready to go."

She pointed the gun at a pot on the counter. "Let's drive somewhere and shoot it."

"There's an outdoor firing range outside of town, but you've got to join this gun club before they let you shoot. Go through this course and everything."

"Let's drive out to the country and shoot it at a fence post or something."

"Okay," I said.

"Really?"

"Sure, let's do it."

She handed me the Beretta, and I slid it back into my holster. I liked the weight hanging off my shoulder, thought I might wear the pistol whenever I was home. Rickie washed the worms down the drain. Said she wanted to shower first.

I walked outside and watched a dolphin arc through the waves. Far out, a ship sailed to the south. Rickie had left the shed door open, and I walked over to shut it. I stepped off the grass to the sandy floor, stepped over oil cans and paint cans and gas cans; stopped at a cross driven into a depression near the rear wall. The grave was a foot wide and two feet long. I knelt and sifted sand through my fingers, watched granules puddle between my knees. The air held the scent of decayed cat, and I did not want to breathe it for long. I walked into open air, shut the door, headed back to the house.

In the kitchen, I peered down at J. Alfred Prufrock, tapped his box, and poked his head. Nothing. I nudged his little bird feet. Still nothing. I picked him up and his head lolled to the side, reminding me of cooked spaghetti. I ran my finger down the neck, and my nail caught on a bone fragment. Blood, a red thread, soaked into the down. I dropped the bird, strode to the bathroom door, pounded until Rickie answered. Naked, she had her hip cocked like this was normal conversation between husband and wife.

"I'm not taking you shooting," I said.

"Suit yourself."

She shut the door, and I stood around in the hall. Hand on the Beretta. I didn't know why I was so upset. My wife had broken the neck of a bird that wouldn't eat. She probably thought she did it a favor.

Chapter 17

"How's she doing?" Miriam said.

Whenever a conversation started like this, Rickie was the subject. Miriam, who wore an orange shirt and white pantaloons, had come to the annual company picnic as a pirate. Skeleton earrings jiggled like marionettes when she turned her head. We stood in my backyard and watched actors mill around as the band arranged instruments on a stage backed up to the house. A wet bar was set up on the beach, and streamers tied to tree branches undulated in the breeze. Miriam repeated her question.

"She's around here somewhere," I said.

I wore a crown of thorns Rickie had woven into my hair, and Jesus-shaped sparkles lit up my robe. Across the lawn a voice boomed, an actor quoting Shakespeare.

"But how is she?" Miriam said.

Rickie walked out of the house, stumbled, hugged a tree trunk. The actors had painted her skin red and glued horns to her forehead. She staggered our way. Apparently, Satan was three sheets to the wind.

" 'Tis all an act," Rickie said. "I'm as sober as any archangel who has walked this earth."

"Honey," said Miriam. "You look marvelous."

Rickie wobbled and caught herself. "I had a pitchfork but goddamn Jesus took it away from me."

"Jesus wouldn't have minded if it was plastic," I said.

Rickie walked toward the wet bar and was soon lost in the crowd. Expecting intense scrutiny after the *60 Minutes* interview, Miriam had retired the actors and ordered replacements from Alton at Pentecostal Hell. A mix of old and new employees cavorted on the lawn. I had not seen or spoken to my mentor since he walked Rickie down the aisle. Miriam said he was using alternative methods to combat mosquitoes. His health had rebounded, and he planned to shut down the boiler forever.

Laney, who arrived in a limo with Chauncey, came as Starlet Walking the Red Carpet, and she wore a dress cut low in the front. The pearls around her neck were glossy and big as grapes. She kissed Miriam on the cheek. Gave her a hug.

Miriam might not have been able to buy her daughter's love, but she'd done a hell of a job with company employees. Miracles, Inc., had paid $3 million buyout bonuses to its original actors, and every one of them would take a bullet for Miriam. Emphasis on Miriam. I was certain, as I surveyed the crowd, one of these sons of bitches was my extortionist. *My* extortionist. How intimate.

The band riffed through several reggae songs, then went inside to play cards in the dining room. They had grown beards and renamed themselves Cucumber Salad. Miriam brought me a scotch and water, and I drank until the glass dried up. Alcohol numbed my lips, my throat, my stomach. Miriam said she was hungry and went to talk to the caterer about getting a nibble before lunch.

I cut Laney from the herd and asked her to come inside.

"I have something I want to talk to you about," I said. "Something important."

She followed me to a room at the end of the hallway, took an offered chair. I lit a cigarette, held out the pack, and she declined. The den was a shrine to Miracles, Inc., and memorabilia covered the walls. Starting at the door and wrapping around the room, photos provided a visual time line, beginning with that first service in Chicago and ending with a revival in Mexico City. I'd preached in twenty-nine countries, and Laney had been with me through it all.

"Before you start," she said, "I should tell you I'm very grateful for everything you've done for me, but if you're going to ask me to unretire, you're wasting our time."

"Yeah?"

"I'm running for mayor of Winthrop, New York," she said. "I'm going to build a civic center to keep kids off the streets."

I stubbed out my cigarette and studied how the pearls fell across her shoulders and curved over the swell of her breasts. Laney had gone up two cup sizes since I'd last seen her. I had no idea she had political aspirations, but what did I know about any of my actors?

"Are you aware," I said, "that there are forces aligned against this empire?"

"You mean like every Pentecostal preacher in the world?"

My voice turned cold. "I mean like someone inside this organization."

I examined her for an involuntary twitch, a spontaneous clench of the jaw. Her eyes widened and nothing more. Laney was one of the best actors to walk my stage, so she could have faked her surprise, but I suspected otherwise.

Laney was not my extortionist.

Determined to send a message, I pulled the Beretta from under my robe. Pointed the barrel in her direction.

"Hey," she said.

My finger sought the trigger, and she darted toward the door. I beat her to it, stood between her and the handle.

"If I find out who is trying to hurt me and my wife, I will shoot them in the head. Do you understand? I will shoot them in the head."

"You're crazy," she said, voice rising.

I stepped aside, followed her clicking heels to the living room, singled out Pastor Yost on the sofa. He walked my way, and I invited him down the hall. Sometimes a guy had to do what a guy had to do.

"The entire company is threatening to quit," Miriam said.

She poked me in the chest and backed me up against the house. The party had subsided, and the only person left was a naked man on the beach. Wrinkled and white haired, he walked in the water and waded in circles, fingers trailing the surface. I thought he came with the caterers, hadn't had time to find out. Rickie was curled in the grass under an oak, and Spanish moss above her head dangled like a bedraggled goatee. I'd changed into Harley gear and had barely thrust my feet into my boots when Miriam barreled into the bedroom and told me to get outside, *pronto.* I clomped my way there, woozy from the afternoon booze. Salmon smell hung in the air, along with a hint of roast beef. In the surf, the naked man fell face forward. His back bowed and his hands slapped the water and he came erect, only to fall again.

"I think I better go help that guy out," I said.

He regained his balance and plodded to the beach, sat his bare butt on the sand. Rickie staggered across the grass and sat next to him. Their faces turned toward the Gulf and its watery expanse, and I wondered what they were talking about. Rickie was probably telling him about the dead cat and the dead bird and the dead horse and whatever else her strange brain dreamed up. A pelican landed on the far end of the beach and faced them. Long beak opening and closing.

The man snuggled up to Rickie, and she pushed him away, stumbled back to her spot under the tree. She squatted and fell to her back. I went over and unwound her legs, and she asked me to help her to bed. I carried her inside, stripped her down, laid her red body on the sheets. She mumbled her thanks, and I went back outside.

"Listen," I said to Miriam. "There's something I should have told you a long time ago."

"This had better be good."

I started my story with the card I found on the sofa while I opened gifts at the reception after the marriage ceremony, told her about the threat to expose the operation, ended by saying five thousand a month was such a small inconvenience it wasn't worth worrying about.

"I did it for the company," I said.

Then I told her Rickie had retained an attorney, who had hired a detective agency that discovered the payments. "She wants a divorce."

"Rickie?"

"She thinks I'm keeping a mistress."

"Why didn't you tell her the truth?" she said.

"She doesn't believe me."

The man on the beach walked to a pile of clothes under one of the awnings, dressed in a white shirt and black pants. I was right, he was one of the servers. He buckled and staggered backward to the stone wall, forced himself upright. I called the caterers, and the woman who answered apologized and said she'd be right there to pick him up. Miriam and I went to the wet bar, and she poured wine for us both. She took off her skeleton earrings, dropped them in a pocket.

"My son-in-law is a romantic," she said. "He's willing to pay a blackmailer to keep a business afloat, but threaten his marriage and he turns into a badass."

We held up our glasses.

"I love her," I said.

"For better or worse."

"For better or worse," I said.

We drank and lowered our glasses.

"You shouldn't have kept this from me," Miriam said. "Especially since I might know who this is."

"What?"

"You stay in a business long enough, you get a feel for things," she said.

"You know who this is?"

"Let me do some checking. I don't want to point a finger unless I'm positive."

Three weeks after the party, I toweled off after a morning swim, then opened the fridge in search of microwavable sausages. Rickie padded up. She wore a blue nightie and still had sleep marks from where her face pressed against the pillow. She broke eggs over a skillet, poured grounds into the coffeemaker, sifted through a drawer for a spatula. I went to the living room and smoked half a joint I found in an ashtray. She brought in two full plates and two steaming cups, sat next to me, and crossed her legs.

"What's got into you?" I said.

"Can't a wife cook for her husband without it being a big deal?"

I hugged her and we kissed. It wasn't one of those tongue explorations that lead to sex. This kiss was less urgent, more symbolic than passionate, like the signing of a peace treaty. We parted and I studied her eyes, watched them peer into mine.

"Miriam called this morning," she said.

I got up and walked to the window. The water was exceptionally blue, and I couldn't tell where the Gulf stopped and the sky began. "I've never fooled around on you, I've never so much as touched another woman."

"Miriam found out who it is. She's one hundred percent positive."

I walked across the room and sat back down.

"It's Alton Pierce," Rickie said. "Daddy Dearest."

"Alton's behind this? Wait, what?! Alton's your father?"

"Miriam crosses her heart and hopes to die." My wife brushed at her eyes like she was expecting tears. There were none.

"He didn't want me to interfere with their careers," she said. "He wanted to abort me. . . . That bastard wanted to kill me before I had a chance to get started."

"Damn."

What else was there to say?

Chapter 18

BUG ZAPPERS RINGED THE perimeter, sent up such a constant array of blue flashes through the darkness the island looked like a Bunsen burner. Lights high on utility poles lit the interior, and the old buildings shone sinisterly in the amber glow. I tugged the shoulder holster under my jacket, and the Beretta shifted away from my armpit. Rickie had her camcorder out.

Miriam told the pilot to stay with the helicopter, and she, Rickie, and I stepped to the ground. From the zappers came a hum, bursts of insects frying in electrical current. Alton had indeed shut down the boiler, and the air smelled fresh and clean. Grass grew where once there was dirt, and alongside the buildings spotlights backlit shrubs in raised beds. No doubt during the daytime Bible Camp was sunny as any beach in southern Florida.

Off to the right were two new buildings, one with a neon sign on a post outside the door. Bible Camp Auditorium. No more than a short walk away, a sprawling cabin loomed in the shadows. It didn't take a genius to figure out what Alton had done with my money. The lights were on in the auditorium, so we walked that way. Rickie, who wore all black—muscle shirt, jeans tucked into boots—swung open the door, took a right, and settled into the rear row. Miriam and I followed suit.

The auditorium sloped toward the front, where Alton stood onstage. Next to him, an actor in a wheelchair shook his legs. In the front two rows, students opened notepads and furiously scribbled. Alton had on the same faded cowboy hat, same worn jeans, same scuffed boots as when I attended his school. He still lit up when he stood onstage, still commanded the attention of his students. I was not surprised he didn't hear the helicopter or see us come in. When he worked, the world faded away.

"Dial back on the movement," he said. "Much less exaggeration. Remember, these days you're performing for a television camera. A little will go a long way."

Miriam whispered in my ear.

"Alton is as tough as they come," she said. "If he confesses, I'll be surprised."

Miriam's detective agency, the same one that tracked down Rickie, had followed the money trail to a Miami bank account opened with Alton's Social Security number. She had pictures of him going into the bank and making withdrawals. I can't say I was surprised. We were all scammers, some more than others.

Thirty minutes after we walked in, the class ended, and the students walked out a side door. Alton looked our way and smiled. Invited us to a dinner of sole and braised potatoes.

"I'm on a seafood kick," he said. "It's good for the heart."

Inside the cabin, sawdust lay like chaff on wooden floors. The windows were open, and a breeze blew through the screens. Alton showed us the bunk room where he slept. A woodstove provided heat during the winter, and he planned to fly in a rick of white oak in a few weeks. I suspected the temperature rarely fell below fifty degrees, so the stove was more for show than anything else. Pictures of Alton during his rodeo days hung on rough-hewn walls. He showed off a gold buckle he won in San Antonio, then walked us to the other side of the house, to the bathroom, where he twisted knobs in a shower large enough to stable a horse. Water streamed out of nozzles and pulsated to a Johnny Cash song. The etched face under the cowboy hat shaped itself into a grin. "These old bones . . . I thought it was about time they deserved a break."

Miriam, Rickie, and I trailed our host to the living room. He switched on a television, and a video of his miracle-faking days brightened the screen. The preacher had a Louisiana accent and wore alligator-skin boots. Alton invited us to a wooden table large enough to accommodate a range crew, said that preacher had poison ivy from screwing the organist in the woods behind the church, and that's why he spent most of the time behind the pulpit instead of working the stage. The cameraman worked a side angle, and sure enough, whenever the preacher's waist was hidden from the congregation, his scratching fingers went to his crotch. The video played out, and we watched a succession of grainy clips showing Alton in various disguises. He kept a running dissection of his performances, pointing out faults only he could see, and fierce pride shone in his eyes. I saw myself in his boots, many years down the line, sitting with Rickie and replaying the best of our lives. I was glad she brought the camcorder—tonight was sure to make the highlight reel.

Royce, dressed in a butler uniform, came in and filled wineglasses, placed serving dishes on the table. The sole was cooked in garlic butter sauce, and I tasted a hint of lemon in my first bite. Rickie picked at hers, and Miriam stuck to the wine.

"I've got this terrific actor you should see," Alton said. "Picks up things at the snap of a finger. Nailed Blind Man Onstage inside of five minutes."

"Better than you?" Miriam said.

Alton placed his fork on his plate. He'd taken off his hat and hung it on the back of his chair, still had a crease in his forehead where the brim had contacted his skin. He seemed at ease, as though he'd made peace with his ghosts.

"He's good," Alton said. "About as good as anyone I've seen."

A mosquito buzzed my ear and settled on my arm. Rickie saw it land, and she grabbed my raised hand. I felt the prick as the insect burrowed into my skin, watched the black body swell with my blood.

"Kill it," Miriam said.

My mother-in-law's violet blouse brought out the green in her eyes. I had not thought about our tryst in a long time, found my mind going to the hotel room where her body had pressed against mine. I forced myself to the present, saw Alton's gaze settle on my arm.

"I apologize for that," he said. "The perimeter works well, but some still get through on the drafts."

Rickie's hand sliced downward, and her palm squished the mosquito. She was crying, uncontrollable sobs, looking from Alton to Miriam, back and forth, like she was stuck in some terrible dream.

"Honey," Miriam said, and slid her arm over Rickie's shoulders.

"I'm tired of the lies." Rickie shook off the gesture. "It's so I can't tell what's real and what's not."

She pushed away from the table and walked out the door. Miriam excused herself, and the two disappeared into the night. I gave Miriam credit. She hadn't given up on her daughter.

"She's been emotional ever since the accident." I unbuttoned my jacket, and the Beretta appeared nestled in its holster. Alton didn't say anything. Miriam was right, this man was cool as they come.

"You're going to pay me back every cent," I said.

Alton quit chewing. "What are you talking about?"

"We know it was you."

Alton wiped his fingers on his napkin, wadded the napkin, tossed it on his plate. "Look, you seem upset about something."

I slid the Beretta from its holster, lowered the barrel, pulled the trigger. An explosion rang out, and the bullet left a high-speed burn in the floor. His eyes registered surprise but no fear. Like the guy was made of stone.

"You almost cost me Rickie," I said.

"I don't know what you are talking about."

He got to his feet, and I shoved him back into his chair. He sat there, seemingly amused, almost as though he were participating in a scene in an acting class.

"Okay," he said. "Happy belated April Fool or whatever, but this is over the top."

A knock sounded.

"If you say anything, I'll shoot whoever that is, then you."

"Mum's the word."

I cracked the door, peered into the night. Royce, dressed in his chef hat, stood on the sidewalk.

"I thought I heard something," he said.

"In here?"

"I thought it came from inside the house," he said.

"It must have been one of the snakes trying to get through the fence."

Royce nodded, shifted so he had a view around my shoulder. I shifted with him and looked him in the eye.

"I suppose I should grab the dishes while I'm here," Royce said.

"We're not done eating."

"I made a carrot cake topped with orange icing. It's Alton's favorite."

I told Royce that Alton wasn't feeling well, and it would be bad manners if we ate dessert in front of him. "He's coming down with something, maybe the flu."

Miriam and Rickie walked up, paused under the porch light.

"Miriam showed me that old boiler room," Rickie said. "It's filthy down there."

"We'll call you if we need you," I said to Royce.

"Okay," he said. "I'll let you folks alone for the night."

Inside, Miriam held her daughter's hand and both seemed happier than I'd seen them in a long time. *Normal* came to mind. My wife was finally acting normal. I had a feeling things would get better for us, that this trip was about healing more than anything else.

When I returned to the table, Alton wore an amused smile. I wondered if I should rough him up. Nothing that would leave a scar, maybe a few slaps here and there. I wasn't *that* mad at the guy. Now that my wife knew the truth, forcing Alton to admit his guilt didn't seem important. Rickie placed the camcorder on the table. Aimed the lens his way.

"Give me the Beretta," she said.

Alton's amusement turned into a laugh. He regained his composure and tilted back in his seat. "Okay, I get it now. You're recording this so you can play it at the next Christmas party. . . . Ooooh, I am so scared. Help me. Help me."

Rickie repeated her request.

"It's loaded," I said.

"Give it," she said.

I wasn't afraid of Rickie intentionally shooting him; it was more like accidentally.

"Do you remember where the safety is?" I said.

She snapped her fingers. "It's that little slide right there."

I handed her the pistol, and she told me to leave.

"Leave?" I said.

"Did he confess to *you*?"

Rickie had a point.

"Miriam and I will take a walk," I said.

"Miriam stays," said Rickie.

I shrugged and walked out the door, to the perimeter of the island. The pole lights had timed off, and stars shone against the black backdrop. This was the first time I had seen the night sky at Bible Camp, and I looked up as if I were a hayseed among New York skyscrapers. I could see the Big Dipper, the North Star, Orion, a number of smaller constellations too blurry to sort out. I faced the fence and peered into the darkness, sensed a wildness that stretched forever.

A white explosion, and on the slope a snake twisted back into the water. A massive swirl and it disappeared. Snakes, alligators, and mosquitoes. The air might have improved but some things never changed. That made me think of Alton and wonder what had prompted him to shut down the boiler. He had seemed ready to sacrifice his life for his penance. Perhaps he had drawn a line in the sand, perhaps enough was enough. Perhaps he was tired of suffering. I had no clue and doubted I would ever find out.

I arrived at the spot where I had found him curled into a ball and covered with sulfur dust. I remembered standing between him and the fence so he wouldn't stumble into it, remembered him getting up and leaving his hat on the ground. I knelt and pressed my palms against the grass. Laid on my back and crossed my arms over my chest. I didn't know how much time to give Rickie, only hoped Alton would confess, Rickie would be satiated, and we could get on with our lives.

Lights brightened dormitory windows, no doubt also illuminating students studying their lessons. I wanted to see this prodigy Alton bragged on; could not believe another actor existed of his equal. I walked back to the cabin, opened the door, and blinked my eyes to adjust to the living room light. Miriam stood at Alton's side.

"Nice night," I said. "It'll be a nice flight back."

Rickie raised the pistol. Something flashed behind her eyes, something horrible, frightening, and beautiful all at the same time.

"No," I said. "Don't do this."

Her thumb flicked off the safety, and her finger curled around the trigger. The barrel pointed my way. She told me to stay where I was, and I stopped in the middle of the room.

"Put it down," I said.

"Honey," Miriam said, skin tightening on her forehead. "Listen to him."

The barrel swung toward Miriam, and I took a step forward. Alton, whose stunned expression suggested he had figured out this was real, blurted something about paying the money back.

"Hear that?" I said. "It's over."

Rickie's words had a bite to them.

"I've fantasized about this moment since I was eight years old," she said. "Do you know what it's like trying to live with that? Do you even have a clue?"

My wife, in her muscle T-shirt and black jeans, seemed to fight something inside her, a mental battle that manifested itself in her body. I'd never seen her like this, so tense . . . so . . . And then I saw something else, the layer beneath the woman so rigid before me. I saw the eyes of a child who realized she'd been dumped like garbage, who realized she was nothing more than a meal ticket to her surrogate parents. I saw the eyes of a child who became so angry she plotted murder when she should have been playing with Barbie dolls.

I talked in a low voice, telling Rickie I loved her, telling her Miriam loved her, telling her Alton loved her, telling her things were never as bad as they seemed, that we'd get through this if she handed me the Beretta, that we'd walk out of here and never come back.

"We have a life," I said.

I thought I was getting through to her, I thought I was making sense, I thought if I could get two steps closer—

A shot rang out, Miriam's head snapped back, and she fell to the floor. I stood there, unable to move. Looked down at blood leaking from Miriam's skull onto the sawdust. A second shot rang out, and Alton's brains splattered on the wall. I leaped forward and snatched the Beretta away from Rickie, jerked her backward. Motherfucker. Motherfucker. Motherfucker. Someone pounded on the front door. A crash, and Royce lunged inside, looked from the pistol in my hand to where the bodies lay bleeding. He came forward, giving me a wide berth, knelt, and took off his shirt. He pressed it against Miriam's head, then Alton's. I held Rickie close and spoke words that changed my life forever. They came in a rush, so quick there was no way to take them back.

"I shot them," I said.

Rickie studied me through her tears, and that's when I believe she understood my love was unconditional. The pain and the anger left her eyes and wonderment took its place. She grabbed the camcorder, and she and I walked outside, down the sidewalk to the helicopter. My mind calmed, and in the midst of chaos, my thinking clarified and became crystal clear. I told her to give me the camcorder, and she handed it over.

"Listen," I said. "I want you to empty your bank account and disappear."

"Where am I supposed to go?"

I grabbed her arm and hustled her onto the landing pad. "I want you to ask the pilot for the latitude and longitude of this island, do you understand?"

She nodded.

"Then," I said, "before you step onto the plane for wherever you are headed, I want you to call the Florida state police and tell them there's been two murders."

She ducked out from under my arm.

"I'm staying with you," she said.

I cupped her chin and forced it upward.

"I want to do this for you," I said.

Rickie nodded, slowly at first, then faster, and we were nodding together and I could see acceptance in her eyes. She told me she loved me and I told her the same, watched her climb into the cabin. The helicopter rose from the ground and started on a northwesterly direction, toward our home in Sarasota. I watched until the blinking rotor light dissolved into the night. Motherfucker, I could not believe this was happening.

I walked past the dormitory and its blackened windows, knew the students were watching. Took a left and entered the old classroom, walked down the steps to the boiler. I twisted knobs, pushed the ignite button, and a flame shot out of the burner. On the floor, a fifty-pound bag of sulfur beckoned, and I ripped it open and shoveled yellow dust into the vat. Air heated, sulfur boiled, and sweat ran off my body. I dropped the camcorder, watched it tilt on its side and sink like a doomed ship into the liquid. Then I held the pistol to my temple. A little pressure and this would be over. Eventually, I laid the pistol on the floor and kicked it out of reach. I had to stay alive, had to convince authorities I was the sole perpetrator. My mind continued to go to my wife pointing the gun at her mother. I should have done something, anything. I should have lunged or thrown a lamp or begged, I should have gotten on my knees and pleaded. Motherfucker. I should have done something. No, worse than that, I should have never handed her the Beretta, should have realized she was not in control of her demons. I should have taken her seriously in the past, should have gotten her help somehow. I thought she was getting better, I truly did. I thought the bad days were behind us.

The rap on the door came hours later, along with a voice announcing the state police wanted to talk to me. I came up the steps, hands in the air, accepted the cuffs without complaint. Men in uniform walked in and out of Alton's cabin. Yellow air shrouded the island, and in every direction bug zappers hummed. A man held up a detective badge and read me my rights, then told me they had eyewitness testimony placing me at the scene, holding the murder weapon, and saying I was the shooter. I was under arrest for the murders of Alton Pierce and Miriam MacKenzie.

"They were going to replace me," I spat. "I killed those bastards and I'm proud of it."

The detective wanted Rickie's statement, and I told him he was wasting his time, that my wife would never testify against me. I knew they would look for her until I was convicted and the State of Florida satisfied its bloodlust. They didn't have a chance of finding her. Rickie was smarter than all of them put together.

The detective loaded me onto a helicopter, and we lifted toward the sky. I looked down on the island, a blur in the morning sun. Imagined Rickie headed to who knew where. I hoped she'd find peace.

Me? The way I saw it, I'd make do.

I always had.

Chapter 19

On this day, June 9, 2009, the view from the window is overcast, and rain falls in liquid sheets from the clouds. A fur-soaked cat scuttles across the field and crawls under a Dumpster. Farther away, on the other side of the graveyard, pipes rise from a slab like slender stalagmites. The contractors do not work in the rain. They have the day off. They are out doing things. Shooting pool, maybe. Maybe out with their families. I am here, I am in this prison. To look beyond my cell is one thing, to imagine myself somewhere else is a luxury I do not allow. I leave the fantasy world to someone with a future.

During one of his visits, Sandoval said the new building will have a break room, a holding cell, a viewing room for reporters and family members, and the Kill Room where the doctor administers the drugs. That's what my attorney calls it—the Kill Room. The only question is if the building will be finished in time for my execution.

Dredge bangs on the wall, rapid knocks that separate into a jaunty beat. I climb on the chair, talk into the vent, ask what he wants. The vent air is fresh and carries the scent of rain. Convicts shout slurs into the hallway, promise to do unspeakable things if only the guard will open the door. Prison life is like living next to train tracks. You grow so accustomed to annoying sound you only hear it when you want to. I allow it to rumble through me.

Noise, the flatness of the chair beneath my feet, these sensations are my world.

"They're buildin' a maintenance shed," Dredge says.

The building has been a source of speculation since the bulldozer thundered across the field and its blade sank into the grass, gouging out a rectangle that grew until it was the size of a basketball court. Everyone has an opinion. My favorite comes from three convicts who took a vote on the opposite side of the hall. They can't see the building, only know it exists because of cell chatter. They say it's a whorehouse for the guards, swear collectively Paris Hilton will visit and get down on her knees twice a week. The convict with the biggest dick on the block will perform nightly, splitting time between the heiress and a donkey. The prime mover behind this gossip is a Frenchman who killed his girlfriend and left her to rot inside a car he abandoned in the Everglades. He would have gotten away with it if two hunters hadn't seen the sun shining off the bumper, cut away the brush, and looked inside. The Frenchman claims to have an eleven-inch dick, says he should have been a porn star instead of a murderer, tells anyone who will listen that the bitch was fooling around and he did what any honorable man would do. He shot her between the eyes, wrapped her in a carpet, and disposed of her like the filth she was.

"It's for diesel maintenance," Dredge says. "It's where they'll work on the tractors."

He is a different man since the heart attack, claims he saw the tunnel and the bright light and Jesus telling him to go back to earth and do something positive with his life. Dredge has become our community organizer, holds tournaments on a bimonthly basis. He's convinced his latest idea will boost morale and make a happier existence for everyone. I picture him in a white robe and a wreath around his head, chanting "*Kum ba ya*" to his toothbrush.

The great State of Florida provides my neighbor with blood-pressure medicine and regular checkups. According to Dredge, prison health care is damn good. I wouldn't know. My knee still aches from when the guards bent it backward during my cell extraction.

"It's a combination chess and talent tournament," he says. "Winner gets an extra dessert for a week."

Every convict on the block plays chess and some are decent. No one can sing worth a crap. I suspect everyone but me has signed up, figure I am Dredge's Mount Everest. I don't know which guard he bribed, don't know what he offered for extra food. Don't care one way or the other.

"I'll schedule you for an afternoon slot," he says. "First round starts next week. That'll give you time to make the pieces."

I don't bother to tell Dredge I play in my head. I don't bother to tell him I can crush every player in the prison system without so much as lifting a finger.

"I told you I'm not playing," I say.

"You need somethin' to do besides work on that book, Preacher. You need somethin' to take your mind off things."

Dredge knows my death warrant has been signed, knows my execution date is around the corner. Hell, every convict on the block knows. I tell him I have things to do. Limp to my desk and heft the manuscript. Sandoval returned my earlier writings and the combined weight feels good, like I've accomplished something. I flip through the pages, skimming, pausing to revisit my favorite scenes. Rickie waking up in the hospital brings a lump to my throat, and I read that passage over and over. I think of her behind me on the Harley the day we got married, feel her legs around my thighs and her arms around my waist.

The first time we made love was in a cornfield outside my hometown. I remember the red blanket she brought from the RV, and the candles she lit in adjacent rows. The corn was green, and long leaves twisted on the stalks. The Milky Way seemed so close I could touch it. The carnival was in full swing less than a quarter mile away, and Pastor Yost barked through the loudspeakers. I'd known Rickie for five days, having met her the first night the carnival appeared, and this was the first time she smelled like strawberries. The scent came from her wrists and the back of her knees, from her slender neck. I wanted to dive into that scent, I wanted to backstroke in it forever.

We came together on that blanket, candlelight flickering around the stalks, corn shadows moving over us in sinuous waves. I orgasmed and she didn't and it was over too quickly. She held me afterward, invited me to leave this Podunk and see what there was to see of the world. Yost's voice changed pitch, the organ music sped up, and the local sinners lifted their voices in joyous piety. She wanted to do it again, and I lasted longer this time. The strawberry scent and the shadows enveloped us, and we kissed for what seemed like an hour. Eventually, she said her break was over, and she had to get back to her Bible booth. I lay on the blanket and listened to her walk through the corn, heard the leaves release her in rustling whispers. I listened until she was gone, and I was alone with a choice. Stay in Silvington and do who knew what, or live an adventure with a girl who smelled like strawberries and preferred lovemaking in candlelight.

I chose the girl.

There are four truths in my pathetic excuse for a life. My failure to kill my sister, my love for my wife, the death penalty, and this manuscript. I flip to where Rickie committed the murders. Study the handwriting. When I began this project, I wrote in tiny letters too embarrassed for the page. Toward the end the scrawls grew larger. Words that demand to be read.

Truth may start out timid, but it finishes bold.

My attorney, in his silk shirts and pressed slacks, black shoes shining below the hems, isn't a bad guy. He's high-strung, a fault he blames on caffeine, cigarettes, and Dunkin' Donuts. In the last year, fat around his belly has swollen to a full-sized inner tube. On my side of the door, I discovered my first gray hair a week ago. I left it alone. I am what I am. Thirty-two and aging fast. He moves his face close to the slot, and his eyes dart in a frantic manner. I stashed the manuscript under the bed, on the end closer to the door, and the pages are not visible from where he sits. Sandoval has signed with a literary agent who is pressuring him to deliver, and he has grown so accustomed to staring at the stack on my desk that he can tell when I've been writing and when I've slacked off. I enjoy his confused look, watch his hands shake, know he needs a smoke. Poor Sandoval, he doesn't smile as much these days.

"Everything all right at home?" I say.

"She wants the LA house or a two-million-dollar buyout."

Sandoval has married, divorced, and remarried, and this last wife is an art dealer who specializes in Persian artifacts. She doesn't need his money, is pissed off she caught him sleeping with a para-legal. Sandoval's firm has swelled to thirty-nine attorneys, and he runs television ads across the nation. Targets court shows because he figures their viewers are litigious. He owns five houses—three in the States, one in Switzerland, and one in Mexico. He's talked about sitting on a deck outside his château. Watching the snow fall in the mountains while he drinks Turkish coffee. The Mexican house is a villa on the west coast, where he pays a señorita to cook and clean and anything else he desires. He tips extra for blow jobs, or, as he calls them, "the amenities."

I am no longer his highest-profile client, was supplanted last year when he took on an actor who cut the heads off his wife and their two children. The police answered a 911 call from the maid, who came back from grocery shopping and discovered the victims propped in chairs around the dining room table. The actor was arrested in the middle of a shoot on a Hollywood set, taping a commercial for a product guaranteed to kill warts.

Sandoval obviously doesn't need the money we'll make off my book. He wants it anyway. He's one of those guys who lives to accumulate ex-wives and wealth. He already has his eye on the literary agent, says they went out to eat, drove back to his hotel room and hit the sheets. I want to tell him he's digging an early grave, so to speak. I figure it's no use pointing out the obvious.

"You shouldn't have married without a prenup," I say.

He looks pathetic. "Love will make a man do strange things."

I agree with him and we're silent for a while. Then I speak up.

"They poured the slab three days ago."

Sandoval wanted to file a "Cruel and Unusual Punishment" appeal when the workers started clearing the land. I nixed that idea, told him the construction is the first entertainment I've had in years, and I was afraid the State would move me across the hall. I hear the view over there is mostly air conditioners and garbage cans.

"You shouldn't watch that," he says.

"It's all right."

"No, you should drape something over the window and try to keep your mind occupied." Sandoval looks down the hall, and I know that urge for a cigarette is growing. Dredge bangs on the wall.

"Prison doorbell," I say.

"You should get it."

"He can wait," I say.

"He's your neighbor." Sandoval still sees my world through civilized eyes. He does not understand ignoring Dredge is one of my few exercises in freedom.

"I don't even know what he looks like," I say.

Sandoval walks out of sight and a few seconds later returns. "He's a skinny guy and has dark skin, olive-colored, like he's part Mediterranean. He has black eyes and a sloped forehead, and he's wearing a T-shirt and boxers."

I thought Dredge was a fat white guy. I don't know why, maybe his name, maybe his voice. I retrieve the manuscript from under the bed. Sandoval licks his lips and extends his hand into my cell.

"I wrote the last part for your eyes only," I say.

"Pardon me?"

"I want you to know what really happened that night," I say. "I want you to know everything."

Sandoval removes his arm from the slot and sits straight in his chair. "Are you suggesting this manuscript doesn't match your confession?"

I must admit I am enjoying this. My attorney based an entire defense on insanity, and he's about to discover that I'm truly innocent.

"I want you to promise you will destroy the murder chapter," I say. "I want you to swear on your mother's life."

"The murder chapter. . . . Sure, whatever you want."

Sandoval will say anything to get his hands on this manuscript, yet I choose to believe him. I'm not sure why. Maybe I'm at the point in my life when I need to believe in *something*, and Sandoval is it. How pathetic is that? Christians have God, Muslims have Allah, Buddhists have Buddha, the ancient Greeks had Zeus, and I have an aging attorney who hops from woman to woman like a horny bullfrog. For a moment, I am incensed and think about throwing the papers into the toilet. I'll destroy them. I'll end this here and now.

"Vernon," he says, "I give you my word. I swear on my mother's life."

I hand him the manuscript, feel a warm wind blow through me. I have faith in my friend, and that faith feels good. Sandoval will do as he says, and the next time he sits on that chair outside my cell, he will look at me with a new perspective. He'll see me as I am, a man wrongly incarcerated.

He gets up, says he'll be in touch, walks down the hall. I stand on the chair and shout into the vent.

"I was talking to my attorney."

"Is that who looked at me?" Dredge says. "I swear to God a pervert looked in my cell. He looked right at me."

"I don't think it was him, it must have been someone else."

"It better not have been your attorney. It had better been someone else."

"What do you want?" I say.

Dredge's tone turns coy. "I know what that building is."

"Yeah?"

"I didn't want to tell you, but everyone on this block knows it's where they're goin' to kill you."

"Dredge," I say, "I thought you were a white guy."

"I'm dark-complected."

"My attorney says you're dark as Martin Luther King."

"You keep him away from me," Dredge says. "That pervert looks in my cell again and I'll kill him."

My neighbor settles down, and I go to the window. The rain stops, and sunlight pushes through the clouds. The cat crawls out from underneath the Dumpster and walks across the field. I press my cheek against the bars and watch as long as possible. The cat is an escapee from cell block A, where prisoners raise felines they get from the Humane Society. In cell block B, prisoners train Seeing Eye dogs, and the State gives them to the blind. Prisoners in cell block C are short-timers, and they work the fields and livestock. The prison raises cows for milk and steers for beef, has a chicken house for eggs, grows vegetables in long rows. Tomatoes, squash, okra, bush beans, anything that thrives in the sun. Most of the convicts would cut off a left nut to live in those blocks. Not me. I'm happy where I'm at.

Clouds ebb toward the east, and white sky appears. Heat burns puddles off the slab, and the concrete loses luster. Two men wearing hard hats drive up in a red truck, remove a tripod and stakes from the bed. They tromp through the field, and it doesn't take long to realize they are surveying the parking lot. I hope it's a big one. No sense attending a small party.

Chapter 20

ONVICTS SCHEDULE A VOTE to name the building. Discussion opens two hours after breakfast, when stomachs return to normal. Dredge suggests Death Awaits, a name that repulses Zach Handover. Zach, who complains he should have received more press for his murders, politics for Handover Manor.

Zach filled us in on what happened that day, claims he purchased the AK-47 to kill the supervisor at Wendy's, who had the gall to dock employees who took extra-long breaks. Zach shot Carlos Sanchez in his supervisor's badge, which was pinned on his shirt over his chest. It felt so good firing that gun, Zach walked past the fryers and shot the drive-in window girl in the head, then turned on the customers, who were running like jackrabbits and jumping over chairs. A Vietnamese guy couldn't move fast enough and got shot under the arm, and two teenagers who went to help him got shot in the stomach. All told, Zach shot seventeen people and killed five, would have kept on shooting if he hadn't run out of bullets. Needless to say, subtle is not part of Zach's character.

"Handover Manor has a certain ring," Dredge says, "but if we're goin' to name it after someone we should consider Vernon Oliver Popped This Cherry."

Dredge is voted down. I'm one of the naysayers. Vernon Oliver Popped This Cherry has too many words for my taste. I'm drawn to the construction in a way that makes me wonder if incarceration has warped my mind. The walls are up, concrete blocks poured solid. Men stand on scaffolding and guide roof trusses into place. The trusses, made of steel, form a skeletonized A-frame. At noon, workers sit in the grass, eat sandwiches, and drink from thermoses. The scene is strangely erotic, graveyard in the foreground, building in the background, fence and guard towers beyond. My hand does not drift below my waist—self-denial is a new concept for me.

I ignore the guard who opens the slot and tells me to come get my lunch tray. The slot shuts, and I know I'll go hungry until dinnertime.

By late afternoon the roof is on and the men are gone, and I'm still at the window watching the prison cast its shadow across the grass. The graveyard darkens first, and the headstones turn dingy gray. The shadow, a horizontal shade drawing over the earth, lengthens. The windows blacken as the shade crawls up and over the building. I bang on the wall.

"I still think Death Awaits," Dredge says. "That one still gets my vote."

"Eternity Beckons."

"That's better than Handover Manor."

"The roof is on," I say.

"They're making headway."

I sense his excitement and do not blame him for it. An execution, one less convict on the block, satisfies his craving for change.

The quarterfinals of Dredge's tournament match him against

Zach Handover. Zach raps a song, words so crushed together I can't make them out, after which Dredge whistles a tune from *Les Misérables*. Dredge is good. I did not know this about him. He wins the talent part of their competition, which means he gets his choice of color on the chessboard. I tell him to take white because white moves first and has a slight advantage over black.

"I don't need an advantage." He picks black.

They call out their moves, and I follow inside my head. Zach opens with the Ruy Lopez and soon gallops his knights all over the place, turning Dredge's defense inside out and upside down. Dredge simpers, hems and haws, claims he isn't having his best day. I see a parry here, a parry there, a sacrifice that involves a rook and two pawns, and Dredge will have a stranglehold on the game.

"Pawn to f4," I say.

Kibitzing is against the rules, and an uproar swells the block. Guards stalk the hall and beat nightsticks against the doors. Quiet returns.

"Pawn to f4," Dredge tells Zach.

I don't know if Dredge trusts me, or if he thinks his position is so hopeless he'll take advice from anywhere. He follows my suggestions, and three minutes later Zach's king is in check with nowhere to move.

Mate.

Game over.

Adios, motherfucker.

"Preacher," Zach says, "that was one beautiful combination."

I am surprised he is graceful in defeat. Dredge screams into the vent. "That's how you do it. That is what I'm talkin' 'bout."

"You should stick to nailing boys on doors," Zach says. "You ain't worth two cents at chess."

Mail arrives at four, and I sit at my desk and sort through envelopes. Pause when I spot a return address I recognize. Nick Wheaton, pastor of Godliness Cathedral, a ministry that no doubt tripled in profitability after Miracles, Inc. shut down, sent me a letter. The handwriting is insultingly large. In a hoarse voice, I read the words aloud, try to see him at his desk, in his pussy pink wardrobe, scrawling out his thoughts.

> *Dear Mr. Oliver,*
>
> *Members of my flock have taken it upon themselves to begin regular prayer meetings on your behalf (they take place every Thursday evening), that you should see the light and confess your sins before you meet God. We have forgiven you for your transgressions and believe you are a good man at heart, and would not have been led astray if it wasn't for your penchant for greed and your love of attention. (These are common failings and have ruined many a man.)*
>
> *I hold no ill will for your hurtful words to Ed Bradley, your insinuation that I am mentally imbalanced. Let it be known that this man of God is not, nor has he ever been, a paranoid schizophrenic.*
>
> *Now, to the point of this letter. (Please forgive my failure to get to the point in a timely manner. It's my Southern background. Ha-ha.) My flock, in their concern that you have every chance to change your stripes, has sug-*

*gested I become your spiritual advisor. If you so desire, I
will arrange my busy schedule to minister to you in person
on the last day of your fated existence.*

Sincerely,
Your loving friend, Pastor Nick Wheaton.

I wad the paper, toss it in the toilet, wonder how much money
it will put in Wheaton's pocket to claim he led me to the Lord
seconds before my execution. Could be worth millions. I give the
guy credit; he knows how to work the angles. I write him a return
letter.

Dear Nick Wheaton,
Kiss my ass.

Sincerely,
Your loving friend, Pastor Vernon Oliver

Dinner arrives. I pick at the mac 'n' cheese. My thoughts have
become increasingly random, like windblown leaves. I rake them
into piles and renegade gusts scatter them across the lawn. It's a
frustrating battle. The wind blows, and my mind goes to a scene
that occurred the night I left home to run away with Rickie.

I stood in the trailer, stuffing clothes into my duffel bag, trying to avoid my mother's gaze. Lucy's death had detonated the
family. Dad no longer went to church, choosing to take jobs that
kept him away for longer and longer periods. He was up near the
Michigan border working on a bridge. Didn't say good-bye when
he left. Grief had descended over Mom's face, and the only emotion she exhibited was immense sadness.

I dragged the zipper along its track until the contents in the bag disappeared. Mom stepped aside, and I walked down the hall to the living room. The legs from Lucy's hospital bed had left indentations in the carpet, and the imprint closest to the door was still visible if you knew where to look. I leveled my gaze, did not stop as Mom spoke over my shoulder.

"It's not your fault she got sick."

I walked out the door and didn't look back. Mom was right. It wasn't my fault Lucy got sick. I blamed that on God.

It was, however, my fault she suffered so long.

In my prison cell, so many years later, I purse my lips and exhale. Rationalization, hammer and tongs of a nimble mind, has beaten my guilt into submission. Yes, I failed my sister, but who among us can kill what he loves?

Not I.

Chapter 21

A PICKUP PARKS NEXT TO the building. Alligator Framing Company, Incorporated. Red letters on the passenger door. Two men strap on tool belts and head inside. To their right, a bulldozer pushes soil between flagged stakes. The road is wide enough for two lanes and will wind around the corner and out of sight. A trustee swings a Weed Eater through the graveyard, edging grass around the markers. Two more convicts have died, one a lifer who had an aneurysm in his cell, the other a young kid who got drunk on rotted apples and hung himself. Their mounds are side by side, a family affair, only there is no family in prison and chances are these convicts didn't know each other.

"Vernon," Sandoval says. "Can you hear me?"

My existence has morphed into a strange dichotomy. I hear Sandoval, I do not hear him. I see the graveyard, I do not see it. My heart beats in my chest. Is it an illusion? Perhaps the great State of Florida administered the drugs, and I am already dead.

"I want you to assume responsibility for my body," I say. "I want you to cremate me and scatter my ashes anywhere but here."

"Your parents—"

"I have not communicated with them in many years."

I turn and stare him down. This is the first time I have seen him since handing over the manuscript. Sandoval's hair has magically thickened, and his receding hairline has disappeared. I walk across the cell and get a closer look. Hair plugs, tiny rows across the top of his forehead, jut from his scalp. He wears golfing attire and the words PEBBLE BEACH adorn a breast pocket. My attorney grew tired of tennis several years back, and now spends his free time on the golf course. He claims to have a wicked sand game, has trouble on the greens. Can't seem to sink putts when the ball is close to the hole. His gaze locks on mine, and I sense his fury. His mood surprises me. I had expected empathy.

I am, after all, an innocent man.

"Vernon," he says, "I wish you'd told me the truth from the beginning."

"How's the putting going these days?"

"Vernon," he says.

"The truth would not have made a difference."

"Maybe yes, maybe no."

"They discovered gunpowder residue on my hands," I say. "They had my confession."

"Do you ever think of her? Do you ever wonder where she is?"

Rickie, no doubt, lives in a seaside tourist villa somewhere in South America. She's had plastic surgery and looks like someone altogether different. She's grown her hair out and wears unassuming clothes, a woman who blends into the crowd. A nun is what I think of when I think of my wife these days. Habit, rosary, the whole works. She might have even put on weight, although I doubt it, basing that theory on slender mother equals slender daughter. If she's fat, that's okay, too. Pleasingly plump is one thing, morbidly obese, though, is something else altogether.

"I suspect she's in Toronto," I say.

"Toronto?"

"That or Paris."

"Do you think they'll ever find her?"

The question surprises me.

"They have no reason to look," I say.

"What if they did?"

"They don't."

Sandoval picks up his briefcase, unsnaps and snaps the lock. Unsnap. Snap. Unsnap. Snap. Unsnap. Like that, for at least a minute.

"What would you say if I told you I had evidence that corroborates your autobiography?" asks Sandoval.

Smoke wafts down the block, and a piercing alarm goes off. The sound cuts through the air loud enough to make Sandoval grimace. I cock my head so my ear is in the slot, revel in the pain that follows. I turn my head and switch ears, lean back when Sandoval gets up and stands close to the door. Guards drag a water hose down the hall and soon the sound of concentrated spray mixes with Spanish curses. We have two pyros on the block, a couple of M13 Hispanics who bound their victims in their living rooms and burned down their houses. Setting mattresses on fire is a monthly event. I have no idea how they get the matches, figure they pay guards to smuggle them in. The water stops, the cursing doesn't, and the guards return to their station.

"Did you keep your promise?" I say. "Did you destroy the last chapter?"

My knee aches, and I shift to take the weight off it. There's no sense in repeating my question. Sandoval's averted gaze says it all.

"My firm received a video after your sentencing," he says. "UPSed from Brazil. It's a five-second clip of a woman shooting two people in the head."

He talks in a terse voice, tells how his staff evaluated the video, then dropped it in the "evidence" box. His staff keeps the box in a closet in his office. My followers have been diligent, although they have slacked off in recent years. A woman named Olivia is the most persistent. She swears I was licking her vagina at the time of the murders. Sends Sandoval letters proclaiming she has indisputable proof I couldn't possibly have killed Miriam and Alton. I do not know Olivia and have certainly never had my tongue between her legs.

"It was too blurry to make out the faces," Sandoval says. "We thought it was just another hoax."

The package came with a short note.

> Dear Mr. Sandoval,
>   My husband is an innocent man.
>   Rickie Oliver

A tingle starts in my toes and works its way through my legs, up the bones in my back, to my scalp. My hair roots are on fire, they're needles dipped in hot sauce. Hope. This is what it feels like. This is what I offered the lost when I was onstage. I replay the murders in my mind, fast forward to Rickie handing me the camcorder, realize I had not checked it for the tape. Suddenly, I am angry. She has made a mockery of my sacrifice.

"Destroy it," I say.

"As your attorney—"

"Incinerate it, drop it into the ocean, whatever you have to do."

"I can't," Sandoval says. "I already sent it and the autobiography to Quantico."

Chapter 22

THE FINALS TAKE PLACE on a Monday morning. Dredge whistles a tune from *Rocky III*, says "Eye of the Tiger" is apropos of the moment. His opponent mumbles through "Amazing Grace" and ends out of pitch and out of breath. Dredge chooses white and opens with e4. I get down and wet a washcloth. Crawl under the bed and wipe down the springs and metal frame. I finger-sweep the floor, toss crumbs in the toilet. Then I strip and run a soapy washcloth over my body. My skin, a sallow tint, has begun loosening from the muscles. The State allows us to shower once a week, in a videotaped room down the hall. I avoid the humiliation and birdbath instead. The closer my execution date, the cleaner I've become. I don't know why. Maybe I don't want to die stinking of prison. Maybe if I scrub hard and often enough I can wash away my past. Maybe there really is a Saint Peter and he does a sniff test at the pearly gate. You there, you smell like a prostitute, off to hell you go. You, sir, you smell like a wino. Turn around and follow that woman in fishnet stockings.

I dry off and shrug into fresh overalls, climb back up on the chair. Dredge shuffles his queen and rook, inches a center pawn forward, slices a bishop on diagonal forays. Not having followed every move, I am unsure of the position. My neck itches and I pull up on the overalls, a movement that tugs the inseam into my crotch. I shrug the overalls back down, live with the itch on my neck. I lick a finger and rub the vent, scrub away dust that has accumulated in a corner.

"Rook to c4," I say, not knowing if the move is even possible.

"Shut up," Dredge says.

There's dirt in the corner over the door, and I run a soapy sock over the block. Sandoval visited twice last week and believes the FBI has begun testing the evidence. He says they'll compare handwriting in the autobiography to letters I mailed from prison. They'll use a computer program to enhance the videotape, try to take measurements between the eyes, pinpoint exact placement of moles and skin blemishes. Then they'll compare that data to pictures of the deceased.

Shouts from the hall and someone yells, "It's a draw." I holler " 'Eye of the Tiger' was ten times better than 'Amazing Grace.' " The block votes for using the talent portion of the contest as the tie breaker, and Dredge is announced the winner.

"Lucky prick," I say, then spend the next hour moving the chair around and scrubbing the ceiling. When I get near the window, I clean it, too. The parking lot comes into sharp focus, along with the asphalt road. Painters in splotched overalls carry in buckets and brushes. I hope they paint the Kill Room a nice quiet color. I'd vote for beige.

Guards march past, a door opens and closes down the way, and through the vent convicts whisper the guards put a trustee in an empty cell. The prisoner screams for mercy, and a guard orders him to cuff up. The marching begins, a determined rhythm. The guards appear, eight strong, dragging the trustee by the armpits. I go to the sink and brush my teeth. Dredge pounds the wall, I get back up on the chair, and he tells me to look out the window. My mouth is full of toothpaste, and I wipe spit on the back of my hand.

"I'm busy," I mumble.

"It's a dry run. That whiny bitch is supposed to be you."

At the window, I peer into lifting fog. The guards, a blue octet, figure contorting in their middle, march into view. The prisoner brings his knees to his chest and kicks outward. The guards are too many and too powerful, and soon he lies in their arms docile as a lapdog. His head turns toward the graveyard, and I know he thinks about lying under that earth. His body bucks, and one arm comes loose and flails about. The guards close ranks, boots never missing the beat.

They carry the man through a door in the rear of the building, and the door closes and calm returns to the field. The sun appears and the headstones brighten, dominoes without dots. I go back to brushing my teeth. Spit into the sink. Blood mixes with saliva and toothpaste, and I realize I've bitten my tongue.

I talk to Dredge later that afternoon.

My neighbor has started a pool on how I'll react come Judgment Day.

"I've got two squares left," Dredge says. " 'Pissin' His Pants' or 'Cryin' Like a Baby.' "

"I'll take 'Crying Like a Baby.' "

It feels good to laugh, wish it was something I had done more in my life.

† † †

Sandoval has on a new ring. This one is wide and diamond-encrusted. He quit dating the literary agent after the sale and has begun shaving his body, including the hairs on his knuckles. He goes out with a young woman who prefers her men like hairless Chihuahuas, and he does his best to accommodate.

"This is the first time I've shaved my testicles," he says.

When you live in a six-by-ten cell, you pick your battles. Sandoval broke the oath he swore on his mother's grave, but I do not hold it against him. My attorney and I have opposite goals. His is to prove innocence, mine is to maintain guilt. He did what any normal human would have done, and I do not hold it against him. Without the tape, I'm positive he would have kept his word.

"She wouldn't go out with me unless I drove a hybrid," he says. "California women are environmentally conscious."

"Rickie was like that. We had a water-saving toilet in the RV."

"She was from Colorado, wasn't she?"

"Boulder."

"Desdemona is from LA," he says. "An aspiring actress."

"You going to get a prenup this time?"

He drops a pen, bends over, picks it up. "I'm through with the vows. My bank account can't afford it."

Sandoval is a perpetual marrier. If not this girl, someone else. Dredge bangs on the wall, and Sandoval tells me I should get it.

"He says the next time you look at him he'll kill you," I say. "He thinks you're a peeping Tom."

My attorney gets up and disappears to my left, and a crash comes from inside Dredge's cell. Sandoval reappears and sits down. Crosses his legs. Hems ride up knobby ankles and expose varicose veins. "Did you know these younger women shave their pubic hair?"

"You shouldn't aggravate him like that. I don't think his heart can take it."

He flexes his fingers. Each digit reminds me of a miniature hot dog; the thumb, wrinkled and bare, looks more like a link sausage. His lips part, a smile that does not force his cheeks upward. Sandoval has Botoxed his face.

"Vernon," he says, lips split wide. "The FBI says they are ninety-eight percent certain the tape is valid evidence."

"Ninety-eight percent?"

"They enhanced it, but it's still too blurry for precise facial measurements. They did find Rickie's fingerprints on the casing." He opens his briefcase. Produces a letter. The paper smells of cigar smoke, and I envision his staff sitting around a table and discussing my case. It must have been a shock to realize I was 98 percent innocent. I hold the letter to the light. My eyes are going bad. If this keeps up, I'll need glasses.

"I'm not signing it," I say.

Sandoval lets out a sigh, followed by a coil and pop of his tongue. I've never heard this chicken cluck, not in all our years.

"Ninety-eight percent verification isn't strong enough for the courts," he says.

The letter requires I renounce my confession and lay all blame on Rickie. The letter requires I testify against her if she is brought to trial. The letter requires I sign an affidavit saying I wrote the truth in my autobiography. I wad the paper into a crumpled ball, stick it in my mouth, chew it up. Swallow. Ink, a chemical taste, coats my tongue.

"You're on your own," Sandoval says.

"You can't do that so close to an execution. The courts won't allow it."

Sandoval, Botox and all, looks twenty years older than his age. This process has taken its toll.

"I'm still your attorney," he says, "but I will not lift another finger to help you."

I stretch out on the bed and close my eyes. For the first time in a long time, I curl into a ball and fall asleep while it's daylight.

Chapter 23

TODAY IS MY BIRTHDAY, and I am thirty-three years old. I have lived nearly a third of my life in prison. I eat a runny pudding I saved from last night's supper, lick stickiness from my fingers. Dredge organizes a serenade from four convicts down the way and strands of "Happy Birthday" wander through the vent. Convicts seldom do anything for free, so I know he paid a dessert apiece for the participation. I stay at the vent hoping for more. I can't seem to stop talking, like I want to get all the words out I would have used in the future. I bang on the wall, and Dredge coughs into the vent.

"What I think," I say, "is once you die, you're dead and gone."

"Preacher, you need to get on your knees and get right with the Lord before it's too late."

"Fuck that."

No last-minute religious contrivances for me. If there really is a hell, and that's where I wind up, so be it.

"You ain't much of a preacher," Dredge says.

I can't argue his point. Still, his words irritate me.

"I hear he has a special place for boy-killers," I say. "I hear you'll get raped a hundred times a day."

Dredge tells me to kiss his ass, and I think that's the end of the conversation. The second year of my incarceration, my neighbor told me a computer chip controls his actions and the murders weren't his fault. Thinks the chip is in his arm and he is preprogrammed. I tried to rationalize him to sanity, and he explained voices in his head tell him what I'm going to say before I say it and that proves they are real.

"I'm ordering pancakes for my last supper," I say. "Maple syrup, lots of butter."

Dredge wants me to order fried chicken, so he can smell it in his cell. That and a shrimp cocktail. He wants me to describe the taste when I get done eating. I haven't decided. Maybe I'll eat whatever Jesus ate for his last supper. I'll conjure up twelve disciples, and we'll hold conversation that doesn't include food or murder. I suppose the conversation is what I miss most about Rickie. We sat around and talked, nothing special, two lovers passing time. That and her touch. She had this way of seeking out my hand, an absentminded gesture that seemed to reassure her I was still at her side. I inhale and fantasize about the strawberry scent she wore so often.

"Strawberries for dessert," I say. "That and a gallon of whipped cream."

"Strawberries are for pussies."

"I'm not getting fried chicken," I say.

"You should at least order a baked potato; sour cream and chives."

"It's my meal." I smack the vent, and ridges imprint my palm. After a while, Dredge mumbles something I can't hear, and I ask him to repeat himself.

"I'll miss you, Preacher."

That's it for morning conversation, so I go to the window and look out at the building. A moving van backs up to the front door, and two black guys get out. They remove a gurney and wheel it down the sidewalk. Straps sway like upside-down cobras. I look from the gurney to the graveyard, back and forth, a tennis spectator too close to the court. The guys wear headphones, and their necks bob up and down. They wear brown uniforms, company issue, and their pants are down around their thighs, exposing boxer shorts. Their slouch says they work for the man and don't like it one bit. I raise two fists in solidarity, watch the workers disappear inside.

A trustee drives a tractor across the field, and grass clippings shoot into the air like organic missiles. I visualize the wheels running over me, whirling blades slicing my body into bite-sized chunks. Lately, I've imagined all sorts of deaths. The guillotine intrigues me the most. On my back, trussed so tight I can't move, a thick metal razor suspended above my head. I hear the executioner breathing deep rasps, see the erection bulging his pants. Sometimes I think about dying between two horses engaged in a lathered tug-of-war. Stretched out. Hands tied to one horse. Feet tied to the other. I wonder which would go first, legs or arms, figure it's the arms because they are smaller appendages. Bloody. That's what I think about when I think about my death. The State, however, will perform my execution with the needle. Sanitized. No muss. No fuss. This is my choice. I'll leave the electric chair to those who don't mind the smell of burning flesh.

They can all kiss my ass. Especially Sandoval, who has not returned since we had it out over my recantation letter. Which suits me fine. Bury me in that graveyard and see if I care. I'll rise in three days and walk this earth in a robe and sandals. I'll minister to my flock one last time and tell them to spread the Good Word around the world, then I'll disappear forever. Maybe I'll go to the Arctic and lead a solitary life. Maybe I'll build a hut and eat seals and make friends with polar bears. I'll sit out in the cold until my bones are so frozen I become an iceberg and float away forever.

I leap across the room and slam my shoulder into the door, back up and do it again. My mouth opens and I scream and I have no idea what I'm saying, but the words come out and the door bucks and my shoulder hurts and my breaths come fast and hard. I slam my head into the Plexiglas, and blood drips down my nose to my lips. The thud is like none I've heard, hollow, ringing, a sound that blurs my eyes. A guard appears. I do not look at him, am determined not to know one of these bastards from the other. I spit a tooth, a crimson Chiclet, to the floor.

"I want my attorney," I say.

The guard disappears, and I drift backward in a fall that takes forever. The ceiling appears overhead, a slide of gray painted blocks and a recessed light, and then the back of my head hits concrete and blackness envelops my soul.

In the morning, I wake to a pounding brain and crusted scalp. I wash up and probe my sore gum, remember the tooth. I set it upright on the sink, stare at it, bow my head. My bloody incisor, a miniature phallic symbol, I will pray to you for guidance, I will bow before you and ask forgiveness.

Sandoval arrives at three o'clock. He has a pleased look, like he knew I would crack. He's dressed in all blue, right down to his loafers.

"You look like hell," he says.

I finger the lumps on my head, watch him open his briefcase. Sandoval wears a new cologne, probably something to please his jailbait girlfriend. He gets out a paper and tells me it's the same as the first. I read upside down as well as right side up, and I know what he says is true.

My equilibrium falters, a car running on bad gas, and I sink to the floor. I'm a bottom dweller, a basement bum, a man in a dark alley with no way out. A pen lands next to my head and spins in circles. It's a blue pen, a Bic, a cheapo from the dollar store, and he wants me to shape the ink inside it, a swirl here, a swirl there, a signature that condemns my wife to my fate.

He moves close to the slot, and his words grow louder. "We lost another appeal.... The Florida State Supreme Court will not grant a new trial based solely on the video. We need this recantation."

I am not surprised Sandoval backtracked on his threat to stop helping me with my case. For all his bluster, he has a kind heart.

"That's not why I asked for you," I said.

"Vernon."

"I want you to contact Nick Wheaton. I want him to be my spiritual advisor. In exchange, I want him to sign a contract saying he'll assume responsibility for my body."

Sandoval's voice washes over me, full of pleading, "I wish you'd reconsider, I wish you'd sign the paper."

"You still don't get it, do you?"

"I'm trying to...."

I sit up so I can look him in the eyes. His face is inches away. We've never been so close, and suddenly I feel sorry for what I've put him through. Overall, my attorney is a generous man. Overall, he is a contribution to humanity.

"I took a vow. I promised to protect her."

Sandoval stows the paper in his briefcase, extends his hand through the slot. I wrap my fingers around his and our palms touch. There is no shaking, just a simple clasp, and I see glistening in his eyes.

That's all I have to say about that.

Chapter 24

THE DATE IS SEPTEMBER 6, 2009. The day before my execution and the crushed peppers on my New York strip are too hot for my taste. I eat them anyway. Blood puddles on the plate, runs toward the dinner roll. I shift knees, and the puddle runs toward the mashed potatoes. The potatoes are mounded and have a dimple in the center, where gravy sits like brown lava. I pour on the salt and eat a bite, swallow, eat another. The sensation of chewing feels surreal; so does the swelling in my stomach. I ordered a stir-fry of onions, carrots, yellow squash, okra, and green peppers. I eat a singed carrot slice and swallow Coke. I thought about ordering Pepsi, stuck with the old standby.

I unfold a napkin and dab at my mouth, fantasize Rickie sits across from me. She had this way of squaring food in the order she wanted to eat it. She would have eaten the veggies first. Twenty-four hours from this precise moment, the State intends to pronounce me dead. I chew on an okra, spit out the stem. Then I eat more steak, chewing faster and faster until I'm swallowing and chewing and chasing with water and stuffing my mouth until it will hold no more. Food drips down my chin to my plate, reconstituting itself into something other than what it was before.

I tell Dredge I ordered shrimp cocktail, I tell him the shrimp tastes like shrimp and the sauce tastes like spicy ketchup and overall the shrimp is cold and the sauce is cold and it's not bad.

"A shrimp cocktail," he says.

I save the Coke for last, sip it so slowly it looks like a black well that never dries up. The Coke fizzes my mouth and I work my lips like I'm going to spit, which sloshes the Coke around my gums.

In the morning, they will come for me, and I know not what I'll do. Tomorrow morning, I'll wake up for the last time.

That night, I look out the blackened glass and watch constellations form against the infinite backdrop. I think of space and how it's nothing and everything at the same time. I think of how stars explode and of how amoebas on other planets begin the cycle that leads to life. I imagine a world where children are born without genetic defects and where wives do not go off the deep end. I think of Lucy and wonder where she is, hope there are cartoons in her life. I don't know why I'm doing this to myself, I mean, motherfucking to hell and back. I wish I was on my Harley with Rickie's arms around my waist. I wish her lips were on my neck and her breasts against my chest, I wish her pelvis moved to the vibration between her legs. I can still feel her coming if I think hard enough, can still hear that groan through my helmet.

My eyelids are weighted, my heart is slowing down. I feel the straps around my chest and the needle in my arm. I smell fear, mine and my executioner's. My executioner. Who will it be? A doctor so deep in debt he moonlights to make a few bucks? What about the Hippocratic oath, Doc? Vows don't mean a thing anymore.

A guard walks the hall, and the rhythm fills my cell. There is no energy to his movement, no anticipation. He walks this walk because he must, because that's what he signed up for when he took this job. Some workers clean teeth for a living, others change tires, this guy walks the hallway. In the morning, they will come for me. Ten, twelve strong, and their walk will be a thing of beauty. The only question will be if that march happens before or after breakfast. I'm voting for after breakfast. It's easier to feed me here.

I study the sky and pray for rain, for a hurricane, for a twister like the one that ripped up Tabernacle Carnival. I pray for a meteorite, a stray comet, an out-of-control satellite to strike this building. Bricks split and convicts scream and I crawl through the opening into the world like an infant emerging from his mother's womb. My life is an hourglass and most of the sand is on the bottom. I wish for a miracle to turn that glass upside down—a new start anywhere but here—think the cruelest death is knowing when it will happen. I close my eyes and relax the fists that were once my hands. I will lie in bed and try to sleep. I will think of jelly beans and cute little girls, I will think of wind in my hair, I will think of Rickie.

Guards stand outside my cell. They have stun guns and tear gas, they have nightsticks and plastic shields, they have the numbers and their faces gleam with desire.

"Where's my breakfast?" I say.

It is nine o'clock, and I am the only convict not to receive breakfast. My stomach collapses into its hollow, and a vast hunger comes over me. I have never been so empty.

"Cuff up," a guard says.

"Where's my breakfast?" I say.

"Turn around and cuff up."

"I want my toast," I say. "I want my eggs."

The guards cinch down their masks, and twenty-four goggle eyes train in my direction. Twelve blue-skinned praying mantises. Gas, an evil hiss, enters through a crack above the door, a traitorous slit I did not know existed. I turn and hold my hands to the slot, and the gas stops. Snick. Snick. Cuffs around my wrists. The door opens, and the plague descends. I have no desire to spend the last day of my life nursing a broken arm or wondering why I'm bleeding out of my ears. Snick. Snick. Cuffs around my ankles. I shuffle out of the cell, take a right, and walk down the hall. Two officers lead, two follow. Four march single file to my left, four march single file to my right. My steps are short; three to their one. Baby steps. I'm an adult taking baby steps. Doors open and close, and I feel sunshine on my skin for the first time in years and suddenly I am glad they waited until now to take me on my walk. The sky is directly overhead, a marvel in itself, clouds so far away they look like toothbrush bristles. I cannot believe Alton and Miriam are dead; cannot believe my life has come to this.

A man perched atop a backhoe drives the machine across the field, a clank of heavy machinery, a roll of rubber tires. The backhoe enters the graveyard, the man works a set of levers on the dash in front of him, and the backhoe arm swings and arcs downward. Removes a shovel full of dirt and dumps it to the side.

We march onward, and I hear the helicopter and for a glorious moment fantasize about Rickie appearing with guns blazing. But then reality sets in, and it sets in on purpose. I have less than nine hours and don't want to waste time on what-ifs. It has not rained in days, and the ground feels solid beneath my feet. I lick my lips, I have never felt so dry. The guards guide me toward the door.

"Please," I say. "Can we stay outside for another few minutes?"

The procession halts. I turn toward the prison, study the gray walls, the guard towers that rise into the sky. There are twenty windows on this side of the block, and nineteen have faces in them. The twentieth, my old cell, is empty. One of the guards says the warden is allowing me a last smoke and asks if I want one. I say yes, and the guard sticks a cigarette to my lips. Lights the end, and I inhale until I think my lungs will explode.

The helicopter hovers overhead. NBC. Out of Orlando. A man leans out the cabin and trains a camera my way. Vernon L. Oliver. Famous to the end. The backhoe digs on, deeper now, dirt spilling over the mound. I spit out the butt and stomp on it with my heel. The backhoe goes silent, and the helicopter lingers like a hungry dragonfly. I thank the guard for his kindness and follow my blue escorts inside. The hallway is long and murky, and we pass a janitorial closet on the left. I had imagined all kinds of rooms in this building, had not thought about cleaning supplies. A guard opens a metal door farther down and motions me inside. He takes off my cuffs, and I flex my hands.

"I'll see what I can do about getting you something to eat," the guard says.

"I'm all right."

"You sure?"

"I'm sure."

I glance at the recessed clock high on the wall. Chrome hands against a black background. It is 9:47 a.m.

"Is that clock right?" I say.

A guard who has not spoken says there are nine clocks in this building and all are synchronized with Greenwich Mean Time. He's saying, without saying it, that the first drug will enter my arm at precisely 6:00 p.m. Not a second before and not a second after.

The door shuts, and I sit on the bed. The cell is green and approximately six by six. There is a Plexiglas window on one end, where a button protrudes from the wall: PUSH TO TALK. On the other side of the window, a guard enters a shadowy observation room. The door closes, and the room becomes dark as before. I am under suicide watch, cannot take a crap without someone knowing. I study the toilet, work the handle, watch water swirl down the drain.

Pastor Nick Wheaton sits where the guard sat. He wants me to call him Nicky, has blue eyes that radiate condescension. His pink suit is too pink and his white shirt is too white, and the mohawk that runs from his forehead to the back of his neck has enough grease to lube a sport-utility vehicle.

"I'm surprised you asked for me," he says, pushing a button on his side of the window.

"Life is full of surprises."

"Shall we pray?" he says.

"Whatever you think is best, Pastor."

Wheaton bows his head and I bow mine but keep my eyes open and watch his lips move, cannot hear the words because his finger slips from the button. He prays for a good five minutes, palms turned toward the ceiling like God hovers in the last coat of paint. I have nothing against this man. I won the battle, he won the war. His hands droop and his lips slow and he seems to be winding down, so I tap on the window and he opens his eyes. I press the button.

"You forgot to press the button," I say.

His index finger arrows forward, the speaker crackles, and he says he'll pick up where he left off. He drones on about sins and sinners and how we all have a place at Jesus's side if we take him into our heart and confess our sins and try to lead a good life from here on out. I have three hours left in mine, so there isn't much time to go astray. He asks if I'm ready to be saved. I nod enthusiastically and say I've never been so ready in my life and how I'm happy God sent him today, and, by the way, here's what I want you to do with my body.

"All in good time," he says.

"I want you to take it somewhere and burn it and drop the ashes from atop a high mountain. I want to drift down into a peaceful valley."

"'Though I walk through the shadow of the valley of death,'" Nicky says, "'I will fear no evil.'"

"That's what I'm talking about, you nailed it on the head."

Nicky places his palm on the window and widens the gap between his fingers. I place my palm on the glass and mirror his. The glass is cold and thick and his palm is an inch away and I do not feel anything. I wonder what I'm supposed to do and decide he needs to see some trembling and thrashing, so I shake my head, hair bouncing in time with my nods. My hand quivers, but I keep it firm against the glass.

"Praise Jesus," I say.

"Repent, sinner. Repent and receive him into your heart."

I stare up at the ceiling, ask the demons to leave my wretched body.

"I repent," I say. "I'm sorry for the things I've done in my life."

Pastor Nick has a satisfied smile. "I'm glad you've seen the light."

"I've seen it, praise the Lord, but now I'm ready to go meet my maker. I'm a better man, Pastor, I'm a better man by a mile than I was before you walked in there."

He gets out a toothpick and digs into the lower reaches of his mouth. His words jumble together. He's headed to Mount Sinai, where he'll scatter my ashes after a morning vigil that will be broadcast on all religious stations. The toothpick picks, his teeth flash, drool runs down his cheek. He wipes away the wetness and leaves a slick behind.

"It will be a media event," he says. "To show that God forgives even the worst of his sinners."

"I'm as bad as they come. I'm the worst of the worst."

He proclaims I should spend the next two hours in reflection, and I thank him all the way out the door. At least I won't lie in that cemetery for eternity, least . . . least . . . my damn hands won't settle down. The guard comes back in and sits in the chair. I will not cry. I will not.

Deputies flank me, hands on my arms. I stand in the Kill Room in front of the glass that separates me from reporters in high-backed seats. Sandoval sits in the rear, head down. Nick Wheaton stands near the exit, cradles a Bible in his arms. The walls that surround them are white and the ceiling is white and the carpet is white. Dressed for the occasion—suits for the men and pantsuits for the women—my last congregation fidgets in silent expectation. The warden, wearing a blue suit and tie, asks if I have any last words, and I try to corral my thoughts. They are scattered, wild mustangs running the range. I try to rope them, desperate to lead them to the stable of rationality.

There have been enough famous last words spoken in mankind's history to fill a book. Maybe I should go the Julius Caesar route, stare at Sandoval and say, "*Et tu, Brute?*" Or perhaps I should go political and quote John Spenkelink, the Florida convict who opined, "Capital punishment: them without the capital get the punishment." Should I leave my flock, those hopeful believers, something to hold on to? Should I forgive my accusers? Should I complain about salty peas, the lack of intelligent conversation coming through the vent?

A body shifts in the rear row, an uncrossing of the legs, and Sandoval gets up and asks if he can have one last word with his client. The warden relents, and Sandoval goes through a door in one of the white walls and a few minutes later appears at my side.

I turn toward the reporters, clear my throat, tell them I have something to say, and they lean forward like my voice is all that keeps them from toppling to the floor.

"I committed these murders. I put a gun to their heads and pulled the trigger. I planned it out, I acted alone—"

"She wants a divorce," Sandoval whispers.

I continue on. "When the State kills me that will end this horrible chapter in Pentecostal history. It will be over and done with, and I am so sorry for my actions. To those who believed in me, I apologize. To those we helped via our clinics, I want to say I wish we could have done more. To Pastor Wheaton, who graciously consented to assume responsibility for my body, I appreciate your humbleness and willingness to help this sinner."

"She sent divorce papers," Sandoval says. "She cites irreparable differences, she says she's in love with another man."

The guards turn me toward the gurney, and I speak over my shoulder.

"What?" I say. "What was that?"

Sandoval is gone, and I am left with the choice of fighting or going peacefully to my deathbed. My heart, beating so fast I can't distinguish the thuds, slows until it hardly beats at all. My limbs become cold, and I draw inward. Guards tighten straps over my chest, my arms, my legs, my forehead. The ceiling is a light color, and in the corner the painter missed a spot. Painters, who can trust them, mostly drunks in my opinion. Least I won't have to sleep in the cell tonight and listen to Dredge dream up some new way to help humanity.

A pinprick in my left arm, a pinprick in my right arm, and I cut my gaze toward a man in a white frock. Dr. Death has hazel eyes and wears a mask that covers him from cheeks to jaw. He has a big stomach, the effort of walking across the room has him breathing hard, and I tell him if he wants to live a little longer he should lay off the sweets or maybe I think that and keep it to myself. It cannot pay to irritate my executioner. The phone rings, a burst of energy that penetrates my thoughts, and I know it is the emperor saying thumbs up or thumbs down and I'm almost wishing for thumbs down because I would hate to go through this buildup again.

The warden announces the execution will proceed on schedule, and on the other side of the glass Sandoval's fist strikes the wall with such impact I know his bones are breaking. The clock strikes six, and the doctor twists a knob that begins a drip into my arm. A numbing sensation, the drug they administer before the kill. I stare at Sandoval and at last fathom what he's trying to tell me.

Rickie is in love with another man.

My wife, the bewitching siren, hath forsaken me. I mumble something, and the warden leans close to the glass. I say it again and he nods at the doctor and the doctor turns off the drip and stands nearby.

"What did you say?" asks the warden.

"I'll sign the paper." My words come out slow, rounded around the edges. "Give me the paper and I'll sign it."

Sandoval stands at the screen and his shoulders jerk. He wads up a handkerchief and wipes his eyes. Reporters clamber to their feet and they stand next to Sandoval and they have their microphones out but they are all watching me. The warden disappears—to make a phone call, I presume—comes back five minutes later. Thumbs up, cut the bastard loose, he's innocent as they come.

I woozily get to my feet, catch Nick Wheaton out of the corner of my eye, force my hand up, and slowly unfurl my middle finger. I am a spiteful Lazarus, and I'm certain Wheaton suspects his bottom line just got smaller. He is wrong; I have no wish to go back into the business. The door opens and Sandoval pushes past a guard and tells everyone to keep their hands off me or he'll sue them for so much money they'll be pissing in a bucket for the rest of their miserable lives. I walk past the reporters who part like I'm Moses and they are the sea, walk out the front door and into open air. The helicopter hovers overhead, presumably to catch a shot of my shrouded body before it's inserted into the hearse, but this is an even bigger story and the metal insect sinks so low wind from its wings ruffles my hair.

The nineteen faces in the cell windows are expressionless, as though the convicts cannot believe what they see. I raise my arms in a V salute, and it's like turning on an animation screen. The backhoe begins to fill the hole, a slow-motion retracing that will go on too long for me to stay and watch. I want my Harley and the open road. I want to think about Rickie and forget her at the same time. I want to forgive her, and I want to forgive myself. These things will be slow in coming, but I've got the time.

Chapter 25

ONE YEAR AFTER MY release, I sit in the back of a movie theater and eat buttered popcorn, sip from a straw jammed into an extra-large Coke. I wear a ball cap low over my brow, but I can't hide my height and several moviegoers in the packed house take extra-long looks in my direction. They forget about me soon as *Biker Preacher* starts, and the fictional car chase scene with me and Lucy trying to dodge the cops rolls across the screen. The movie is two hours long, and ninety minutes in, Rickie flicks off the safety and shoots her parents. Women dab at their eyes when I sacrifice my freedom. Men shift uncomfortably. It is a touching movie, me as the villain, then as the hero, then finally deciding my life is not worth sacrificing for one-way love.

The movie ends and the crowd cheers and I exit while credits are still onscreen. I do not stop until I am out of the theater and down the street to the subway, where I step through the doorway of the train and take a seat. I look at no one and hopefully no one looks at me. I am tired of the attention—first this book, now this movie—which has been out three weeks and is still atop the box office.

I've met a woman who works as an attorney in Manhattan. She has a kid and a German shepherd. The dog no longer tries to bite me and the kid stays with his father half the time, so the house is fairly quiet. I've had arthroscopic surgery on my knee, dental work to replace my knocked-out teeth, go to the gym four times a week. I'm toned and have a full smile, walk without a limp. Physically, I'm normal in every way. The woman, the kid, and I live in a gated community, and all in all it's not a bad life.

The subway goes aboveground, and New York in all its drabness slides past the window. Rain falls, and cars below splash through widening puddles. People scurry across sidewalks, umbrellas over their heads. I position my face close to the glass, same way as back in prison, and for a nightmarish moment am transported to those walls. I force myself to the present and a familiar smell comes to me, that sweet scent Rickie wore so often. I do not turn around. I am tired of looking for her, no longer seek out the cut of her hair, the tilt of her shoulders, no longer follow strangers until I get a look at their faces.

The glass is cold, and New York is gray and moldering. I watch it until the subway goes underground. The scent is stronger and still I press against the window. Tunnel lights appear, flash past so quick it's like they never existed. I feel vibration in my soles, sense the stops and starts, people moving up and down the aisle. Papers rustle and shoes click on the floor, words in different languages sprinkle the air. The smell is strong. I feel her essence flow through me, and for the first time in years I feel alive. I smile into the glass, wanting to prolong this olfactory hallucination, wanting to hold her one more time. A voice comes over my shoulder. The words are soft, almost a whisper.

"Don't turn around," the voice says. "Don't acknowledge my presence in any way."

My heart stretches out, so thin it might snap.

"They follow you," the voice says. "They watch you hoping I'll try to make contact."

My hands shake and my knees weaken and I fight the urge to turn. My lips compress into painful lines. The subway is on the elevated tracks again and it is still raining and the clouds are still low and people still scurry among the puddles. A neon light flashes something I can't read, something in Spanish.

"Are you okay?" I say. "Are you doing all right?"

"I miss you, if that's what you're asking."

Was I?

People shuffle past, and I realize we've stopped moving. More people get on, and the subway continues up the tracks. The smell is still there, still strong. My body aches to meet hers and still I face the glass. I feel her sit, see her squeezed-down reflection in the chrome pole that runs floor to ceiling. She wears some kind of green outfit. The subway accelerates and my hip presses against hers, a tingle that shoots to my spine. I listen to her talk—in that same quiet voice—about going underground and changing her address once a year. I sense a loneliness strong as my own and dream about my arms around her. The quiver in her voice suggests it's been a long time since she cried.

"I can't believe you fell in love with someone else," I say. "I can't believe you wanted a divorce."

"That never happened. That was something your goddamn attorney made up."

I stare at the rushing wall so close, hear the groaning brakes.

"The divorce papers were fake?"

"His lie saved your life; I wouldn't hold it against him."

I tell her I am too tired to hold anything against anybody, close my eyes, and rest my forehead against the glass.

"I wanted to let you know I'm not like before," she says. "Miriam and Alton made me who I was but your sacrifice changed all that. You saved my life in more ways than one."

I don't know what to say to that, so I keep my mouth shut and listen. She's started an orphanage in a location she won't disclose, says it's a satisfying feeling to know she's helping kids who remind her of herself. One of the boys graduated high school and starts college next year. I tell her it's a good thing she's doing, that I do not hold the murders against her, that we all deserved to die.

"That doesn't make it right," she says.

"No . . . no it doesn't."

"I guess the main thing," she says, "is I wanted to see if your life is going all right. If you're doing okay."

My desire overwhelms me, and I turn in her direction. She is already gone. She is already gone, and I am alone. She is already gone, and my heart free-falls with no landing pad in sight. I look down the aisles, peer over heads. The doors are closing and I take two leaps and I am on the platform into the humid air. I see her in the distance, a swell of people between us. I run in her direction, dodge a baby stroller, push past a startled Chinese man. I run and it feels good to feel sinew pull against bone, to hear my shoes contact the pavement. I run and I call out her name and yet she does not turn. A policeman jerks my arm and spins me around, and I shove him to the ground and gallop forward. I see that familiar walk, the way her legs glide along, and then I am beside her, arms entangled around her body, and she is screaming and hitting me and I raise my hands to block the blows.

"I thought you were someone I knew," I say.

The woman strides away, and I duck down a hallway and step out into the rain. The drops feel good against my face and I stand there, allowing the water to soak me to the skin, allowing it to run down the crack of my ass, to fill my shoes. I spread my arms and raise my face to the heavens. Time, that great desensitizer, has not diminished my feelings for Rickie. Yes, I still love her. Yes, I still love her despite the murderer that she is. Who can choose love?

Not I.

Acknowledgments

During the writing of this novel, I lived for eight years in an attic, in an unheated room that has a plumbing pipe rising floor to ceiling in one of the corners. My landlord fed me when I was without food and allowed me to work off rent when I got behind. I will never forget her kindness.

For her professionalism and keen insight, I acknowledge my agent, Leigh Feldman. Michele Mortimer, a staff member at the agency, played a key role in this process.

Many thanks to Kerri Kolen, senior editor at Simon & Schuster, for her patience in shaping my words. I could not have asked for a better advocate.

I must not forget Francis Ford Coppola and his philanthropy in offering Zoetrope.com to the creative community. Without this online workshop I'd still be figuring out how to string sentences together. I am indebted to Terri Brown-Davidson, who offered me encouragement from the day we met, which was ten long years ago. To Bonnie ZoBell, a faithful reader who gets to the point. And to Thea Atkinson, who is always willing to offer suggestions on my manuscripts.

Special thanks to the following writers, friends, and editors. All of you touched my journey.

Cezarija Abartis, Mary Akers, Ann M. Amodeo, Stephanie Anagnoson, Hobie Anthony, Wesley Arnold, Beebe Barksdale-Bruner, Rusty Barnes, Jensen Beach, Diane Hoover Bechtler, Matt Bell, Karen Berger, Sarah Black, Shari Blume, Barrett Bowlin, Mark Budman, Aaron Burch, Mike Burrell, Daphne Buter, Gary Cadwallader, Don Capone, Jessie Carty, David Caruthers, Tania Casselle, Louis E. Catron, Ginger Hamilton Caudill, Elaine Chiew, Kim Chinquee, Dave Clapper, Jai Clare, Stephan Clark, Martin Cloutier, Peter Cole, Myfanwy Collins, Ramon Collins, Ronald F. Currie Jr., Tommy Dean, Jason DeBoer, Terry DeHart, Katrina Denza, Lucinda Nelson Dhavan, Viet Dinh, Susan DiPlacido, Trisha Dower, Scott Doyle, Neal Durando, Xujun Eberlein, Pia Z. Ehrhardt, Anne Elliott, Pamela Erens, David Erik Erlewine, Kathy Fish, Glen Fleagle, Marko Fong, Heather Fowler, John Matthew Fox, Stefanie Freele, Avital Gad-Cykman, Scott Garson, Cliff Garstang, Carla Gericke, Maggie Gerrity, Alicia Gifford, Ricky Ginsburg, Marcus Grimm, Natasha Grinberg, Sue Haigh, William Reese Hamilton, Jim Harrison, Martin Heavisides, Susan Henderson, Hannah Holborn, Mark Hubbard, Frank J. Hutton, Debbie Ann Ice, Beverly Jackson, Raul E. Jimenez, Liesl Jobson, Jeffrey N. Johnson, Len Joy, Roy Kesey, Cheryl Kidder, Nausheen Khan, Jonas Knutsson, Susan Lago, Laila Lalami, Michael Leone, Joe Levens, Richard Lewis, Julia Mary Lichtblau, Jessica Lipnack, Linera Lucas, Antonios Maltezos, Ravi Mangla, Steven J. McDermott, Sharon McGill, Mitzi McMahon, Lisa McMann, Mike McManus, Ellen Meister, Kirsten Menger-Anderson, Mary Miller, Barbara Milton, Roger Norman Morris, Justine Musk, Sequoia Nagamatsu, Sam Nam, Darlin' Neal, Ray Norsworthy, Sandra Ramos O'Briant, Elsie O'Day, Daniel A. Olivas, Sue O'Neill, Melissa Palladino, Ellen

Parker, Anne Leigh Parrish, Shari Pierce, Meg Pokrass, Mary Lynn Reed, Carol Reid, Sharon Mauldin Reynolds, Jordan E. Rosenfeld, Max Ruback, Jim Ruland, Monideepa Sahu, Tom Saunders, Kay Sexton, Myra Sherman, Marie Shield, Danna Layton Sides, Barry Simms, Robin Slick, Simon A. Smith, Mithran Somasundrum, Kelly Spitzer, Maryanne Stahl, Jill Stegman, Donna Storey, Lauran Strait, Craig Terlson, Lena Thomasson, Jim Tomlinson, Ania Vesenney, Donna D. Vitucci, Julie Wakeman-Linn, John Warner, Holly Wendt, Lesley C. Weston, Dan Wickett, Joan Wilking, Evan Morgan Williams, Regina Williams, Wayne E. Yang, Mike A. Young, Laurie Zagorski, and Bonnie ZoBell.

Printed in the United States
By Bookmasters